ALSO BY ROBERT VAUGHAN

LEGEND OF A GUNFIGHTER

ROBERT VAUGHAN

WOLFPACK
PUBLISHING
— EST 2013 —

Legend Of A Gunfighter
Robert Vaughan

Wolfpack Publishing
6032 Wheat Penny Avenue
Las Vegas, NV 89122

wolfpackpublishing.com

Paperback ISBN 978-1-64119-551-5
eBook ISBN 978-1-64119-550-8

Library of Congress Control Number: 2018965399

LEGEND OF A GUNFIGHTER

When gunfire erupted in the Longhorn Saloon all conversation stopped while the piano music faded. Gun smoke hung in the air and four men lay face down on the saloon floor. The gunman was dressed in white, and at the moment there was a smoking gun in each hand as he stood looking down at the carnage he had just caused. He was showing, by the expression on his face, that he was ready to take on anyone else who might have the courage to challenge him.

Two beautiful bargirls approached him and standing on either side, they looked up at him with adoring eyes.

"You are wonderful!" the blonde said.

"I was so frightened!" the brunette said.

"The town is safer with their kind gone," the man replied.

"You are so brave," the blonde said.

The man turned to the woman who spoke last, and lashed out at her.

"You stepped on my line, you stupid . . . ! 'The town is safer with their kind gone' is the last line of the scene!"

"Cut! Cut!"

The cameras stopped rolling.

"Clive, I didn't mean to. I'm so sorry," the blonde said with a look of fear on her face.

"Guy, we're going to have to shoot that scene over," Clive Malone said.

"It's a good scene," Guy Lashlee protested.

Clive shook his head and pointed to the actress who was portraying one of the bar girls.

"This idiot blew it. I've got the last line in the scene, and since I'm one of the producers, I say we shoot it again."

The director let out a discernible sigh. "All right, reset," he said as he waited for everyone to get into position.

"Picture is up," the assistant director announced, "Everyone settle please. Camera ready?"

"Camera ready," the director of photography said.

"Sound ready?" the AD asked.

"Ready," the mixer replied.

"Boom in, slate it, roll sound," the assistant director said.

"Speed," the mixer said.

"Scene five, take two. Roll camera."

"Marker," the director called.

The clapper was brought down on the slate.

"Action."

Clive came in through the swinging bat–wing doors.

CLIVE

You outlaws ran, but you didn't run far enough. Now you'll have to pay.

OUTLAW NUMBER ONE

It's Clive Malone! Shoot him! Shoot him!

The scene continued as before and this time the blonde didn't step on Clive's lines.

"Cut!" Guy called, when the scene was completed.

The cameras stopped rolling, and the "dead" villains got up from the floor.

"Too bad this isn't a real saloon," one of the villains said, "I could sure use a beer."

"The crafty has beer."

"That's only for cast, not for day players," one of the other 'dead' outlaws said, "Anyhow it isn't real beer; it's near beer."

`"Well, at least near beer is better than lemonade."

The two actresses who were portraying the bar girls were still standing next to Clive.

"I'm sorry I yelled at you darlin'," Clive said to the blonde, as he pulled her to his side, "but I'm serious about my work and I just want to get everything right."

"That's why you're the best actor in Hollywood," the blonde said turning toward him.

Clive smiled. "I can see right now you want a role in my next picture, and sweet talking me is just the way to do it."

"Clive, before we're back in, Mr. Harris wants to see you in the production shack," Guy Lashlee said.

"What does he want? You know I don't like to break the creative flow."

"He's my boss just like he's your boss, and if he wants to see you, you'll just have to get back into the mood when we start shooting again." Guy smiled, "But you're a pro, and I know you can do it."

Clive Malone was one of the most popular Western actors in the movies, and though he rivaled Tom Mix in popularity, that was where the comparison ended. Tom Mix had been a genuine war hero in Cuba and the Philippines, an actual Texas Ranger, and a United States Marshal who had been wounded in a gunfight.

Clive Malone had no personal history to match that.

The door was opened by a very attractive young woman in revealing garb.

"Hello, Velma," Clive said his eyes drifting downward. "Guy said the boss wants to see me."

"Yes, come on in!" A man called out, even before Velma could answer.

Alcy Harris was sitting on a leather couch openly drinking a glass of liquor despite the fact that national prohibition made drinking illegal. He motioned for Clive to join him.

"Velma, bring Clive some refreshment," Harris said.

"No, no—not while I'm working," Clive said holding up his hand.

"What do you know about Buck Elliot?" Harris asked.

"I think I've read about Buck Elliot. Isn't he supposed to be some old `gunfighter or something? But then maybe he's a made up character like The Virginian or Hopalong Cassidy."

Harris shook his head. "No, for sure, he's not made up. The stories about Buck Elliot are real."

"Wait, are you telling me there really was a Buck Elliot?"

"Not was—is. I've just hired the real Buck Elliot for *Legend of a Gunfighter.*"

"You've just hired him to do what?"

"Be a technical consultant for my next movie. It'll be called *Legend of a Gunfighter*, and it's about Buck Elliot, who just happens to be one of the most famous gunfighters of the old West," Harris said. "So who better to be my technical consultant to you, than the actual man who lived it?"

"What do you mean consult me about it? What do I have to do with it?"

"I just told you. I bought the rights to the book, *Legend of a Gunfighter*, and Starburst Motion Picture Studios will be

4

making it into a movie. You'll be portraying Buck Elliot in the picture."

"No, Mr. Harris," Clive said shaking his head. "I think you'd be making a big mistake there."

"Why do say that?" Harris asked, surprised by Clive's reaction.

"I'm famous and well-loved as a cowboy actor because I always play myself. My fans like to see Clive Malone get the better of the bad guys; then I get the pretty girl and ride off into the sunset. These are all fiction with lots of action. They don't want to see me portraying some old man who might've done something a long time ago. They want entertainment; they don't want a dry history lesson."

"I thought you said you'd read about Buck Elliot."

"Well, sort of, I mean I recognize the name, just like I recognize Jesse James or Wild Bill Hickok. But I don't really know anything about any of them, except that they're dead."

"Well, Buck Elliot isn't dead, and I intend to do the picture, so as long as you're under contract with Starburst Motion Picture Studios, you *will* take the roles I give you."

"Yes, sir, I'll do as you say, but you'll see that I'm right. Nobody's going to pay good money to watch me play some dried up old has-been, who not that many people have ever even heard of in the first place."

"Didn't you just tell me that you've heard of him?"

"I did, but what does that mean?"

"Clive, you're one of the least-read men I've ever known, and your grasp of history is abysmal. You barely know the difference between Christopher Columbus and George Washington. So if you've heard of Buck Elliot, then we can be certain that millions more know about him."

"All right, but I still say you're going to lose a lot of money." Clive pointed his finger toward Alcy Harris. "I'm telling you right now, if this fool idea destroys my career, I'll sue you for so much money that I'll wind up owning Starburst."

"You just fulfill the terms of your contract, and let me worry about the money," Harris replied.

Clive withheld any further remarks, but was still fuming when he returned to the studio.

"Good, you're back," Guy said, "I think we can get in one more scene before lunch."

Clive waved him off. "I don't think so. I'm not ready, and I need a couple of hours to get back in the mood."

"Clive, you know we're on a tight shooting schedule here, and we have to pay for studio time whether we're using it or not."

"Then shoot a scene that doesn't have me in it," Clive said, angrily, "I told you, I'm not ready!"

"All right, all right, have it your way." Guy forced a smile. "After all, you're the star."

"Yeah, I am. And don't you ever forget it."

"AD, we're going to have to reset," Guy called as Clive left the studio.

Who the hell is this Buck Elliot guy, anyway? Clive wondered as he headed for his dressing room. The son of a bitch has to be damn near a hundred years old. Hell, he'll probably drop dead right in the middle of production. Clive smiled at his thought. Yeah, he just might drop dead during production. Then there won't be a problem. He wondered if there was any way he could help that along.

Meacham Field—Ft. Worth. Texas - 1931

He had been clean shaven in his younger years, but now Buck Elliot had a full moustache that matched his silver hair.

And although he was eighty years old, no one could guess Buck's age by a casual glance because he had the health, wit, and physique of someone who was considerably younger.

"Passengers for Transcontinental Air Transport flight three – oh – four, please be advised that your plane is now on final for two seven," the augmented voice over the public enunciator system said.

"On final? My, that sound ominous," a woman said.

"It just means that the airplane is coming in for a landing on runway two seven," a knowledgeable passenger explained.

Buck, who was waiting for flight 304, moved to the window and watched as the Tri-motor Ford touched down, completed its landing roll out, then left the runway and trundled down the taxiway toward the terminal building where the arriving passengers could deplane. After that, Buck and the other outgoing passengers could board.

When it turned to present its side to Buck, he could see the TAT in bold black letters, then superimposed over the TAT in a long, narrow, red outlined arrow, the smaller letters, "Transcontinental Air Transport."

"Passengers for Abilene, El Paso, Las Cruces, Lordsburg, Phoenix, Palm Springs and Los Angeles may now board," the same augmented voice announced. Seven passengers left the plane, and Buck was one of the six who boarded; the other passengers being three men and two women. Once he stepped in through the door, bending to accommodate the interior to his height, Buck took a look around. There was a row of seats on each side of the aircraft where he saw five additional passengers. The wicker seats were brown and yellow, and the ceiling and walls of the airplane were pine paneled.

Buck was sitting next to the left engine nacelle that hung like a big, silver pine-cone from beneath the high wing. Shortly after he was seated he heard the whine of the inertia starter, then the cough as the fuel mixture ignited in the exposed cylinders and the propeller began to whirl. With all three engines turning, the airplane taxied out to the runway, sat at the end for a moment as first the left engine, then the engine on the nose, then the engine hanging under the right wing were run up for pre-takeoff checks. That done, the airplane started down the runway, gathering speed until it lifted into the air.

Ten minutes later Buck was looking down at the compact farm and ranch units, the small houses, barns, and outbuildings passing far below. The flight, he had been told, would be fourteen hours in the air, though the fourteen hours would not be uninterrupted. Eight hours from now the plane and its passengers would spend the night in Lordsburg, New Mexico.

2

BUCK HAD READ THAT SEVERAL OF THE AIRLINES NOW HAD women stewardesses, and TAT flight 304 was one that did. As the flight winged west, an attractive young woman came walking down the aisle speaking to each of the eleven passengers.

"Sir, would you like coffee, or would you prefer tea?" she asked having to speak rather loudly to be heard over the roar of the three engines.

"Coffee would be nice," Buck replied.

"Cream and sugar?"

"Black."

The young stewardess smiled broadly. "You are my kind of passenger," she said. "Black coffee is easy to serve."

Buck watched her walk back to the front of the cabin where a shelf stuck out from the forward bulkhead.

While waiting for her to return, he stared through his window, looking down at the ground between the engine, which had a strut containing the three engine instruments, and the fairing-covered wheel. The ground was fifteen hundred feet below. Although they were doing better than

120 miles per hour, from this altitude the ground seemed to roll out very slowly.

"Here you are, sir. Enjoy," the stewardess said as she handed him the hot coffee.

As Buck drank, he wondered why he was making this trip. He had been asked to be a consultant on a movie about his life, but more than likely they would get it all wrong just like the dozen or so books that had been written about him. They were all figments of some author's imagination.

But that wasn't entirely true. There had been one author, Ernest Haycox, who had taken the time to come to Arizona and interview him. And the book that was the result, *Legend of a Gunfighter*, was a damned good book.

And now there was to be a motion picture made based upon the Ernest Haycox book. If they followed the book they would get it right, and Buck hoped that his being there would assure that that happened.

Eight hours after taking off from Ft. Worth, and with stops in Abilene, El Paso, and Las Cruces, the airplane landed in Lordsburg, New Mexico. This would be the last stop of the day. A six hour flight remained that tomorrow would fly on to Los Angeles. In the meantime, the flight would be interrupted for a night's rest. The through passengers were met at the airport, and taken by motor coach to the Hidalgo Hotel.

The exterior of the hotel, which was Lordsburg's newest, was Pueblo-Spanish in design. It was stucco, while brightly colored log ends set off the front facade of the building.

Buck smiled as he stepped into the lobby with its comfortable leather chairs placed in groupings to facilitate conversation. He took a seat while the other passengers were assigned their rooms.

The last time he had been in Lordsburg he had arrived by stagecoach. In fact, he had been driving the stagecoach, because in a holdup attempt, both the driver and the shotgun guard had been shot and wounded. The shotgun guard had managed to kill one of the two would-be outlaws, and Buck, who had been a passenger on the coach, had killed the other one.

At that time, Railroad Avenue had been a dirt road littered with horse apples, and crowded with wagons and horses. Today the road was paved and filled with automobiles. Buck marveled at the big changes that had occurred within his life-time. Airplanes, automobiles, telephones, radio, and of course, motion pictures which just in the past few years had learned to talk, were quite common now.

"Mr. Elliot?"

Buck, who was sitting in one of the big leather chairs in the spacious lobby, looked up at the bellboy who had just addressed him.

"Yes?"

"Are you *the* Buck Elliot?"

Buck laughed. "I am Buck Elliot, but as I'm sure there may be others with my same name I don't know that I'm ready to say I am *the* Buck Elliot."

"Did you once drive a stagecoach into Lordsburg because robbers had shot the driver and guard?"

Buck was stunned by the question as he had just been thinking about that very event.

"Well, yes, yes I did," Buck answered

A huge smile broke out on the bellboy's face, "I *knew* it was you! You saved my grandpa's life!"

"Oh?"

"He was a shotgun guard for the Lordsburg Stagecoach Company and when his coach was held up you . . ."

"Your grandpa's name was Green O. Prouty?"

"Yes! You remember him! He would have been so proud to know that you remembered him."

"He has passed?"

"Yes, sir, he died two years ago, but he told me all about how you saved his life and the lives of everyone else on the coach that day."

"What's your name, son?"

"Prouty. Leonard Prouty."

"Well, Leonard, did your grandpa tell you that he got one of the outlaws himself? Mr. Prouty did himself proud that day, and I hope you remember that about him."

"Yes, sir, I do remember that. But because of what grandpa told me about you, well, I've read ever' thing I could get my hands on about you."

"I hope you don't believe everything you read about me."

"Well sir, I read *Legend of a Gunfighter*, 'n there's a paragraph in that book that says you say Mr. Haycox got ever' thing right. Did you say that?"

"I did say that, and I must confess that of everyone who has ever written about me, Ernest Haycox has been the most accurate."

"What are you doing in Lordsburg, Mr. Elliot?"

"Well, you may not believe this son, but I'm on my way to Hollywood. It seems they are going to make a motion picture from that book."

"Wow!" Leonard said, excitedly, "I'll sure be lookin' for that one when it comes out!"

After dinner that evening Buck bought a newspaper and took it up to his room to read before going to bed.

NEW TALKING PICTURE TO STAR CLIVE MALONE
Raised on a ranch near Chugwater, Wyoming, Clive Malone

was herding cattle by the time he was twelve years old. He joined the army as a young man of 17, and was with the American Expeditionary Forces on the Western Front. Later he was a deputy sheriff in Idaho, and a U.S. Marshal in South Dakota.

In 1923, Clive Malone was hired by Starburst Motion Picture Studios to break horses to be used in western films. His first movie, The Great Stagecoach Robbery, was a silent film, as were his first nine pictures.

Clive Malone's newest film, Texas Shootout, has just been released, and he is currently in negotiation with Starburst Motion Picture Studios to do a new movie. Although Starburst is keeping the project a secret, it is said that the new picture will be a departure from Clive Malone's normal fare. It is also believed that in the new picture Malone will not play himself but rather will bring to the silver screen the indomitable exploits of an authentic hero of the American West.

Clive Malone's popularity eclipses that of nearly every other great cowboy star including Hoot Gibson and William S Hart. Only Tom Mix is more popular, and earns more money. "However," Alcy Harris, head of Starburst Motion Picture Studios says, "Clive Malone's next movie will clearly establish him as the most popular cowboy star of all time."

Grand Central Airport – Glendale. California:

Clive Malone parked his brand new, dark blue Cord in the parking lot across from the terminal. Alcy Harris had said he would send a studio car and driver to pick up Buck Elliot, and at first Clive agreed. Then he changed his mind and decided that he would rather pick up Elliot himself. The earlier he could get to him, the more opportunity he would have to make Buck Elliot his ally.

Clive had read through the script and, in his opinion, it needed a drastic rewrite. He might have been asked to play an authentic historical character, but when it came right down to it, Clive intended to portray Clive Malone.

Clive had worked hard to develop and to promote himself as the quintessential American cowboy, and he had been enormously successful. The studio hired people whose only job was to measure the amount of impact his name had on the public. Those people told him that, for the moment at least, his name was as well-known as that of Tom Mix. Clive didn't want to do anything to jeopardize that position.

"I'll lose ground if I don't play myself," Clive told his agent.

"Not necessarily so. Clive, sweetheart, think about it," Jay Garand said in a mincing and slightly lisping voice. "You will be portraying one of the best known Western figures in our history, but who is it the audience will see? They'll see you, dear boy, and from now on when they think of Buck Elliot, they will also think of Clive Malone.

"Why, it is the perfect opportunity to double your fame. You'll be able to build upon both Buck Elliot's exploits, and your own screen charisma, and in so doing steal whatever fame Elliot has and add it to your own luster."

"Yeah," Clive had agreed, "Yeah, that's right, isn't it? Okay, I'll take the role, but in the meantime, I'm goin' to tell Harris that I'll pick this guy up at the airport. I can tell him that I need to start studying Elliot, if I'm going to be him."

Clive left his car and walked from the parking lot to the terminal, thinking about the conversation he had had with Jay. He knew that his career might well hang on what happened in this next picture, so he intended to do whatever it took to make himself look good. And if it meant augmenting, or even changing the script so as to direct more attention to the Clive Malone his fans knew, and less to the Buck Elliot he would be portraying, then he perfectly prepared to do so.

3

BUCK HAD BEEN TOLD HE WOULD BE MET BY A STUDIO CAR AND as he was looking over the people who had greeted the flight, he expected to see a uniformed chauffer, but was surprised to see Clive Malone himself. He had never met the movie star, but even if he hadn't seen Clive Malone in the movies, he believed he could have picked him out.

While everyone else in the terminal was dressed as one would expect, one man stood out from the others. He was wearing white pants, stuck down into tooled leather boots that were nearly knee high. The trousers were held up by a belt buckle that was a huge turquoise and silver oval. He wore a blue and white vertical striped shirt with a bright red bandana at his neck. The outfit was topped off by a high-crowned ten gallon hat that was encircled by a turquoise-studded silver band.

Smiling more from amusement than social grace, Buck walked toward the man.

"Clive Malone?" he asked.

Clive waved him away with a dismissive motion of his

hand. "I don't have time to sign autographs right now; I'm here to meet someone."

"I imagine that would be me."

"What?"

"You're here to meet Buck Elliot, aren't you? Well, I'm Buck Elliot; I'm here to help you with your next picture."

"You can't be Buck Elliot, you aren't old enough."

"Really?" Buck's smiled grew larger. "I'm sorry I can't be any older than I actually am, but this is all I have."

"I'll be damn. You mean you really are Buck Elliot?"

"I am."

Clive Malone extended his hand. "Come on then. My car is just outside."

As they started through the terminal a young, bright-eyed boy came up to them holding a pen and paper. "Mister Malone, would you sign your autograph?"

"Go away, kid, can't you see I'm busy?"

The star-struck look left the boy's face to be replaced first by an expression of disappointment, then by anger, "That's all right, you ain't Clive Malone anyhow, 'cause the real Clive Malone ain't mean like you," He turned and hurried off.

"I swear it's gotten to where I can't go anywhere without some little brat like that coming up to pester me," Clive said. He sighed, "It's all the price of fame, I suppose."

Buck's first reaction was one of disapproval. Kids had been coming up to him for most of his life, having heard of him, or having read one of the dime novels written about him. Often they would hold out a well-read book asking him to sign it. And even though Buck knew the novels were exaggerations or total untruths, he never turned a kid away.

Of course he had never experienced the fame and instant recognition of someone like Clive Malone who, in addition to all the movies, had his picture published in magazines and newspaper all over the country. Perhaps always being in the public eye could begin to wear on a person, and considering that, Buck decided to withhold judgment.

Clive drove the little Cord as if he had exclusive right to the road, honking only a little more often than he shouted expletives at the other drivers. When they reached The Brown Derby Restaurant, Clive stopped in front of the building.

The Brown Derby looked exactly like its namesake, being in the shape of a big, brown, round-domed hat.

"Have you ever been here before?" Clive asked as he pulled the car to the curb in front of the restaurant.

"No, I haven't," Buck replied.

"Then you're in for a treat."

"The food is good, is it?"

Clive laughed, "Food? Don't be silly, nobody comes to the Brown Derby for food. We come here to see and to be seen." Clive stepped out of the car.

"The sign says no parking."

"Don't worry about that. The valet will take care of the car," Clive replied, as he tossed the keys to a uniformed man who approached them.

"Mr. Malone, it is so good to see you, sir," the *maître de* said, his greeting dripping with obsequiousness. "Mr. Harris is waiting for you at his table."

"Thank you, Royce, I can find my own way."

"Very good, sir."

As Buck followed Clive through the dining room, Clive pointed out some of the people.

"That's Douglass Fairbanks talking to Joan Crawford and Gloria Swanson. And that's John Barrymore with King Vidor and Erich von Stroheim."

"I've heard of John Barrymore, but I don't think I recognize the other two names," Buck said.

"They're just two of the most important directors in Hollywood."

As they made their way through the room, there were effusive greetings between Clive and several of the other patrons, some of whom, like Lon Chaney and Lillian Gish, Buck recognized. Many, he did not.

When they reached a table in the corner two men stood to greet them. One of the men was rather plump, with a red face, bulbous nose, and heavy eyebrows over pale blue eyes. The other man was thin, almost to the point of being skinny. He had thinning hair and brown eyes that were enlarged by the thick glasses he was wearing.

"Meet Alcy Harris," Clive said, indicating the red-faced man. "He's the head of Starburst Motion Picture Studios. And this is Ryan Gilmore, the screenwriter. Gentlemen, I give you Buck Elliot."

Buck shook hands with both men, and when he was offered a chair at the table he hesitated for a moment, then pointed to an empty chair on the other side of the table.

"If you don't mind, I'd rather sit there. It's just an old habit of mine," Buck said, shaking his head, "and I'm too old to break it now."

"Wild Bill Hickok," Gilmore said, raising his finger and smiling at the observation.

"Wild Bill Hickok?" Harris asked, confused by the comment.

"Wild Bill Hickok was sitting with his back to the room when Jack McCall slipped up behind him and shot him in the back," Gilmore explained.

"You're quite right, Mr. Gilmore," Buck said. "And Wild Bill had asked for a chair that would have had his back against the wall. I never forget that."

Harris laughed. "Mr. Elliot, surely you don't expect someone in The Brown Derby to shoot you in the back "

"As I said, I'm too old to break the habit now," Buck replied.

"Then, by all means, sit here," Harris invited pointing to the vacant chair. "I'll have the place setting moved."

"Thank you," Buck said, walking around the table and sitting so that his back was against the wall. This seat afforded him a good view of the dining room.

"Now that we're all settled I want to thank you for agreeing to be the consultant to our picture," Harris said. "We'll pay you a thousand dollars per week while the film is in production, and I expect it will take us at least eight weeks to shoot the picture. Is that compensation agreeable?"

"Yes," Buck said, his eyebrows rising. The truth is he hadn't even considered that he would be paid. His principle reason for accepting the position was to make certain that his life's story would get a creditable telling.

"Well then, gentlemen," Harris said with an agreeable smile, "I would say that we have just established the beginning of a most productive relationship." Reaching for a stack of paper, Harris handed it to Buck. "Here is Mr. Gilmore's latest screenplay. I trust that his interpretation of your story will meet with your approval."

"Mr. Elliot, how many men have you killed?" Gilmore asked.

"I haven't killed anyone today," Buck replied, taking the script, "but then, today isn't over."

"What?" Clive Malone asked with a shocked expression on his face.

Harris laughed, "Clive, I think our friend is just having some fun with us."

Clive Malone's remark that people came to the Brown Derby to see and be seen was soon evident. More than half a dozen times someone came to the table to speak, with Tom Mix being the latest star to stop by.

19

"So, Clive, I hear you're to portray Buck Elliot in your next film," Tom Mix said and then he laughed. "Does *Elliot* know it's you who's going to play him?"

"Of course he knows," Clive answered, barely able to keep the irritation from his voice, "This is the man, himself." Clive gestured toward Buck.

"Buck Elliot," Mix said with a broad smile on his face. He extended his hand across the table and standing, Buck took it. "I'm very pleased to meet you."

"Thank you, but the pleasure is mine," Buck said.

"No, sir, it is I who should thank you," Mix said. "Clive and I get to try to portray heroes on the screen, but you have lived the life of a genuine hero." He looked directly at Clive. "We're both phonies and we know it. Perhaps I'll see you again sometime, but I must be going now."

"I would like that," Buck said as he sat down.

"What an arrogant buffoon he is," Clive muttered after Tom Mix was out of earshot. "I've never seen anyone so full of himself. He loves to brag that he's lived the roles he now plays, but that doesn't make his acting any good. Have you ever seen a more wooden actor than Tom Mix?"

Although Buck could tell by the expressions on their faces that neither Harris nor Gilmore agreed with Clive, they said nothing to dispute his remark.

"I was thinking you and I might have a friend in common," Buck said as Clive was driving him to his hotel.

"Oh? And who would that be?"

"I read that you grew up near Chugwater, Wyoming," Buck said. "I have a good friend there, a fella by the name of Mike Lindell."

"The name doesn't sound familiar."

"Well, Mike is considerably older than you are, but the Double Diamond is the biggest ranch in the Chugwater Valley. I just thought you might have heard of him, or at least his ranch."

"I've come a long way since then," Clive said, "and I've met a lot of people. It's not unusual, I suppose, that some of them have dropped by the wayside. The Double Diamond you say?"

"Yes."

"Hmm, now that you mention it, I do know about that ranch." Clive chuckled. "But I was just a cowboy then; I didn't run in highfalutin' company."

Alcy Harris had arranged for a suite for Buck at the Hotel Normandie. It was the most elegant hotel Buck had ever visited, and as he walked through the three room suite, with its gold plated fixtures, plush carpeting and heavy draperies, he couldn't help but compare it to some of the bunkhouses he had lived in starting at the age of twelve.

Buck chuckled as he made the comparison. "Yes, sir, I've come a long way since then." He repeated the phrase Clive Malone had used.

When Buck went to dinner that evening, the opulence of the hotel carried over into its restaurant. A white jacketed waiter who walked as if he had a board tied to his back, poured water, then handed Buck a menu, which was encased in a blue leather cover. The words, *Café de l'hôtel Normandie* were written in gold script on the outside.

"As you can see by the menu, sir, our *Spéciale du jour is poulet cuit dans du vin avec des champignons, servi avec pommes de terre rôties et crème sure.*"

"Yeah, that sounds pretty good," Buck said. He smiled at the waiter, "What the hell is it?"

"Our specialty of the day is chicken cooked in wine with mushrooms, served with roasted potatoes and sour cream."

"Wine? With prohibition?"

"It is a special cooking wine, sir," The waiter looked around to make certain he wasn't being overheard, then he leaned over so he could speak quietly. "Cooking wine is supposed to be salted to prevent it from being drunk, but our cooks have developed a special way of removing the salt. The results are quite pleasing."

Buck closed the menu. "I think I'll just have beans, bacon, and a biscuit."

The waiter's eyes grew large, "I beg your pardon, sir?"

Buck chuckled, "On second thought, bring me a steak and baked potato. And you can cook the steak in some of that unsalted wine."

The waiter smiled. "Yes, sir."

The steak was cooked to perfection and Buck didn't know when he had enjoyed a meal more. As he ate his dinner, though, he realized that he had become the object of attention for several of the other diners. He was able to over-hear the conversation from one of the closer tables.

"Buck Elliot? That's Buck Elliot? Isn't he some old U.S. Marshal, or gunfighter or something?"

"Something like that. Anyhow, I hear that Starburst is making a movie about him."

"No kidding! You mean he's going to be an actor?"

"I don't know, I haven't heard what his deal is. I really don't know why he's here."

That was a good question, Buck thought. He wasn't a hundred percent sure why he was here, either.

The first thing Buck did when he returned to his room was to pick up Gilmore's script and begin to read.

Legend of a Gunfighter
Screenplay by
Ryan Gilmore

PRODUCTION DRAFT

TITLES AND CREDITS
FADE IN:
INT. SHACK -NIGHT

The CAMERA MOVES through a small room. The room is dark, but not too dark to see what is inside. It is empty except for a saddle, a pair of boots, and a holstered pistol lying on the wide-plank floor. A man is sleeping, his only protection from the floor being the saddle blanket and bedroll. This is Buck Elliot.

The door of the shack bursts open and a Gunman crashes in. He has a six gun in each hand and he is blazing away.
CAMERA ON Buck Elliot, who has been awakened and rolls away from his blankets. He has a gun is his hand and from the floor is returning the gunman's fire. The bullets from the intruder's gun smash into the floor near Buck, but none of them strike him. Buck's return fire is more accurate, and the gunman is slammed against the wall, then slides down to the floor, dead.
CAMERA ON blood on the wall.
Buck gets to his feet, then walks over to have a look at the body.

BUCK
Who are you. Mister, and why did you come in here a' shootin' like you just done?

CUT TO:

23

EXT. Buck rides (various shots) - showing passage of day and night.

CUT TO:
DAY: Buck rides through the desert with the sun beating down on him. He dismounts takes a short pull from his canteen then pours some water into his hat and gives it to his horse.

CAMERA ON horse drinking from hat

BUCK (talking to his horse)
I don't see a damn thing but sand and sun.

SOUND: Horse whinnies
Buck remounts.

BUCK
I wonder who that fella was. Was he someone who wanted to kill me on his own? Or did Nigel Smythe send him? If he was sent by Smythe, I'm sure there will be more.

SOUND: Horse whinnies

BUCK
So, you agree with me, do you?

Buck sighed, then lay the script aside. If what he had read so far was indicative of how the movie was going to be, then he was going to have his work cut out for him. He had no idea where the writer had come up with the opening scene. Buck had a very good memory and could recall in great detail significant events of his life. And never, at any time, had he been sleeping in a small shack and been surprised by a gunman sneaking in on him.

Buck laced his hands behind his head and stared at the ceiling as he recalled the event that Ernest Haycox had written correctly as the first event of a series of incidents that would lead to what ultimately came to be the book called *Legend of a Gunfighter*.

MOGOLLON RIM, ARIZONA – 1885

The man who was stringing barbed wire was wearing worn jeans, a faded red shirt, and an old hat. This was Isaac Mitchell, the owner of the Bar M Ranch. At the moment, he was pounding one nail into the fence post while holding three more nails in his mouth. He was so involved in his task that he didn't see the two riders until they were within a hundred yards of him.

Isaac watched as the two riders approached. One was tall and round shouldered with a face that was carved by lines of cruelty and harshness, the other had the look of someone who had travelled down many a hard trail.

When they were close enough for conversation, Isaac took the nails from his mouth and addressed them.

"Howdy, fellers. You men lookin' for directions?"

"This here's the Bar M Ranch, ain' it?" one of the men asked.

"Yes, this is the Bar M," Isaac answered.

"Then we don't need no direction." At that both men pulled their guns and began firing. Isaac pitched forward but the fence prevented him from falling all the way to the ground. His left arm was draped over the barbed wire, and he was still grasping the hammer with his right.

"Isaac?" A woman screamed running from the house after hearing the gunshots. She saw her husband draped over the fence and the three mounted men, with smoking guns in their hands, "What have you done?" she called out, more aggrieved than frightened.

The two men fired again and the woman fell at her husband's feet.

From the *Canyon Diablo Brimstone:*

Local Rancher Killed by Cattle Rustlers

On the 5th Instant, a person or persons unknown visited the Bar M Ranch, said property belonging to Isaac Mitchell. It was not a social call for Mr. Mitchell and his wife, Matilda, were both killed.

That the killings were murder is not in dispute, for the deceased was found to be unarmed. It is believed that this was the result of cattle rustlers, as Mr. Mitchell's herd was noticeably depleted. Mr. Mitchell was a former sergeant in the U.S. Army having served with General George Cook in the campaign against the Apache Indians.

When informed of the murder of one of his neighbors, Nigel Smythe issued a statement. "Our valley is being devastated by this rogue band of cattle thieves. Why, my own ranch, Eagleshire on the Sherlons Fork, has suffered grievous losses in cattle as a result of the rampant lawlessness. It is my hope that whoever committed this foul deed be found and punished to the fullest extent of the law, and to that end I shall personally offer a reward of five hundred dollars."

Sheriff Jones has announced that he has no leads and has asked anyone who might have some knowledge as to the identity of the outlaws to come forth with the information.

Albuquerque, New Mexico Territory:

A tall, slender young man dismounted in front of the post office. The features of his face, light blue eyes, narrow nose, and a clean-shaven, square jaw line, were such that women found handsome. His men friends considered him to be honest and honorable, a man "to ride to the river with." When he stepped inside, the postal clerk greeted him with a smile.

"It's good that you dropped in today, Mr. Elliot. I just received a letter for you."

Buck Elliot thanked the clerk, retrieved the letter, then headed for the Pronghorn Saloon. He ordered a beer, found a quiet table that was remote from the others, and there, began to read his mail.

Dear Buck,

It has been almost twenty years since you and I hunted up more than five hundred head of cows and hired a couple of drovers to help us drive the herd to Kansas. We've both gone our own ways since then, but I have fond memories of that time.

I have been told that you are a man who moves from state to state in a restless drift which proposes no particular destination nor has a sense of purpose, but that you often right wrongs when such are encountered.

The purpose of this letter is to solicit your help in overcoming a wrong that is being directed not only toward me, but toward many of my friends and neighbors as well. If there resides in you the memory of an old friend with whom you once shared hardship and danger, and if that friendship moves you to charity, I beg of you to come to my aid now.

You will find my ranch, Trailcross, seven miles west of the town
of Canyon Diablo, Arizona Territory
    Your friend in hope,
    Sean Kelly

After reading the letter Buck went immediately to the tele-graph office to inform Sean of his intention.

I HAVE RECEIVED YOUR LETTER AND I AM COMING
- Buck Elliot

When Buck stepped down from the train the next day his first impression of the little town of Canyon Diablo was one of incredible heat. It bore down on him like some great weight, and heat waves shimmered up from the streets so that Buck wondered what kept the town from just melting.

Buck stood by as his horse, Scout, was unloaded from the stock car which had accompanied the train. After the train pulled away, he saw that the tracks seemed to be a dividing line for the road that crossed the track had two distinct identities. South of the tracks there were a dozen or more abode build-ings and the few signs that were visible were in Spanish. North of the tracks the road had a much more American flavor with the buildings primarily of wood or brick construction and the signs all in English. There were two cross-streets which consisted mostly of dwellings; some were substantial, while others were ramshackle structures. He saw the steeples of two churches: St. Francis Catholic Church on First Street, and the Church of Salvation, on Second Street. The line of business buildings facing each other across the main street, which was called Hell Street, included two saloons, a feed store, a hotel, a courthouse and the city hall. Wedged between these business-es were a couple of cafés, a general store, and a hardware store, that also served as the mortuary. At the far end of the street, set aside from the other buildings, was a sheriff's office.

Buck tied his horse off at a hitching rail in front of the Mogollon Saloon, so named because of the nearby Mogollon Rim, a range of mountains that connected Arizona with New Mexico.

The cool interior of the Mogollon Saloon beckoned him. A sign outside promised cold beer, and after a long, hot train ride, Buck thought nothing could be better than that. He pushed his way through the bat wing doors and went inside. It was so dark that he had to stand there for a moment or two until his eyes adjusted. He learned, quickly, that the "coolness" promised by the shadowed interior of the saloon was only an illusion. It was just as hot inside as it was outside. There was, however, no sun beating down on him and that at least, was welcomed.

As his eyes gradually adjusted to the decreased light, he was able to examine the saloon and saw that the bar was made of burnished mahogany with a highly polished brass foot rail. Crisp, clean white towels hung from hooks on the customers' side of the bar, spaced every four feet. A mirror was behind the bar, flanked on each side by small statues of nude women set back in special niches. A row of whiskey bottles sat in front of the mirror, reflected in the glass so that the row of bottles seemed to be two deep. A bartender, with a waxed handlebar moustache, stood behind the bar indus-triously polishing glasses. He was wearing a red vest with a red and white striped shirt.

"Is your beer cool?" Buck asked.

"Cooler 'n horse piss," the bartender replied.

Buck smiled at the response. "That's good enough for me. I'll have a beer." He put a coin on the bar.

When a mug of golden brew was set before him, Buck picked it up, then with Adam's apple–bobbing gulps, drained the entire glass before setting it down.

"Another one," he said, wiping the foam from his lips with the back of his hand.

"You like our beer, do you?" the bartender asked.

"I don't know, I didn't taste it," Buck replied, "That one was for thirst; this one will be for taste."

The bartender chuckled as he set another one before him.

Buck picked up the second beer, took a swallow, and nodded appreciatively before he turned to look around the place. He was sipping, rather than drinking this beer. There were two bargirls working the floor, moving from table to table to smile and make flirtatious comments to the men. At the back of the room a piano player was playing the plaintive strains of *Lorena*. At one of the tables a card game was in progress and he watched it for a few minutes.

The back door opened and a tall, broad-shouldered, bearded man wearing a lawman's badge stepped in through the door. He was holding a pistol in his hand and he pointed the gun toward the table where the men were playing cards.

"Lon Etherton, I am Deputy U.S. Marshal Abraham Johnson, and you're under arrest."

"What is it you're arrestin' me for?"

"For the murder of Isaac Mitchell."

"You aint got no . . ." Etherton paused in mid-sentence looked toward one of the men he had been playing cards with.

"Jurisdiction," the man said, and though he spoke quietly, Buck could hear him.

"Jurisdiction," Etherton said. "Yeah, you ain't got no jurisdiction in this county. Sheriff Jones is the only one that's got 'ny jurisdiction here."

"That's where you're wrong, Etherton. As a deputy US marshal I can arrest you here, in California, in Texas, or in New York. My jurisdiction covers the whole country. Now you can either come peaceably alive, or you can come peaceably dead. Either way, you're goin' to be comin' with me so which will it be?"

Buck, like the others, was watching the drama unfold when he heard something—a soft squeaking sound as if weight were being put on a loose board. He looked up toward the top of the stairs and saw a man standing there, aiming a shotgun at Johnson's back.

"Marshal, shotgun above!" Buck shouted. When he shouted the warning the man who was standing on the upstairs overlook turned his weapon toward Buck, and without so much as a word, pulled the trigger.

The shotgun boomed loudly.

The moment Buck saw the shotgun move in his direction he reacted swiftly, almost automatically dropping his beer, jumping to one side, and drawing his pistol as he did so. He pulled the trigger within an instant after the man at the top of the stairs fired. The heavy charge of buckshot tore a large hole in the bar right where Buck had just been standing. The shotgun blast also smashed some bottles and broke the mirror. The mirror fell except for a few jagged shards which hung in place to reflect distorted images of the dramatic scene before it.

Buck's shot had been more accurately placed, and the man with the shotgun dropped his weapon and grabbed his neck. He stood there for just a moment, clutching his neck as blood spilled between his fingers. Then his eyes rolled up in his head and he started down twisting around as he fell so that, on his back and head-first, he slid down the stairs, following his clattering shotgun to the ground floor. He lay motionless below the bottom step with open, but sightless eyes staring up toward the ceiling.

The sound of the two gunshots had riveted everyone's attention to that exchange. While attention was diverted from him, Etherton took the opportunity to go for his own gun. Suddenly the saloon was filled with the roar of another gunshot as Etherton fired at Johnson, who had made the mistake of being diverted by the gunplay between Buck and the shotgun shooter. It was a fatal mistake. Etherton's bullet struck Johnson in the forehead and the impact knocked him back on a near-by table. Johnson lay on the table, his head hanging down on the far side as blood dripped forming a puddle below him. His gun fell from his lifeless hand and clattered to the floor. Etherton then turned his pistol toward Buck. Seeing that he was about to be a target, Buck fired first and Etherton went down, dead before he hit the floor.

"What's goin' on in here?" a voice asked, "What's all the shootin'?"

When Buck turned toward the sound of the voice he saw a man standing just inside the open door. Because the brightness of the light behind him contrasted with the darkness of the room, Buck couldn't make out his features.

"Move out of the door, the light is behind you," Buck growled.

"You don't tell me what to do, I . . ."

Buck pulled the hammer back and his pistol made a deadly metallic click as the sear engaged the cylinder.

"Mister I told you to move and if you don't do it, I'll kill you where you stand."

The figure moved out of the light. When he did, Buck saw that he was wearing a sheriff's badge.

"I didn't know you were the law," Buck said as he put his pistol away.

"Sheriff Jones, I'm glad you came," one of the men who had been playing cards said, "This here fella just shot Wilson 'n Etherton, down in cold blood."

"You lying son of a bitch," Buck said, bristling in quick anger, "I don't know who you are but . . . "

"That's Lanny Parker," the sheriff said. "He's my deputy and if he says you kilt them two men then I'm goin' to have to take you in."

5

ALTHOUGH BUCK HAD ALREADY HOLSTERED HIS PISTOL, IT suddenly appeared in his hand again, the draw as fast as the wink of an eye.

"Sheriff, I don't know what this man saw, or thinks he saw, but apparently that man lying belly up on the table over there is a US marshal who had come for this man," Buck said. He pointed to the man who had been identified as Etherton.

"When the lawman announced his intention of taking Etherton in, this man," Buck pointed to the man lying at the bottom of the floor, "aimed a shotgun at the lawman. I shouted an alarm, and this man turned his shotgun on me. I killed him. Etherton killed the lawman, then Etherton and I exchanged shots and I killed him."

"So you admit that you killed two of them," the sheriff said.

"My involvement in this was strictly self-defense. Before this started I didn't know the name of either one of these men, and I still don't know the name of the man with the shotgun. I had no motive for killing either one of them, other than self-preservation."

"Sheriff Jones, this here fella is telling the truth," one of saloon patrons said. "Wilson started shootin' first, usin' that scatter gun that's lyin' there on the floor beside 'im. Take a look at the bar there and you'll see what I'm talkin' about. Then Etherton killed the lawman that's lyin' over there on the table 'n after he done that, why he turned on this here feller. But this here feller managed to kill Etherton a' fore Etherton could kill him."

"And that suited you just fine, didn't it, Wilkerson? Correct me if I'm wrong, but Etherton and Wilson both rode for Nigel Smythe. And you 'n Smythe don't get along all that well, do you?"

"Who the hell does get along with Smythe?" Wilkerson asked. "That son of a bitch owns half of the Mogollon Valley, 'n he's tryin' to gobble up all the rest of us smaller ranchers by runnin' us out of business. But that don't have nothin' to do with what happened here. I'm tellin' you the gospel truth about what I saw."

"Wilkerson ain't lying, sheriff," the bartender said.

"What are you sayin', McDaniels?"

"I'm sayin' that this feller," the bartender pointed to Buck, "was in the right. And except for Lanny Parker, you can ask anybody in here and they'll all say the same thing."

There was a general buzz of agreement from all the other patrons in the saloon.

Sheriff Jones glared at Wilkerson for a moment longer, then he looked back at Buck.

"What's your name, Mister?"

"Elliot. Buck Elliot."

"Buck Elliot," someone said in a low, but awe-struck voice. "Lord have mercy, I've heard of that feller."

A brief widening of the eyes and a tightening of the cheeks indicated that Sheriff Jones had also heard of Buck Elliot.

"All right, Elliot, with all these witnesses I don't reckon I can make any kind of a case against you," the sheriff said as he pointed to Buck. "But I'm tellin' you right now, I'll be a' keepin' my eye on you." He turned, and walked out.

"Sheriff Jones, wait!" Parker called. He hurried to join the sheriff in making an exit.

"Sheriff Jones didn't seem all that interested in what happened to Marshal Johnson," Buck said after the sheriff left.

"I'm the one that sent a letter to Marshal Johnson," Wilkerson said. "Isaac Mitchell was my friend. I know damn well Etherton kilt him, but when I told the sheriff, he didn't do nothin' about it."

"What did you expect? Emile Jones is in Nigel Smythe's pocket," the bartender explained. He drew another beer and set it in front of Buck. "You didn't get to finish your beer. My name is Ben. Ben McDaniels and this one is on the house."

"Thanks, Ben," Buck said. He looked at the young cowboy who had backed him up. "And I want to thank you, too, Mr. Wilkerson, for telling the sheriff how it was."

"Call me Dub, 'n truth to tell, you prob'ly made yourself a lot of friends around here, today."

"How's that?" Buck asked.

Dub Wilkerson nodded toward the bodies which were now being carried out of the saloon.

"Like the Sheriff said, Etherton 'n Wilson both worked for Nigel Smythe, and Jones is in Smythe's pocket. If it had been up to the sheriff, Marshal Johnson would've been shot down today, and nothing would have happened to Etherton or Wilson. I reckon the town folk are all goin' to figure justice was served."

"Why don't you tell him the rest of it, Dub?" Ben asked.

"Yeah, well, when word gets around about what happened, you'll wind up having made yourself about as many enemies as you have friends," Wilkerson said. "And Simon Lodeen, Adam Stillwell and Frank Corbett aren't the kind of enemies a man wants to have. Smythe tries to pass 'em off as cowboys, but what they really are is . . ."

"Gunmen," Buck interjected before Wilkerson could finish his sentence, "Yes, I've heard of them."

"I thought maybe you had. They've got themselves quite a reputation."

"You see, Elliot," Ben continued, "what you have stumbled in to, is sort of a war."

"A war?"

"Yes, with Smythe and all his hands on one side, and the smaller ranchers and the townspeople on the other side."

"Not all the townspeople," Dub corrected.

"Sheriff Jones?" Buck asked.

"And Teasdale, who owns the holding pens," Dub added. "He makes it really hard for us to ship our cattle out, because he charges us three times as much as he does Smythe. He says Smythe gets a break because he does so much more business with him than the small ranchers do."

Tristan James Clay was the owner, editor, and publisher of the newspaper, *The Canyon Diablo Brimstone*. Buck's arrival in town occurred at exactly the right time because Clay was just putting the next day's newspaper together and what had been the lead . . . a story about a new organ being installed in the Church of Salvation . . . was replaced with a story of the gunfight.

Yesterday's Fateful Events

Yesterday in the Mogollon Saloon, Deputy U. S. Marshal Abraham Johnson attempted to serve a legitimate warrant of arrest upon the

person of Lon Etherton, and in less time than it will take you to
read this article, three men were hurled into eternity.

In the story that followed, the editor of *The Brimstone* left
no doubt as to where he stood. Although all good men of the
town would lament the passing of Marshal Abraham Johnson, there would be no tears shed over the deaths of Bill
Wilson and Lon Etherton.

Viscount Nigel Smythe, who lived ten miles from town on
his ranch Eagleshire on Sherlons Fork, received two visitors.
In England Smythe would be addressed as "My Lord", and
though he could no longer use the title, he was quick to point
out to others that he was a member of the Peerage. Smythe
was but a couple of inches under six feet tall, had rusty hair,
very light blue eyes, and a face that was free of beard or
moustache and unremarkable except for a somewhat
red tint.

After receiving his two visitors, Sheriff Jones and Deputy
Parker, Smythe removed a cigar from a silver humidor, cut
the end off with a gold snipper, ran his tongue down the side,
then lit it and took several puffs until the end of the cigar
was well aglow. Once his head was wreathed in aromatic
smoke he took the cigar from his mouth and held it out to
look at it, admirably.

"I would offer you lads a cigar," he said, speaking for the
first time as he closed the humidor, "but these are from
Cuba, *Canaria d'Oro*, which are the finest and most expensive
cigars in the world. I'm afraid it would be a shame to waste
such a gem on someone who lacked the total appreciation
one might need to enjoy it. It would be rather like feeding
swine. Whether you set before a *porcus* a fine chef-prepared
meal on a plate of china, or offer for his meal the leftover

food tossed away by the cook, a pig will eat with equal enjoyment."

"Yeah, well I smoke cigarettes," Parker said, not quite understanding the insult Smythe had just delivered.

"Why are you gentlemen here?" Smythe asked.

"We're here on account of Etherton 'n Wilson got themselves kilt," Jones said.

"Yes, I have heard. Do you know the particulars?"

"Do we know what?" Jones asked.

Smythe sighed in frustration, "Do you know what happened?"

"I know, 'cause I seen it," Parker said. "I seen it all. The feller that done it was named Buck Elliot."

"Then please do tell me what happened," Smythe said.

Parker began to give a full account, though he was speaking very slowly and enunciating every word.

*"Deputy Parker, you needn't speak so slowly, I understand English, and the patois you are using is close enough to English that I believe I will be able to follow you."

"Yes, sir. Well, the thing is, Etherton, why, he wasn't expectin' no stranger to take a hand in a private fight, 'n while the stranger was killin' Wilson, Etherton was a' killin' the marshal. But by the time he got done a' shootin' the marshal, this here Elliot feller, why, he already had the drop on Etherton. I seen that myself. 'N Elliot just up and pulled the trigger."

"Was this Elliot that good? Or was he just lucky?" Smythe asked.

"Well, sir, I couldn't rightly say that he was all that good," Parker said, answering the question, "I mean, seein' as he already had his gun out. But he was good enough, I reckon."

"Why didn't you take a hand in it?" Smythe asked. "You were there."

"I didn't have no idea none of this was goin' to happen, I

mean, it all happened so fast 'n all. First thing you know there was all this shootin' goin' on, and the next thing you know this here stranger was standin' there holdin' a gun in his hand. What was I supposed to do?" Parker asked, defending himself.

"Why was the federal constabulary there?"

"The what?" Parker asked.

"Why was the U.S. marshal there?" Smythe asked, clarifying his earlier question.

"Well, what he said was, he was there to arrest Etherton for the murder of Isaac Mitchell."

Smythe took several more puffs from his cigar, squinting through the smoke his puffing had created.

"The question that concerns me, you see, is how did a U.S. Marshal get involved in the first place? I thought you had cleared Etherton."

"No, sir, Mr. Smythe, now I couldn't actual clear him," Sheriff Jones said. "What I done was, I told the judge that I didn't have enough evidence to arrest 'im."

"You know what I'm thinkin'? I'm a' thinkin' that someone must of told Marshal Johnson about it," Parker said.

"What a brilliant deduction," Smythe said, sarcastically. "Of course someone told Marshal Johnson about it. The question is who did it?"

"Yes, sir, but that ain't the only question we got to worry about," Sheriff Jones said. "The other question is who sent for Buck Elliot?"

"Elliot? You are talking about the man who killed Etherton and Wilson?" Smythe asked.

"Yes, sir."

"What makes you think someone sent for him?"

"Well, when it first happened I didn't know who the man was that shot your men, but I found out pretty quick that it was Buck Elliot. And I don't figure a man like Buck Elliot would just happen to drop in on a little town like Canyon Diablo without he had some sort of reason. 'N I'm pretty sure the reason is because someone sent for him."

"You speak of this Buck Elliot as if you know him."

"No, sir, that is, I don't actual know him, but I sure do know who he is. Truth is, I'm kind of surprised you haven't never heard of 'im neither. Why, he's one of the fastest men with a gun there is."

"I have not been in America long enough to know of all the aficionados who are so proficient in the art of the rapid withdrawal and shooting of a pistol, that they become folk heroes," Smythe said. "But you gave me cause to believe that Lodeen, Stillwell, and Corbett were such men. Have I been misled?"

"No, sir, you ain't been told wrong at all. Them three is three of the best there is."

"Are they better than this man, Buck Elliot?"

"I . . ." Sheriff Jones paused for a moment before he answered, "Well, the truth is that I don't know as any one of 'em is as good or better than Elliot, but they's three of 'em, 'n Elliot is all by hisself. So there ain't no doubt in my mind but that the three of 'em won't have no problem with Buck Elliot, no matter who it is that sent for 'im."

"There is only one problem with that scenario you just presented, sheriff."

"What problem is that?"

"If I were Buck Elliot, and my shooting skills were equal to, or even superior to each of them, I would make certain to arrange any encounter on a one to one basis."

"Yeah," Jones said, I'll have to tell them that."

6

Hollywood, California – 1931:

Buck was awakened by a telephone call.

"Buck, have you had your breakfast yet? This is Clive."

"No." Buck didn't want to say that he wasn't even out of bed yet.

"Grab a bite to eat, and I'll pick you up in an hour."

True to his telephone call, Clive showed up in front of the hotel within the hour.

"How was your night?" Clive asked as they turned off Normandie Avenue onto Wilshire Boulevard.

"I was tired from the trip, so I slept well."

"Yeah, at your age I can understand how traveling could be tiring," Clive said.

Buck was offended by the inference that he was some-how, physically limited because of his age. Buck had kept himself in good condition, and he was reasonably certain he could handle any activity as well as Clive could.

"Did you read the script Gilmore gave you?"

"Just a few pages before I went to sleep," Buck replied.

"I would ask you what you think about it, but if you didn't read more than a few pages, I doubt if you have any opinion about it. But I can tell you right now, that script isn't going to stay the way it is. I plan to see to it that there are some major changes."

"Really? Well, I have to tell you from what I've read so far, it could use some changes," Buck said.

"Good! I'm glad you and I agree on this, Buck. We can be partners in seeing to it that the script is rewritten in a way that suits us both."

Twenty minutes after they left the hotel, Clive pulled up to the gate that led onto the Starburst Studio lot. He parked his car in a spot that was marked for him.

Buck had never been on a movie lot before, and he was amused by all the activity.

Two men walked by, engaged in spirited conversation. The two men were wearing buckskin shirts and trousers, and Buck could almost believe he was back in Colorado attending a fur trappers' Rendezvous.

"Damn!"

"What is it?" Clive asked.

"Those two men they're wearing . . ."

"Oh, you mean the buckskins? They're in costume for a movie we're doing about mountain men. Surely you met some mountain men in your time," Clive said.

"Quite a few, actually," Buck said, "But these are the first two mountain men that I've ever seen with eye makeup, painted cheeks and lip rouge."

Clive laughed. "I expect you'll be seein' a lot of that before this trip is over. You need makeup for the camera. Otherwise all the lights will be so bright that it'll wash out the faces so that their own mama wouldn't recognize them."

A pirate came walking by then, followed a moment later by two beautiful young women in short dresses and cloche hats with two men wearing gangster-like pinstripe suits.

"We'll be doing a story conference in here," Clive said, pointing to one of the buildings. A sign showed a background of stars, with one much larger and brighter that the others.

STARBURST PICTURE STUDIOS ---Where Dreams Come to Life

There were four men inside, two of whom Buck had already met: Alcy Harris and Ryan Gilmore. Clive introduced Buck to the other two.

"This is Guy Lashlee; he'll be directing the picture," Clive said, indicating a tall, thin man. "And this is Stan Cooper, our AD."

"Did you get a chance to read any of the script, Mr. Elliot?" Harris asked, in a repeat of Clive's earlier question.

"I read the opening scene," Buck replied.

"What did you think of it?"

Buck shook his head. "I've never been in a shootout in a cabin in the middle of the night."

"Oh, don't mind that. It isn't meant to be literal," Guy Lashlee said.

"What do you mean it isn't meant to be literal? This is about my life, isn't it? From the book Ernest Haycox wrote? Why don't you use his book? He got the story right."

"That's what is called the exposition, and it's used so that the audience learns the setting and the characters. It's a technique that is frequently used at the very beginning, where the conflict is first introduced," Guy Lashlee said.

"Principle photography begins next Monday. You'll see how the story develops and you'll like what you see. In the meantime, you and Ryan can work out any differences you may have, and with Clive's approval, we can get this thing in the can," Harris said.

"Mr. Elliot," Ryan Gilmore said as the meeting broke up, "would you let me buy you a cup of coffee so we can talk for a moment or two?"

"Yes," Buck answered, "I think that's a good idea."

When the two men left the conference room, Buck started toward the cantina.

"No," Gilmore said, "that's not a good place to talk—too many ears there. I know a place on Wilshire where we can go."

"All right, but you'll have to give me a ride. I've been depending on Clive to take me everywhere."

"Clive didn't tell you about the car rental service?"

"I know I can rent a car, I just haven't gotten around to it yet."

Gilmore shook his head. "You don't need to rent a car. The studio has an arrangement with Hertz to supply cars to visiting dignitaries and, as a script consultant, you certainly qualify to have a car furnished for you. And believe me, you don't want to be beholding to Clive Malone for anything."

"I'm beginning to think that," Buck said. "Thanks."

A few minutes later Buck smiled as the waitress in the coffee shop put not only a cup of coffee in front of him, but also a piece of apple pie.

"The Purity Café makes the best apple pie in LA and I don't even have to ask for it anymore. Janice brings it to me automatically."

"Well, I thank you for the coffee and the pie."

"You know, Buck, Clive Malone isn't your friend." Gilmore chuckled, "But then, he isn't a friend to anyone, except Carroll Luscombe."

"Carroll Luscombe?"

"Yep, that's his real name. He was born and raised in New York."

"Wait, are you saying he grew up in New York?"

"That's right."

"That explains it," Buck said.

"Explains what?"

"I read that he grew up near Chugwater, Wyoming. It so happens that I have a good friend who is from Chugwater, in fact, he has the biggest ranch in that part of Wyoming. But when I asked Clive about him, he said he'd never heard of him."

"Is this what you read?" Gilmore asked. "*Raised on a ranch near Chugwater, Wyoming, Clive Malone was herding cattle by the time he was twelve years old. He joined the army as a young man of 17, and was with the American Expeditionary Forces on the Western Front. Later he was a deputy sheriff in Idaho, and a U.S. Marshal in South Dakota.* Is that the article you're talking about?"

"Yes, you read it too?"

Gilmore chuckled, "Read it? I wrote it, and I made all of that stuff up, I work for the studio, remember, and when you're promoting a cowboy star, the fans don't want to know that when their Western hero was in his teens he ran numbers for one of the biggest crime bosses in New York City."

"Really," Buck replied. "Well, I have to give him credit for coming as far as he has; I mean from a kid on the streets of New York to a cowboy star in the movies. How was he able to do that?"

"It was what you call a happy coincidence. He met and

befriended Rudolf Valentino and when Valentino became famous, Clive traded on that friendship to get his own break in the movies."

"The funny thing is, I think that would make a better story than the one you made up," Buck said.

"Oh, I agree with you. But like I told you, I work for the studio, so I write what they tell me to write, which brings me to the reason I invited you to have coffee with me. How much of the script have you read?"

"I must confess that I've only read the opening scene."

"And it wasn't like anything in the book by Ernest Haycox, was it?"

"No."

"Read this," Gilmore said, handing a file folder to Buck, "Don't worry, it isn't the entire script, it's only the opening scene."

"I read the opening scene, remember?"

"Huh, uh, you didn't read this opening scene."

Legend of a Gunfighter
Screenplay by
Ryan Gilmore

PRODUCTION DRAFT
TITLES AND CREDITS
FADE IN:

EXT. ENTERING CANYON DIABLO – DAY
The CAMERA MOVES down the street of the town, pausing long enough to identify some of the buildings; SIKES HARDWARE, the

newspaper office, CANYON DIABLO BRIMSTONE, the
MOGOLLON SALOON.
There are PEOPLE walking on the boardwalks. A BUCKBOARD,
being pulled down the street meets a lone rider going in the opposite
direction. The rider is BUCK ELLIOT.

CONTINUOUS
Buck Elliot rides through the town, stops and dismounts in front of
the Mogollon Saloon.

SOUND – Music and conversation, a woman's laugh, a man's
guffaw.

CUT TO:
INT SALOON – DAY
Camera on bat wing doors, looking outside. As Buck Elliot steps in
through the door he pauses for a moment.

CUT TO:
BARGIRL reacts to the handsome young man who has just entered
the saloon.

CONTINUOUS
Buck Elliot steps up to the bar, and signals to the BARTENDER

BARTENDER
What'll it be, Mister?

BUCK
I'll have two beers.

BARTENDER
Two?

BUCK
One for thirst and one for taste.

Buck drains the first beer quickly, then sips the second one as he turns his back to the bar to watch FOUR POKER PLAYERS. A man wearing a star, steps in through the back door of the saloon. This is ABRAHAM JOHNSON

"Yes," Buck said, looking up from the script, "This is just how I told it to Haycox, and this is the way he wrote it. But I don't understand. Why isn't this the opening scene?"

"It *was* the opening scene," Gilmore said, "but Clive Malone convinced Alcy and Guy to change it. He decided it would play better if he didn't have to share the screen with anyone else in the opening."

"I see."

"Buck, he's going through the entire script, rewriting it so that it's nothing more than another Clive Malone movie. By the time this movie is in the can it won't have anything to do with what really happened, or with what Ernest Haycox wrote."

"But you're the screenwriter, aren't you?"

Gilmore chuckled. "Believe me, Buck, in the movie business the writer is at the very bottom of the totem pole, but not all writers. As it turns out, I saw something in Haycox's contract that says he has the right to provide input into the screenplay. So if you and Mr. Haycox and I put up a united appeal to Alcy Harris, we just might be able to prevail over Clive Malone."

"All right, if you think that will work, it sounds like a plan," Buck said.

"Good, I'm going to need you to get in touch with Haycox and ask him to come out here."

"Wouldn't it be better coming from you?"

"You do have a lot to learn about this business, don't you?" Gilmore replied with a chuckle. "There is a natural enmity between an author and the screenwriter who is adapting his book. Each of them has their own proprietary interest to protect. It's my understanding that the two of you got along very well while he was writing your book."

"We did," Buck said. "I enjoyed spending the time with him."

"Your relationship with him might come in handy at some point. By the way, do you have anything to read tonight?"

"You mean other than the movie script?" Buck asked.

"Yeah, here's a copy of *The Hollywood Reporter*. It's a new feature out here, a daily entertainment magazine. There's an article in this issue about you."

"About me? I'll never understand how someone can write about me without ever speaking to me," Buck said as he took the magazine. "I'll read it tonight, and find out what other exploits I've done."

True to his promise, the *Hollywood Reporter* became Buck's reading when he went to bed that night.

Authentic Western Hero to Consult on Clive Malone Film
By
Jasper Darnell

Sometimes in the tinsel of Hollywood we lose sight of reality. Were there really such aviators as the Rutledge Brothers in Hell's Angels? Was there really a legionnaire named Tom Brown who rode his horse across the burning sands in Morocco? In New York in 1980, will airplanes actually replace cars, numbers replace names, pills replace food, as in the movie, Just Imagine?

We are able to suspend reality when we see such films but now,

Starburst Motion Picture Studios is about to begin production on Legend of a Gunfighter. This is a story about an authentic part of our history, and the principle participant in the exciting event, Buck Elliot, has been selected to act as consultant for the movie. And that, dear readers, means that when Clive Malone, portraying Buck Elliot in the movie Legend of a Gunfighter lights up the silver screen, all viewers can be assured of the story's accuracy.

7

Arizona Territory - 1885

Without telling anyone in Canyon Diablo why he had come, Buck abandoned the town and rode about six miles west, then stopped to read a sign beside a lane that turned off from the main road.

TRAILCROSS RANCH
The Kellys
Sean, Rosaleen, Nola, Finn, Timothy

So this was Trailcross. It had been in the late sixties when he and Sean Kelly had ridden all over Southeast Texas gathering up maverick cattle. The cattle drive to Kansas had been their first, and the money they made was good. Buck was sure a good part of that money had been used to buy this ranch. He was proud of his friend, and he was anxious to see Sean again.

Buck smiled when he saw a rider coming up the road

toward him. Sean was more than likely sending one of his sons to meet him. But as the rider got closer he could see by the hair that it was a young girl. And though she was dressed like a boy, Buck thought that the girl, who was around sixteen years old, was a very attractive young woman.

"Are you Mr. Elliot?" the girl called.

"I am."

The young girl's face lit up with a broad smile as she urged her horse closer. "I'm Nola Kelly," she said, extending her hand to Buck. "Papa sent me down here to wait for you. There are a lot of bad things going on, and he said you can take care of it."

Buck's mind flashed back to the shootings in the saloon. "So I've heard," he said without being more specific.

Buck couldn't tell how large Trailcross Ranch was just by casual observation from the road. But when he arrived at the house, he saw that there was no bunkhouse, and no out buildings except for a barn. He did see a swiftly moving stream of water running through the property.

The man who stepped out onto the porch to greet them was a couple of inches shorter than Buck, with brown eyes, and a clean-shaven, oval–shaped face.

"Am I happy to see you," Sean Kelly said as he came down the steps.

"It's been a long time," Buck said.

Two boys stood on the porch, one Buck guessed, would be about fifteen, the other a couple of years younger.

"These are my boys, Finn and Timmy," Sean said. "You've met Nola."

"I did," Buck said. "You have a fine family."

Sean nodded his head. "Now, Finn, why don't you take care of Mr. Elliot's horse?"

"Yes. Papa," the young man answered agreeably, and he hopped down to stand by the horse as Buck dismounted.

Buck removed the saddlebags hung them over his shoulder, then snaked the rifle from the saddle sheath.

"Thank you, young man," Buck said.

Nola accompanied Finn to the barn, leading her own horse.

Sean Kelly reached out to take Buck's hand as he chuckled. "I remember the last time I saw you; you had your cow money and you was hoppin' on board a train out of Kansas City headed for who knows where."

"My share was seventeen-hundred and fifty-seven dollars. I remember it well because, at the time, it was the most money I had ever had."

"Where'd you go?"

"St. Louis, Memphis, New Orleans, Galveston, Houston, and a lot of places in between."

"You've never wanted to settle down anywhere?" Sean asked. "Put down roots?"

"Not yet. Someday I might find a place, but not now."

"You know how I found you," Sean said. "Alice Kirby."

Buck smiled. "I ran into Alice a few years back."

"She said you helped her out of a bind."

"I like to think that I did."

"Well, that's why I sent you that letter," Sean said. "I need you now."

"Oh, for heaven's sake, Sean, you don't have to talk business standing out in the open. Come on inside," an attractive woman said stepping out onto the porch then, "I've got coffee brewing."

"Buck, this is my wife, Rosaleen, and Rosaleen, this is the man I told you about."

"Yes, your partner from the cattle drive to Kansas City," Rosaleen said. "To hear Sean tell it, the two of you had enough adventures on that drive to fill a book."

"Well, if that's how Sean tells it, it must be so," Buck replied with a wink.

"I'll get the coffee," she said.

"By the way, your Nola is a beautiful young lady and, I noticed, a good rider," Buck said. "How old is she?"

"She's the oldest at sixteen, then Finn is fifteen and Timmy's thirteen. They're good kids," Sean said, "All three of them."

Rosaleen set the two cups of coffee on the table, then opened the pie safe.

"I know it's only mid-morning, but are you two ready for a piece of pie?" Rosaleen asked. She had high cheekbones, wide-set green eyes and hair that was so light a brown, as to almost be blonde. She was quite an attractive woman.

"Thank you. Mrs. Kelly, I'd love a piece of pie."

"Oh, for heaven's sake, my name is Rosaleen."

"All right, Rosaleen it is," Buck said.

After the coffee and pie were served, Sean continued with his discourse.

"I heard about Marshal Johnson being killed. It was Moe Peters who sent for him. Moe had the idea that if we could get us a US Marshal in here, he could establish some law. And if we had some law and someone to enforce it, I believe we could stand up to 'His Lordship.' "

Sean screwed up his face when he spoke the words, 'His Lordship' to prove that he was saying it in a derisive, rather than a laudatory way.

"Would 'His Lordship' happen to be this Smythe I heard about?"

"That's him. He's got some sort of title back in England, but I don't know what it is. Anyhow he came out here with a lot of money and somehow he got his hands on some quit claims. The next thing you know he'd put together a ranch the size of Delaware."

"I don't see how owning a big ranch could be a problem," Buck said. "I have friends with mighty big ranches and they all get along quite well with their neighbors."

"Well in Smythe's case, he's got no intention of being a good neighbor," Sean said. "Actually he doesn't want any neighbors at all. He's trying to get control of every drop of water in this whole valley, and he doesn't care what it takes to get the job done. That's why he's got almost as many gunfighters as he does cowboys."

"Would you be talking about Lodeen, Stillwell, and Corbett?" Buck asked, repeating the names Buck had heard mentioned in the saloon.

"You know them?" Sean asked, surprised to hear Buck mention them.

"A man named Wilkerson told me about them," Buck replied.

"That would be Dub. He's a neighbor, and a good man," Sean said.

"To answer your question, I've never met these three men, so I don't know them, but I do know of them."

"I wish I could tell you they were the only ones Smythe has, but they're just the tip of the iceberg. I wouldn't be surprised if he didn't have half a dozen more gunfighters working for him who are just about as good."

"Why do you think he has so many hired guns?" Buck asked.

"Because he wants our water. He calls his ranch Eagleshire on the Sherlons Fork, and like the name says, the Sherlons Fork is the largest creek under the Mogollon Rim," Sean said. "But there are other creeks and streams here as well, and that water is what makes this land ranch land, instead of desert. All of us let these creeks flow through our land, so that others can use the water, too. But Smythe don't think the way we do. He figures if he can get control of all these creeks, he can divert the water wherever he wants it to go, and he'll force us all out."

"You say he had a title back in England?"

"That's what he says."

"He might be thinking he wants a fiefdom," Buck said. "In England whoever had this much land, and with as many people working for him as he has, had the title and the authority to govern his neighbors."

"That sounds like something Nigel Smythe would want."

"How large is Trailcross?" Buck asked.

"I've got a little over three thousand acres, and I'm running about fifteen hundred head of cattle."

"You have any hands?"

"You've already met all of 'em—Nola, Finn, and Timmy. And don't laugh, but even though she's a girl, Nola is good around cattle. Truth to tell," Sean stopped and looked around to make certain he wasn't likely to be overheard, "she's a might better even, than Finn."

"Well, I can see where the four of you can handle a ranch this size, but if you get many more head you'll most likely have to put on another hand or two."

"Yeah, that's part of the problem," Sean said, "I haven't expanded the herd, even though I've got enough water and grass that I could. But there aren't any hands available. Smythe has just about every able-bodied cowboy in the entire valley working for him, and he's payin' wages that none of the rest of us can afford."

"How many smaller ranchers are there?" Buck asked, "And how many of you are having trouble with Smythe?"

"There are eight of us, and we're all havin' trouble with him," Sean said.

"Where do the other ranchers stand, in size to yours?"

"We're all about the same size," Sean said, "Two of them, the Mountain Shadow and the T Bar X each have one hand working for them, and the Tumbling R has two grown sons. The other four are worked by the owners."

"Eleven more men?" Buck said, having done the math.

Sean shook his head. "Ten men," he said. "The T Bar X is owned by Sara Sue Tanner, and the man she has working for her, Pete Connors, has worked for her since before her husband died."

"All right, that makes twelve, counting the two of us."

"I don't know what you're figuring, Buck, but I've tried, and Wilkerson has tried, and we've never gotten everyone to agree to pull together. And even if we could gather everyone, we'd still be outnumbered by more than two to one. Smythe has at least twenty men working for him, and half of them are more than just cowboys. And then there's the sheriff," Sean said. "He's on Smythe's side and that put's the law on his side, too."

Buck smiled, "Well, then, it looks to me as if our work is cut out for us, doesn't it? Uhmm, uhm," he said with an appreciative smack of his lips, "I'm going to have to tell your wife that this is some of the best apple pie I've ever tasted."

Sean laughed.

"What is it? What's wrong?"

"It's Nola. She might look and act like a tomboy, but she's also a good cook. She made this."

8

Hotel Normandie – Los Angeles. California - 1931

There was a radio in the room and Buck had it tuned to KGFJ, Los Angeles. The song playing was Ruth Etting's *Ten Cents a Dance*.

In the song, the singer was lamenting the fact that she worked at a dance hall, and every night her eardrums burst to the sound of the trumpet and drum while she danced with "fighters and tailors and bow-legged sailors."

Buck liked the song because it reminded him of the percentage girls who used to work the saloons. Some were young and pretty, some had lost their looks to the dissipation of their profession, some were hard women made even harder by their long life on the line, and some were young and vulnerable. All were a part of Buck's past.

Buck had just finished shaving when the phone in his room rang.

"Mr. Elliot? Ryan Gilmore here," the voice on the other end said. "They're going to shoot a scene from *Legend of a*

Gunfighter on location this morning. If you'd like, I'll pick you up and you can watch."

"I'll be ready," Buck said.

An hour and a half later Buck and Gilmore reached Agoura Hills near Malibu Creek. Here, Starburst Motion Picture Studios owned 2,700 acres of land in the mountains. They had built several sets including ranches and an Old-West town.

Ryan moved Buck into position where both could see a stagecoach in the distance, waiting for the call to action.

"So, the first scene is going to be with a stagecoach?" Buck asked.

"This is the first scene to be shot, but it isn't the opening scene of the film," Ryan said. "We don't shoot the pictures in a linear order."

"Interesting."

"Action!" Guy Lashlee called.

Buck watched as the stage coach started toward them. Four outlaws were chasing the coach. The shotgun guard was "shot" and, dramatically, he stood in the seat, threw his arms out to either side, and fell from the speeding coach. Next, the driver was hit, and like the shotgun guard and in just as dramatic a fashion, he too fell from the coach. Then Buck saw a horse and rider, the rider dressed all in white, as he clenched the reins in his teeth. He was firing with both pistols at the outlaws. After a few more shots from the cowboy, all four outlaws were gunned down.

There was a truck with a camera, driving along beside the runaway coach, getting close up pictures of a young woman who was inside. Her head and arms were pushed out through the window as she was reacting in fear to her perilous situation.

Galloping up so that he was between the coach and the camera truck, the man in white jumped from his horse to the coach, then from the front of the coach he began leaping out onto the six horse team, the first pair, then the second, until he was at the lead pair. There he climbed onto the off-lead horse and pulled on the reins until the coach was brought to a halt.

"Cut!" Guy Lashlee said.

"I don't know where this scene came from," Buck said during the lull in shooting, "I never did anything like that, and don't know anyone who ever did. But I have to give Clive credit; that was one slick piece of action."

"Wait," Ryan said.

"Wait? Wait for what?"

"You'll see."

"Cameras move up!" Guy called. "Clive! We're ready for you!"

Clive Malone emerged from a nearby trailer, dressed all in white, as had become his signature look; then he walked out to the coach.

"Hold on here, you mean that wasn't Clive Malone?"

Guy laughed. "It was Yakima Canutt. He's the best stunt man in Hollywood."

Yakima Canutt jumped down from the front of the team and a small step ladder was moved into position to allow Clive to climb up into the same position Canutt had just occupied. The step ladder was removed.

"Action."

The camera moved in on Clive, as he petted the horse on its neck.

BUCK
Easy, boy, easy.

"Cut!"

The step ladder was moved back into position and Clive climbed down while Yakima climbed up. When the camera began rolling again, Yakima leaped down from the horses and turned his back to the camera. Once again he and Clive exchanged places, and once again the camera began rolling.

Woman Passenger
Oh, you saved me, I was so frightened. May I ask your name?

Camera ECU Buck's face

BUCK
The name is Elliot ma'am. Buck Elliot. And I'll always come to rescue a beautiful woman who is in distress.
TWO SHOT - Woman passenger embraces and kisses Clive

"Cut! That's a wrap!" Guy shouted.

Another man stood up from the forward boot of the stagecoach, and jumped down.

"I didn't see him before. What was he doing?" Buck asked.

"If you walk up to the coach you'll see a second set of reins coming through a slit. He was the one who was actually driving the coach." Again, Ryan laughed. "It's called movie magic."

"Ryan, I'll have to admit that was exciting, but where the hell did that scene come from?" Buck asked, "I know damn well I never jumped from my horse to rescue a runaway stagecoach, and I know it didn't come from Haycox's book."

"No, and it didn't come from my film script either," Ryan

said, "I'm afraid this is something that the prima donna put into the script."

"You need to talk to Lashlee or Harris."

Ryan shook his head, "It won't do me any good to see them alone. But perhaps if we both talked to them we could accomplish something. Would you be willing to come with me to talk to Harris?"

"All right, let's go see him."

———

"It was a good scene, fellas," Harris said, "and we got it in one take. It'd be a shame not to use it."

"But it isn't true," Buck complained. "I thought this was supposed to be a story based upon Ernest Haycox's book about something that actually happened. What was this business today about chasing down a stagecoach, then leaping onto it, then leaping out onto the horses? Even if I had done such a thing, which I never would have, the reins were right there. Why wouldn't I just grab the reins instead of leaping from one horse to the other?"

"Because Clive Malone's fans like to see him in exciting situations," Harris said. "They expect to see him do something like that in every movie."

"You mean they expect to see Yakima Canutt do something like that," Ryan added.

Harris shook his head. "As far as the viewing audience is concerned, it's Clive Malone doing that. For crying out loud, Ryan, you've been in the business long enough to know what goes on."

"You've just made my point. Mr. Harris," Buck said.

"What do you mean?"

"You said as far as the viewing audience is concerned, it's Clive Malone doing that. Clive Malone, not Buck Elliot."

"Well, of course. Clive Malone is portraying Buck Elliot."

Buck shook his head. "No, he isn't. Clive Malone is portraying Clive Malone."

"You don't understand, do you?" Harris said.

"Understand what?"

Harris sighed, then shook his head before he spoke.

"Look, Buck, Clive Malone isn't just the biggest star Starburst Motion Picture Studios has; you might say that he is our franchise. Clive Malone's pictures are responsible for sixty percent of our total income. Sixty percent!" he added with even more emphasis.

"Do you gentlemen understand what I'm saying? If we lose Clive Malone, Starburst will go bankrupt. And if we don't give him his say on this picture, we *will* lose him."

"Do you intend to follow any of the story?" Buck asked.

Harris shook his head. "I don't know. Clive has taken over the story and is giving us one scene at a time. And of course, since we're shooting out of linear sequence, and from what we have seen, we really have no idea if he's following any of the story or not."

"I thought I was supposed to have some input into this picture," Buck said.

"You do, that's why we've hired you as our historical consultant."

"And yet, so far, I have had virtually no input."

"May I make a suggestion? Let's just give Clive a little room here—let him establish himself with the picture, then maybe we can rein him in a little later," Harris suggested.

"You know, Alcy, Buck and I *do* have a weapon we can use," Ryan suggested. "We can resign, and then go to the press and tell them why we have resigned. That kind of negative publicity will have a devastating effect on the marketing."

"No, no, don't do that, please!" Harris begged. "Look, let

us get some of his scenes in the can; then we'll come back to the true story. Once we begin to assemble the picture, we can take some of the more outlandish scenes out."

Half an hour after their meeting with Harris, Buck and Ryan were having coffee in the Purity Café.

"Can we trust Harris?" Buck asked.

"Well, the suggestion that we would go to the press with a very public resignation did seem to get a rise out of him," Ryan said.

"Yes, but if Clive Malone is sixty percent of their total revenue, then it seems to me like he may have a hold that Harris can't break."

"Let's see what we can do about getting some of the real story shot. It's like Alcy says—the pictures are never shot in order from first scene to last, so it's really easy to lose track of where you are and what's going on. And if Alcy really will take out some of Clive's self–aggrandizing scenes, we may be able to salvage the story."

"What about Haycox?" Buck suggested.

"What do you mean?"

"You said my relationship with him might come in handy at some point. What if we get him here? He's a nationally known, best-selling author, and I'm pretty sure he won't be pleased to see his story so ignored."

"That's a good idea," Ryan admitted. He chuckled. "I think that the natural enmity between screenwriter and book author could be set aside in this case. We would both have the same goal in mind, the perseveration of the truth. Do you think you could get him here?"

"Yes, I think I can. He lives in Portland, Oregon. I'll get in touch with him."

Ryan followed Buck back to his hotel room where Buck made the telephone call.

"I would like a long distance operator, please," Buck said. Then, when he got the operator he said, "I would like to make a person to person telephone call to Mr. Ernest Haycox in Portland, Oregon."

Buck held the telephone as he heard the telephone operators go through all the exchanges. Then he heard a woman's voice answer the phone. This, he knew, was Ernest's wife, Jill.

"Hello?"

"I have a person to person telephone call from Mr. Buck Elliot to Mr. Ernest Haycox," the operator said in her very professional voice. "Is Mr. Haycox available?"

"Yes, he is," Jill said.

"Hello, Jill."

"Hello, Buck."

"Sir, please wait for your party," the operator said.

Buck waited quietly.

"Hello?"

"Mr. Ernest Haycox?"

"Yes."

"Sir, your party is on the line," the operator said to Buck.

"Thank you. Ernest? This is Buck, and I'm calling to tell you that this movie is making a mockery of your book. If you can, I'd really like to see you come down to Hollywood."

"You can't trust a screenwriter," Haycox said.

"Believe it or not, the screenwriter is on our side," Buck said. "Can you come down?"

"I'll be on tomorrow's plane," Haycox promised.

As Buck lay in bed that night, he hoped Haycox could salvage the story. And if not, then he hoped the film would be dropped, or at least produced under another title, and with all allusion to him removed.

Ernest Haycox had thought the truth of what had happened made a good enough story. Why didn't Hollywood?

9

CANYON DIABLO. ARIZONA – 1885

Canyon Diablo, unlike many of the towns and villages in the Arizona Territory, did not exist prior to the annexation of Arizona to the United States. Founded by Americans in conjunction with the railroad, it was much more American in nature than most of the other towns of the Southwest. However, it did have a Mexican presence in the form of a small barrio on the south side of the railroad tracks.

Here, in the adobe buildings that housed the Mexicans and their families, the nights were darker for only the cantina was well lighted. The other structures were either in total darkness, or barely illuminated by burning embers of mesquite wood or fat-soaked rags, because few could afford candles, and fewer still, kerosene lanterns.

There were no hotels in the barrio, and no restaurants except for the food served in the cantina. Some of the Mexican women earned money as prostitutes, and many of their customers were American, some attracted to the women because of their dusky beauty, others because a Mexican whore cost less than half as much as an Anglo.

An American habitué of the Mexican whores was sitting in the lone chair in the small room watching as the woman began undressing before him.

"Do you like?" she asked.

"Yeah, I like" he answered, his voice thick with passion as he moved toward her. "What's your name?"

The woman lowered her face.

"Look, whore," he said, grabbing her long dangling earring and forcing her to look up at him. "When I ask a question, I expect an answer."

"Stop pulling. It hurts," the woman said as she put her hand to her ear.

At that moment, the man yanked the earring, ripping the earlobe as he pulled it free. The woman cried out in pain.

"Gold," he said as he turned the medallion over in his hand.

"Please, senor, do not take my earring," she whimpered. "They belonged to my *abuela*."

"Is that so?" the man said. "Do you think your *abuela* is proud of her granddaughter? All you have to do is tell me your name, and you can have it back."

"Frederica."

The man smiled. "Now, that wasn't so hard was it?" He slammed the woman down on the bed.

It was early morning, and though most self-respecting roosters had announced the fact long ago, half-a-dozen or so were still trying to stake a claim on the day. The sun had been up for quite a while, but the disc was still hidden by the mountains in the east. The light had already turned from red to white and here and there were signs of Canyon Diablo awakening.

A pump creaked as a housewife began drawing water for her morning chores, and somewhere a carpenter had already begun hammering.

Buck was awakened by the early morning sounds, and he poured a basin of water for his shave. As he stood by the open window, he could look out on the town. He had been here for nearly a week now, long enough for him to measure the intensity of the disagreement between Smythe and the smaller ranchers. The town itself was divided; the larger merchants who did a lot of business with Eagleshire on Sherlons Fork sided with Smythe, while the smaller businesses and many of the ordinary workers sided with the rest of the ranchers.

But even those who for business reasons sided with Smythe, considered the cowboys who worked for him to be nothing but a bunch of ruffians . . . hell-raisers who had grown wild on the range and were only too anxious to let off steam when they came into town. Often, letting off that steam meant shooting their guns, if not at each other in some spontaneous duel, then at any target that might catch their fancy.

As Buck was shaving, a couple of freight wagons rolled slowly through the streets, just beginning their journeys to the nearby towns which, unlike Canyon Diablo, were not serviced by a railroad. The shop keepers were very busy on the wooden porches and boardwalks, sweeping them clean, the better to attract potential customers. A cowboy, who had just awakened from a drunken night on the street, was wetting his head in a watering trough.

After his morning ablutions, Buck started toward the Dutch Skillet Café, passing the general store on the way. A

Mexican was picking through the fruits and vegetables the store owner had on display on the front porch of his store.

"*Buenos días. Senor,*" Buck called, cheerily.

"*Buenos días. Senor,*" the Mexican replied with a polite tip of his hat, surprised that he would be addressed in such a friendly fashion by an Anglo.

At breakfast a few minutes later Buck was having a second cup of coffee with his pancakes, when three men approached the table, all of whom were wearing suits. None were wearing guns. Buck recognized one of them. He was Tristan James Clay, publisher of the *Canyon Diablo Brimstone.*

"Mr. Elliot, excuse us for disturbing you at your breakfast, but I wonder if we might have a few words with you?" Clay asked.

"Sure. Would you gentlemen like to join me for breakfast?"

"No thank you, but perhaps we could drink a cup of coffee with you."

Buck held up his hand and signaled to the waitress to bring coffee for the three men.

"Mr. Elliot, this is Paul Cravens, the mayor of our town," Clay said. "This gentleman," the newspaper publisher added pointing to the third man, a tall, thin man, dressed all in black, "is Leo Ponder. Mr. Ponder is our mortician."

"Mr. Ponder, Mr. Cravens," Buck said, acknowledging the introductions.

"Leo, tell Mr. Elliot about the, uh, customer, you received this morning," Clay said.

"When I walked down to open my store, I found the body of a young Mexican woman lying in front of my door. She'd been brutally beaten, but that wasn't the cause of her demise. Her throat had been cut, and she bled to death," Ponder said.

"Anyone who'd do such a thing is pure evil," Buck said.

"I agree, even if the woman is a prostitute," Ponder said.

"Which is why we've come to you," Clay said.

"I'm afraid I don't make the connection. Why is it that you would come to me?"

"We'd like for you to become our city marshal," Mayor Cravens said.

"What?" Buck replied, surprised by the request.

"As mayor of the city, I have the authority to appoint you to the position," Cravens said. "And the way you dealt with Etherton and Wilson proves that you can certainly handle the job."

"Mexican or not, that woman's death shouldn't go unpunished," Clay said.

"What about Sheriff Jones? Doesn't a death like this come under his jurisdiction?"

"I assure you, you will find few in this town who are acolytes of Sheriff Emile Jones," Mayor Cravens answered. "In my opinion, he represents the interests of Nigel Smythe and Eagleshire at the expense of the citizens of this town."

"Does the sheriff represent the interests of the small ranchers of the county?" Buck asked.

"No, he does not," Mayor Cravens said, "but of course, as marshal of Canyon Diablo, that wouldn't be your problem."

"That's the problem," Buck said.

"I beg your pardon?"

"The fact that as city marshal, the situation between Smythe and the small ranchers wouldn't be my problem *is* my problem."

"Excuse me, Mr. Elliot, but I don't have the slightest idea what you're talking about."

"Mayor, I didn't just happen to drop in on Canyon Diablo. I was invited here by one of the small ranchers."

"Which one?"

"I'd rather not say, but I'm going to be meeting with a group of them this afternoon. If I accept the position of city marshal, though I might be able to help out some of the city folks, I would be restricted from doing anything to help the small ranchers. So I'm afraid I'm going to have to turn down your offer."

"Not necessarily," Clay said, "there might be a way to do both."

"How?" Mayor Cravens asked.

"You all know I worked with Governor Tritle when he tried to get the Arizona Rangers going. Like the Texas Rangers," Clay said.

"We know, but he didn't get the bill passed," Cravens said.

"It doesn't matter. It didn't pass because he couldn't get the funding," Clay said, "but that doesn't mean he can't appoint a law officer with authority over the whole territory. I'm pretty sure that we could get him to appoint Buck to such a position."

Cravens smiled, and nodded. "Yes, yes, that would work. What do you say, Mr. Elliot? Would you accept a position as territorial ranger?"

"Of course it would be an unpaid position, I'm afraid," Clay added.

"Not necessarily," Mayor Cravens said, "I can appoint him as city marshal, and then he could be both a marshal and a territorial ranger. The city can pay fifty dollars a month and we'll board you at the hotel. You'll have to pay for your own food, of course."

"Gentlemen, that *is* an interesting offer. Not very lucrative, I'm afraid, but interesting," Buck said. "But I need to go to my meeting this afternoon before I make any kind of decision."

"We understand," Mayor Cravens replied. "We'll have to send a telegram to Governor Tritle to get his authorization anyway."

"I'll let you know my decision after I've had my meeting

with the ranchers," Buck promised.

Later that morning two Mexicans showed up at the sheriff's office holding their sombreros in their hand.

"Frederica Gomez," one of the Mexicans said.

"What?" Sheriff Jones asked, confused by the visit.

"The woman who was killed last night," the Mexican said. "Her name was Frederica Gomez."

"Why are you telling me this?" Jones asked, "If you're wantin' the whore's name on the grave marker, you should be tellin' the undertaker."

"Si, this we have done. But we have come to you to find," he stopped and looked at his companion, "*Justica?*"

"Justice," his companion said.

"Si, justice. We have come to you so that you may find justice for the killer of Frederica."

"Do you know who killed her?" Sheriff Jones asked.

"No, Senor."

"Then how is it that I'm supposed to find justice?"

"You are the sheriff, Senor. Is it not your job to find the guilty so that they may be punished?"

"Yeah, all right," Sheriff Jones said with a dismissive wave of his hand, "I'll see what I can do."

"Are we going to do anything about this?" Parker asked when the two men were gone.

Jones shook his head. "No, what the hell can we do about it? She was a damn whore, and a Mexican whore at that. Let 'em work out their own problems. We all know it was probably one of 'em anyway."

"Yeah, that's what I say," Parker said. "Let 'em work out their own problems."

THE MEETING FOR THE SMALL RANCHERS WAS HELD AT Trailcross and though the house wasn't big enough for everyone, tables and benches had been set up outside to accommodate all the guests. The ranches represented in addition to Trailcross were the Bar 20, T Bar X, Tumbling R, Mountain Shadow, Baker Ranch, Sundown, and Circle J. Entire families had come to the meeting so that the gathering took on the atmosphere of a picnic, rather than a business meeting. Sara Sue Tanner of the T Bar X, a rather stout woman in her forties, was the only woman present at the business meeting part of the gathering.

"Lady, and gentlemen," Sean said, "to get this meeting started, I'd like to introduce my friend, Buck Elliot."

Buck nodded to the group, but didn't say anything.

"I don't have to tell you that Smythe is making things mighty difficult here. Just in the last six months, he's taken over three ranches, and with those ranches, he got access to Cottonwood Creek. Now, he's diverted that water away from our creeks."

"And he didn't just take over the land," Dub Wilkerson said. "He had Lon Etherton kill Isaac Mitchell."

"Now, Dub, Sheriff Jones looked into that," Moe Peters said. "He claimed it was a fair fight between Mitchell and Etherton."

"What about Matilda?" Sean asked. "Did she put up a fair fight too?"

"It wasn't a fight. It was a murder—two murders," Dub insisted. "And we all know Nigel Smythe is the one behind 'em."

"There's no doubt in my mind but what he didn't have Isaac Mitchell 'n his wife kilt," George Baker said. "We all seen how quick he took over the Bar M."

"You're right, George. How is it Smythe could just walk in and take over somebody's property like that?" Dub asked.

"I know how he did it," Roan Roberts said. "Johnny Wellman over at the Cattleman's Bank said Isaac had a loan against his ranch, and then old man Felker sold the loan to Smythe. With Isaac and his wife both gone and nobody knowin' how to find any kin, Smythe just up and paid off the loan. So now the Bar M belongs to him."

"What if Smythe *is* behind these murders? If the sheriff won't do anything about it, what are we supposed to do?" Clyde Jamison asked.

"That's why I sent for Buck," Sean said.

"I've heard about you, Mr. Elliot," Stan Emerson said. "And from what I've read, you're a pretty remarkable man. But you are just one man."

Sean shook his head. "Not just one, there are eight more of us."

"Nine," Sara Sue Tanner said holding up her hand.

"Sara Sue, you're a woman," Emerson said.

"You noticed that, did you, Stan?" Sara Sue said in a wry voice that brought a chuckle from the others.

"What I mean is, you can't be expected to . . ."

"I kilt four Apache my ownself when me 'n Larry first come out to my pa's ranch. 'N if you think I can't handle anyone that works for that damned Englishman, well, you've got another think comin'."

"All right, nine," Emerson said.

"Eleven," Roan Roberts said. "I've got two grown sons."

"And we can count on Howard McGill," Stan said. "He works for me."

"And don't forget my hand, Pete Connors," Sara Sue added.

"Pete's too old," Emerson said.

Sara Sue chuckled, "I wouldn't advise you to tell Pete that."

"All right, all told, that gives us thirteen men, uh, twelve men and Sara Sue," Sean said.

"We'll still be outnumbered by merely two to one," Clyde Jamison said.

"There's a saying about that," Buck put in. "It's from a fella named Euripides, and the saying is: 'Ten men, wisely led, are worth a hundred without a head.' "

"I go along with that," Sean said, "and the first thing we have to do is elect us a leader so that we are wisely led."

"Hell, Sean, there ain't no need for an election," Dub Wilkerson said. He pointed toward Buck. "There he is, right there."

"Anyone opposed to that?" Sean asked.

"I'm not opposed to Buck Elliot leadin' us," Roan Roberts said, "but I do have a question about somethin' that might cause us a problem."

"What's that?" Sean asked.

"Well sir, we all know that Smythe has Sheriff Jones right there in his hip pocket. And while we know Jones isn't worth a gob of warm spit, he *is* the law, and that means the law is going to be on Smythe's side. If we start this battle, we won't be fightin' against just Smythe; we'll also be fightin' agin' the law."

"Not necessarily," Buck said with a smile.

"What do you mean?" Wilkerson asked. "Do you have a connection with another deputy U.S. Marshal?"

"Not exactly, but if what I have in mind works out, we'll have the law on our side."

————

When Buck returned to town, he saw an elegant coach sitting in front of the hotel. The coach was white, trimmed in gold, and there was a driver sitting on the seat. Four matched white horses stood quietly in harness. On the side of the door was a family crest in gold and blue, a shield with a bend sinister, supported by lions rampant, and a helmet helm. The motto was *In Honorem Service.*

Above the crest were the words, EAGLESHIRE ON SHERLONS FORK RANCH, and below the crest the name, Nigel Smythe.

As soon as Buck stepped into the hotel lobby, he saw a well-dressed man wearing a maroon–colored cravat. The man approached Buck with an artificial smile on his face.

"My good man, would you be Buck Elliot?" the man asked in a cultured British accent.

"I'm Elliot," Buck replied, purposely omitting his first name.

"I am Viscount Nigel Smythe. Oh, forgive me sir, I realize that in this country I'm not allowed to use my title, but sometimes it slips out. Force of habit, you understand."

Smythe extended his hand and though Buck had a notion to refuse it, he put the notion aside. Smythe's hand was soft and his grip, weak.

"What do you want, Smythe?"

Smythe's eyes narrowed slightly in response to the way Buck had addressed him.

"I don't know if you are aware, but the two men you killed were in my employ."

"So I heard."

"Well, that leaves me in a bit of a pickle, you see. I am now two men short, and a ranch as large as Eagleshire on Sherlons Fork requires a great number of employees to maintain functionality. I came here today, to offer you a position on my ranch."

Buck shook his head. "Sorry, I've tried punching cows, and I don't particularly enjoy it. I wouldn't make a very good cowhand for you."

"You haven't heard my offer," Smythe said, the smile returning.

Buck started to say he didn't care what he was offering, that he wasn't interested. But he realized that he was interested in just how much Smythe would be willing to pay. The more he knew about this man who was about to become his adversary, the better off he would be.

"All right, what's your offer?" Buck asked.

"I will pay you one hundred dollars per week, and a bonus of one hundred dollars for every, uh, *obstacle* that you remove."

"That's a hell of a lot of money for punching cattle," Buck replied.

"Indeed it would be, if you were being hired to punch cattle. But I have been led to believe that you possess a talent that might be unique to my needs. I am told that you are exceptionally good in the employment of your pistol, and the result of your encounters with Mr. Etherton and Mr. Wilson would seem to validate that claim. I would be hiring you, Mr.

Elliot, not for your acumen with cattle, but for your skills as a gunman."

"Why do you need a gunman?"

"Why, indeed?" Smythe replied. "Mr. Elliot, I am a very wealthy man, and I am a most successful rancher. And unlike in my own country, where wealth and station alone are enough to earn the respect and admiration of your inferiors, here, success tends to breed jealousy and hostility. That puts my life in jeopardy, and I must hire people like you, to defend me against attack."

"I've heard you already have some gunmen working for you," Buck said.

Smythe smiled. "Indeed I do. You see, I have decided that the best way to keep any gunfighter from attacking me is to put him on the payroll. You would be but one of many, but from what I have heard, you would be my Sir Lancelot, or in the colorful language of the Mexicans, my *pistolero número uno.*"

"Well, I thank you for the offer, Smythe, but someone else has offered me a job, and I've decided to accept it."

"You have another job offer?" Smythe asked, surprised by Buck's response. "May I ask who has made the offer?"

"Mayor Cravens," Buck answered. He smiled broadly at Smythe. "I'm going to be the city marshal."

"You! You can't be serious!" Smythe sputtered. "You would take a job as city marshal over the position I am offering you?"

"I would."

"Why?"

"Why, the money of course," Buck said. "That fifty dollars a month looks pretty good to me."

"But I don't understand; I've offered you one hundred dollars per week!"

Buck walked away before Smythe could say another

word, leaving the Englishman with his mouth agape. He couldn't contain the laugh as he hurried up the stairs to his room.

Buck's room overlooked Hell Street and through the window he saw Smythe's carriage driving away. With it gone, Buck left the hotel and walked down the street to the city hall.

"Ah, Mr. Elliot, have you made a decision?" Mayor Cravens asked.

"I have," Buck said.

"Before you answer, I want to tell you I've received the authority from Governor Tritle to appoint you as an officer with authority throughout the entire territory of Arizona. You'll be an Arizona Ranger."

"That's good," Buck said. "I wasn't sure you'd be able to get the governor to do it."

"He says he doesn't have authority to establish an official organization of Rangers similar to what Texas has, but he does have the authority to appoint a single ranger as a special law officer answerable only to him." Cravens finished his report with a wide smile.

"As both positions will give me the legal authority I'll need to deal with Smythe, and the sheriff, I'll take it."

"I'm afraid you may have to deal with the sheriff first," Cravens suggested.

"That's my intention," Buck said.

"So what if he is the city marshal, we'll still have authority over him, won't we?" Lanny Parker asked, after learning that Buck Elliot was to be the new city marshal.

"Well, it's not really all that clear," Sheriff Jones said. "We'll have authority over him outside the town limits, and that means most anything that might have something to do with Mr. Smythe. But it might be that anything that happens in town would be Elliot's responsibility."

"That ain't right," Parker complained. "Hell, ever' body knows that a sheriff comes over a city marshal."

Jones chuckled. "Well, what are you worried about? All that means is that when the cowboys come into town 'n get drunk 'n start raisin' hell, why it'll be Elliot's problem, not ours."

"What about that murder that happened to the Mexican whore?" Parker asked.

"Seein' as she was kilt here in town, that makes it Elliot's job." Jones laughed out loud. "Let's see how the famous gunfighter solves this case. You know damn well it was a

Mexican that done it, 'n he sure as hell ain't goin' to get one of 'em to snitch on another 'n."

"Yeah," Parker said. He giggled. "Let's just see how the city marshal deals with that."

Shortly after he returned from his fruitless attempt to recruit Buck Elliot, Smythe asked Simon Lodeen, Adam Stillwell, and Frank Corbett to come to his office.

"Yeah," Lodeen replied to the question posed by Smythe, "I've heard of Buck Elliot."

"I have been led to believe that he is quite proficient in the use of firearms. Have I been misled?" Smythe asked.

"No, you ain't been told nothin' wrong," Lodeen said. "The son of a bitch is good." In a nervous gesture, Lodeen stroked his scarred and drooping eyelid. "Why is it you're askin' about 'im? You plannin' on hirin' 'im?"

Smythe started to tell them that he had made an attempt to recruit Elliot, but decided it would be better to keep that particular effort to himself, especially since it had failed.

"Quite the contrary, I fear he has become an adversary. I need to know if you gentlemen are sufficient to the task of eliminating this potential impediment to the attainment of my goal."

"I ain't quite sure I know what it is you're a sayin'," Lodeen said, "Are you askin' if we are as good as Elliot?"

"You do get to the point rather quickly," Smythe said, "Yes, that is precisely what I am asking."

Lodeen looked at the other two gunmen before he replied, "Yeah," he answered. "We're good enough." He chuckled. "That is, if we can keep Frank away from the Mexican whores long enough to do the job."

"Mr. Corbett's propensity for the Latina ladies of the evening notwithstanding, I am quite pleased to hear that you

consider yourselves sufficiently skilled to deal with the problem. And to make certain that this man does not become an
impediment to my ultimate goal, I am prepared to offer a
bonus of one thousand dollars to effect the removal of Buck
Elliot."

"What?" Corbett asked, unable to understand the implied
request in Smythe's dissembled response.

"He says he'll give us a thousand dollars to kill Elliot,"
Lodeen explained.

"I didn't say that . . . exactly, for to say such a thing would
make me an accessory to murder," Smythe said, quickly.
"However if your attempt to reason with Mr. Elliot should
provoke some sort of confrontation that would prove fatal to
him, I would regard the requirement for the payment of one
thousand dollars as having been met."

"What?" Corbett asked again.

"Like I said, he says he'll give us a thousand dollars to kill
Elliot," Lodeen repeated.

That night Lodeen, Stillwell and Corbett were in the Cow
Palace Saloon.

"Truth is, I think I can take the son of a bitch by myself,"
Lodeen said.

"Why take the chance?" Stillwell asked. "They's three of
us, 'n any one of us might be as good as Elliot is. But you
know damn well all three of us can take him."

"Yeah, you're right."

"I'll see you boys tomorrow," Corbett said, shoving his
empty glass toward the middle of the table.

"Where ya goin'?" Lodeen asked.

"You really have to ask?" Stillwell added with a chuckle.

"Frank, what do you see in them Mexican whores,
anyhow?" Lodeen asked.

"I just like 'em," Corbett replied, believing that was a good enough answer. He left the saloon.

"You know what's goin' to happen to him, don't you?" Lodeen asked.

"What?" Stillwell replied.

"He's goin' to pass out drunk in some *puta's* bed one night and wake up dead the next mornin' 'cause some jealous jackass slit his throat."

Stillwell laughed. "Hell, if you're dead, you ain't goin' to wake up a' tall."

"Stupid, that's what I said."

"Here he comes," Imelda said. "It's your turn, Jacinta."

"No, it is Manuela's turn," Jacinta said.

"Mierda," Manuela said. "Why does he not visit the *putas Americanas?"*

"Because they are so pale they look like paste," Imelda said, and the other two laughed.

"Don't worry, Manuela. His *pene es tan pequeño* that he can't hurt you," Imelda said, and she held up her hand measuring the distance with her thumb and forefinger. Manuela laughed as she walked over to greet the gringo. The gringo lifted his hand to pat her face.

"You like, Senor?" Manuela asked, smiling flirtatiously at him.

"Yeah. I like."

The next morning, Simon Lodeen found a place on the bank of the Sherlons Fork and because it was a fast moving stream, when he tossed pinecones into the water they were carried along swiftly. He threw a cone into the water, then drew his pistol and fired. At the impact of the bullet, pieces of the cone flew off. He did that for five cones and hit every one of them. Then, after reloading his pistol, he was ready to go.

"Here's the thing," the infamous gunfighter, Wild Bill Longley, had told him when they were talking about gun fighting. "It ain't how fast you are. Hell, I've kilt people that was faster on the draw than me."

"It's how straight you can shoot," Lodeen had said, interrupting his mentor.

Longley held up a finger, "Now, don't be gettin' ahead of me boy. Yes, it's about shootin' straight, that's for sure. But the most important thing is to be willin' to kill someone. You see, most people ain't got it in 'em to actual do it, 'n that'll make 'em stop 'n think maybe for just a heartbeat a'fore they pull the trigger. 'N while they're a thinkin', the other feller is a shootin'. But if you know for sure that you're willin' to kill the other son of a bitch when you start your draw, you'll win most ever' time."

Now, as Lodeen recalled that conversation with Longley, he knew that he was absolutely willing to kill, and he was about to make himself a thousand dollars.

That same night in Canyon Diablo, over on the Mexican side of town, a man stood in the alley behind the cantina hiding in the shadows of the *letrina*. The stench emanating from the toilet was overpowering, but the man was so consumed with the malevolent craving that had invaded his soul, that he was oblivious to the odor.

He had been there for at least two hours, and though the smells no longer bothered him, he was getting tired of standing in one place. Several people had come out to use the toilet during the course of the evening, but because there was only one serving both men and women, the women had come together, one standing guard for the other.

Then about midnight, his luck changed. A woman came out of the cantina alone and started toward the toilet. She walked with a weaving, staggering gait, indicating that she was already drunk.

She was ideal for his purposes. She was alone, and because she was drunk, if she didn't return to the cantina right away, her absence might go unnoticed.

He looked around and seeing that he was not being observed, started toward her.

BUCK WAS HAVING BREAKFAST IN THE DUTCH SKILLET CAFÉ the next morning when Sheriff Jones came in to see him. He walked up to the table.

"Elliot?"

"Mornin' Sheriff, what's on your mind?" Buck replied.

"Have you ever been a law officer before?" Sheriff Jones asked.

"A few times. Why do you ask?"

"You're wearing that marshal's badge now," the sheriff said. "Are you serious about bein' a marshal, or did you take a job that don't hardly pay nothin' for some other reason?"

"Sheriff, I have a feeling you're taking a long way around to try and say something," Buck said, "Why don't you just come right to the point?"

"I figure that anything that happens in this town is your responsibility," Sheriff Jones said. "Ain't that the way you see it?"

Buck nodded, "I'd say you're right."

"Well, sir, I hate to spoil your breakfast, but we had another one last night."

"Another one what?"

"Another whore got herself kilt."

"I see."

"'N like I say, I sort'a figure this here one in the barrio, 'n the one that was kilt a couple of nights ago is both of 'em your responsibility now, seein' as you're the new town marshal."

"When did you hear about it?"

"Not more 'n a few minutes ago. Lanny Parker—he's m' deputy you already know, well sir, while he was doin' the rounds, one o' the Mexicans come up 'n told him about findin' her body behind the cantina. So he got a couple o' hombres to carry her over to Ponder's place."

"I wish he would've left her there," Buck said. "It's best to leave everything alone until you've had a chance to investigate the crime scene."

"Why?"

"Because most of the time someone who murders another person will leave something behind, some sort of clue that helps in solving the case."

Jones gave a derisive laugh. "Hell, there ain't no need for investigatin' anything. I already know she's dead 'n I know how come it is that she's dead. Her throat was cut. But if you need to see her, she's lyin' out down at the funeral parlor right now. Come on, I'll go with you."

"I appreciate that," Buck said. He shoved his plate of uneaten eggs, bacon and biscuit aside. "I wish you could have waited until after I had eaten my breakfast."

"Hello, Marshal Elliot," Ponder said when Buck and Sheriff Jones entered his place of business. "I thought I might see you this morning."

"I'd like to see the body if you don't mind," Buck said.

"She's in the back, but it isn't a pretty sight. Her head was cut nearly clean off."

Buck and Sheriff Jones followed the undertaker into the back of his shop where they saw the young woman lying on a table, covered by a sheet. When Ponder lowered the sheet, Buck could see the deep, pink slash in her neck.

"If you ask me, the same person who killed the other whore is the one who killed this one," Ponder said.

"That may be so."

"There's no maybe about it," Ponder said. "Look." He pointed to the girl's left ear. She was wearing an earring on her right ear, but no such jewelry adorned her left ear. Instead there was a bloody gash in her earlobe where the earring had been.

"It looks like her earring got jerked off in the struggle," Buck said.

"You might think so, but the earring was missing from the other girl as well, same ear, same type of wound. That seems just a little too strange for it to be a coincidence."

Buck nodded. "I'd have to agree with you."

When Buck and Sheriff Jones left Ponder's place, they went over to the barrio, then walked back to the toilet where according to Parker, the body had been found. Even though the body had been taken away, there was still a puddle of blood, which was now providing a veritable feast for hundreds of flies.

Buck had no real idea what he was looking for and the heat and the odor from the toilet were terrible. As a result, he and Sheriff Jones stayed for less than a minute.

"What have you found out about the first one?" Buck asked.

"I ain't found out nothin' 'bout the first one, but then again, I ain't actually looked for nothin' neither."

"You didn't investigate at all?" Buck asked.

"What the hell was there for me to investigate?" Sheriff Jones asked. "It warn't no time at all after it happened 'till you was made the city marshal which meant the investigatin' was your business, not mine, which is why as soon as Parker told me 'bout this one, I come to see you. But, to be honest with you, I figure this is all Mexican business anyway."

"What do you mean it's all Mexican business? Aren't the people who live here in the barrio covered by the same laws that apply to the rest of the town? Aren't they entitled to our protection? And if one of them commits a crime, like murder for example, aren't they just as guilty and just as liable as any man who lives on the other side of the tracks?"

"Yeah but you'll find out soon enough. You can try 'n find out what happened to these two whores, but you won't get no help from anybody. There don't none of 'em ever know nothin', 'n they won't none of 'em hardly talk to you even if they did know somethin'."

The very fact that Buck would even bother to come to the scene of a crime in the Mexican part of town was enough of an event that it aroused the curiosity of nearly every resident of the barrio. While Buck and Sheriff Jones were at the toilet, the Mexicans stood around, holding handkerchiefs to their noses, speaking to each other in Spanish, watching as Buck went through the motions of "investigating" the crime.

"We can go into the cantina 'n talk to Juan Bustamante if you want to," Sheriff Jones suggested. "He's the one that owns this place."

"Do you know the girl's name?" Buck asked Bustamante after he and Jones stepped inside the cantina.

"Her name was Manuela."

"Any idea who killed her?"

"No, Senor, I do not know who killed her."

"We have reason to believe that Manuela and Frederica were killed by the same person," Buck said. "Did you ever see someone with Frederica that you also saw with Manuela?"

"I cannot say, Senor."

"You can't say, or you won't say?"

"I cannot say, Senor," Bustamante repeated.

Buck couldn't get over the impression that Bustamante knew more than he was saying, but he didn't get the idea that Bustamante was involved in any way. It was more a feeling that the cantina owner was too frightened to share what he knew.

Buck had missed his breakfast so he was hungry enough for a pretty substantial lunch and when he stepped into the Dutch Skillet Café he saw the publisher of the Canyon Diablo Brimstone seated alone at the table. Tristan James Clay beckoned for Buck to join him.

"Do you have anything to report on the Mexican woman who was killed last night?" James Clay asked.

"No, I talked to Bustamante, but didn't get anything from him."

"Ponder says an earring was jerked off her ear just like the other one."

Buck nodded his head.

"I agree with Ponder. That's too strange to be a mere coincidence."

"I'd rather you not put that in the paper. Right now it's the only lead we have."

"All right," Clay agreed, "I'll leave that part out of the story."

From the Canyon Diablo Brimstone:

Another Grisly Find

The body of yet another young woman has been found, and she, like the first murdered lady of the evening, was Mexican.

Sheriff Jones, correctly believing that an all-out effort should be launched to locate the fiend who is committing such wanton deeds, has enlisted the services of our newly appointed city marshal, Buck Elliot.

Both the marshal and the sheriff say that they have no leads.

After two weeks of investigating the murder of the two women, Buck was about ready to believe Sheriff Jones when he said that the investigation was futile. Despite his best efforts he had gotten no help from those who lived in the barrio. The only good thing to come of the two previous weeks was that no one else had been killed.

Buck, frustrated by his lack of progress in the case, walked into the Mogollon Saloon.

"I'll have a beer, Ben," he said to the bartender.

Ben McDaniels drew a beer and handed it across the bar to him. "Nothin' on them two whores that was kilt?"

Buck shook his head, "No, and to be honest, unless somebody says something, or I get a break, I don't see this case being solved. I'm not a detective."

"The sheriff sure as hell ain't been able to do nothin' about it," McDaniels said.

"Well, to be fair, he doesn't have any more insight into it than I do. And he warned me that I wouldn't get much help from any of the Mexicans. As it turns out, he was right."

"You think one of them did it?" McDaniels asked.

"I don't know for sure, but it probably is one of their own.

Whoever it is, he's got everyone over there too scared to say anything."

"Well I'll say this. Anyone who'd go around killin' women for no reason is one mean son of a bitch, no matter that they were whores," McDaniels said. "'N if you catch 'im, I want to be on the front row to watch 'im hang."

"I'm not sure someone like this would let himself be taken alive," Buck said.

"Yeah, well, I don't reckon it matters that much to me, just as long as the son of a bitch winds up dead."

13

WHEN SIMON LODEEN RODE INTO CANYON DIABLO THERE WAS only one thing on his mind: he was going to kill Buck Elliot. Smythe had offered the thousand dollar bonus for anyone getting rid of the man who would interfere with his plan to take over the remaining small ranches. He was sure Smythe intended that the bonus be shared among his three top gunhands, but Lodeen had decided to do it alone. For one thing he wouldn't have to split the money. But even more important than the bonus, would be the recognition he would get for being known as the man who had killed Buck Elliot.

In a world without guns, the small, gnarled-looking man with a disfigured eye would barely draw a second look, let alone command fear and begrudging respect. But this was a world *with* guns, and Lodeen had to be taken seriously because he had proven his skill with the pistol and a propensity, almost an eagerness, to use it. He enjoyed watching bigger, stronger men quake in their boots when he addressed them. And so far he had come out on the standing side of every gunfight in which he had been a participant.

Deciding to have a beer before he looked up Elliot, Lodeen tied his horse off in front of the Mogollon Saloon, then stepped inside. He smiled when he saw Buck Elliot standing at the bar. *Well*, he thought, *I ain't goin' to have to look hard to find you, 'cause there you are.*

"Hey, you, Buck Elliot." The shout, loud and angry, came from just inside the batwing doors.

Buck didn't turn.

"I'm talkin' to you, Elliot."

Buck turned then, and saw an incredibly ugly man standing in the door. He lifted his beer toward him.

"What can I do for you?" Buck asked

"I've come to kill you."

"Is that a fact?" The question was in a conversational tone.

"Yeah, that's a fact." This was a new experience for Lodeen. At this point in any previous confrontation his adversary was showing fear. Buck Elliot was not.

"Did you come alone? Or did you bring others with you?"

"Why would I need anybody else?" Lodeen asked the question more to boost his own confidence than to intimidate Buck Elliot.

"Why indeed?" Buck replied.

"I've got a bone to pick with you. Mr. Buck Elliot. Mr. famous . . . gunfighter." He set the last word apart from the rest of the sentence, and said it with a sneer.

By now the little man's belligerence told the others in the saloon that they should get out of the line of fire, should shooting break out.

"May I give you a word of advice? Don't try me," Buck said.

"Don't try you? Don't try you?" The gunman turned to address the others. The saloon had grown deathly still now as the patrons stood quietly, nervously, and yet titillated, by the life and death drama that had suddenly begun to unfold in front of them. "Did you folks hear that? He said don't try me." Lodeen stopped in mid-sentence then shook, exaggeratedly, to emphasize his point. "I suppose he thinks I should be quakin' in my boots 'cause I'm in the presence of the great Buck Elliot."

"Did Smythe send you here to challenge me?" Buck asked.

"Smythe? No, he don't even know I've come to town. But he'll know about it before this day's out. Ever' body'll know about it, and I figure by killin' the great Buck Elliot in a fair fight, why the price of my gun is going to go way up."

"What's your name?"

"What's my name? Are you kidding me, Mister? Are you telling me you don't know who I am?"

Buck knew exactly who he was, but he also knew that Lodeen was a very vain man, and to think that he wasn't recognized would agitate and unnerve his challenger.

"That's what I said. Should I know who you are?"

"The name's Lodeen, Simon Lodeen. I reckon you've heard of me."

"Yes, now that I think about it, I have heard of you," Buck said.

Lodeen's smile broadened. "Yeah? What'd ya hear?"

"I've heard that you are a dried up little piss ant, trying to make a reputation for yourself by killing old men, drunks, and boys."

Lodeen's smile quickly turned to an angry snarl, "Draw, Elliot!" he shouted, but he had given himself an advantage by going for his own gun even before he issued the challenge.

Lodeen was quick enough to justify the reputation he had established. But midway through his draw Lodeen realized he wasn't quite fast enough. The arrogant confidence in his eyes was replaced by fear, then the acceptance that he was about to be killed.

The two pistols discharged almost simultaneously, but

Buck had been able to bring his gun to bear a split second faster, and his bullet plunged into Lodeen's chest. The bullet from Lodeen's gun smashed the mug on the bar that held Buck's drink, sending up a shower of beer and tiny shards of glass.

Looking down at himself, Lodeen put his hand over his wound, then pulled it away and examined the blood that had pooled in his palm. When he looked back at Buck there was an almost whimsical smile on his face.

"Damn, you're good. I thought I could beat you, I really thought . . ." Lodeen's sentence ended with a cough, then he fell back making an attempt to grab onto the bar to keep himself erect. The attempt was unsuccessful, and Lodeen fell on his back, his right arm stretched out beside him, his pistol still connected to him only because his forefinger was hung up in the trigger guard. The black hat, with its silver band and red feather, had rolled across the floor and now rested on a half-filled spittoon. The eye-burning, acrid smoke of two discharges hung in a gray-blue cloud just below the ceiling.

Buck turned back to the bar where pieces of broken glass and a small puddle of beer marked the spot where his drink had been.

"Looks like I'm going to need a refill, Ben."

"Sure thing, Marshal, coming right up, and this one's on me," McDaniels said, holding a new mug under the keg spigot to draw another beer.

Deputy Parker came into the saloon less than a minute later and he stopped when he saw the body lying on the floor.

"I'll be damn," he said, "That's Simon Lodeen."

"Deputy," Buck said recognizing Parker, "would you like to join me for a beer?"

"Who killed Lodeen? Did you kill him?"

"I did."

"Why'd you kill him?"

"It seemed to me the appropriate thing to do at the moment."

"What you talking about? At what moment?"

"At the moment he was trying to kill me," Buck replied.

"The marshal's telling the truth, Deputy," McDaniels said, "Lodeen drew first."

Half a dozen others backed up the bartender.

Parker shook his head slowly as he stood there, staring at the body. "Simon Lodeen," he said, "I never thought anybody could beat him in a fair draw."

"Are you going to have that beer or not?" McDaniels asked, from behind the bar.

"Yeah," Parker said as he stepped over Lodeen's body to get to the bar. "I don't think Smythe's going to like this very much."

Infamous Gunman Killed in Gunfight

Simon Lodeen, a man who had acquired a much deserved reputation as a gunfighter, met his match yesterday. The disputatious gentleman presented himself as a belligerent in a battle of his proposal with Marshal Buck Elliot.

Unfortunately for Mr. Lodeen, he had more confidence than intelligence, for he was unaware of the brevity with which Marshal Elliot could put his gun to work. As a result of Simon Lodeen's miscalculation, Eagleshire on Sherlons Fork, the ranch owned by Nigel Smythe, is now short one more hand.

It was an angry Nigel Smythe who addressed Stillwell and Corbett, and the other six hands who had been hired for their ability with a pistol. That skill was at various levels with

Lodeen, Stillwell and Corbett being the most adept. Now, there was no Lodeen.

"I don't want to see anyone else be so foolish as to try something like this again," Smythe said. "Mr. Stillwell, just how good was Lodeen with a pistol?"

"He was better 'n me or Corbett. Fact is, he was the best I've ever seen, 'n I've seen some really good guns: Hickok, Masterson, Hardin, Billy the Kid, 'n I ain't never seen nobody that I thought could hold a candle to Lodeen," Stillwell said.

"And yet, Lodeen was bested by Elliot," Smythe said.

"I just can't hardly believe that," Stillwell said.

"Do you doubt that Mr. Lodeen is dead?" Smythe asked.

"No, sir, I don't doubt that none a'tall on account of I seen his body standin' up down in front of the hardware store," Stillwell said. "It's just that I can't hardly believe that Elliot beat 'im without cheatin' in some way."

"I am not a man of chivalry, and I have no intention for my future to be determined by affairs of honor, gentlemen, and I do use that term fatuously. Please do not lose sight of the reason I have placed such men as you in my employ. I have not hired you to test your skills against Buck Elliot; I have hired you for one purpose and one purpose only. It is my intention to increase my holdings in the Mogollon Rim, and you are to help me achieve that goal."

Smythe paused for a moment to allow that statement to sink in, and then the stern expression on his face was eased with a smile. "And believe me, as I attain my goal of total ownership of all useable land in the Rim, the rewards will accrue to you as well. When I am successful in my endeavors I am a happy man. And when I am happy, I am a generous man. The more contented I am, the more generous I shall be.

"Now, if you are to share in these plans, you will make no effort to embellish your reputation by engaging Buck Elliot in a gunfight. I think Mr. Lodeen's experience should be a warning to all."

"But, Mr. Smythe," Stillwell said, "I've heard that Elliot is more than a city marshal, I've heard that he has some kindly of a job workin' for the governor, 'n he intends to help out the small ranchers. If that's true, that means we're bound to run acrost him sometimes."

"That may be so," Smythe said. He held up his index finger to make a point. "But if such an event takes place, we shall manage all the details so that we will face him with a significant numerical advantage."

"Yeah," one of the other men said, "That's the only way I ever want to face the son of a bitch."

"What are you goin' to do about Lodeen?" Corbett asked.

"What do you mean, what am I going to do about Lodeen?"

"Are you goin' to see to his buryin'?"

"My good man, Lodeen acted upon his own," Smythe replied. "I feel no obligation toward the disposal of his remains."

WHEN SEAN KELLY CALLED ANOTHER MEETING OF THE SMALL ranchers, word of the showdown between Buck and Lodeen had already reached everyone. It was the main topic of discussion as they waited for the meeting to get started.

"Ben McDaniels said he ain't never seen nothin' like it," Moe Peters told the others. "He said Simon Lodeen made the fastest draw he'd ever seen."

"Lodeen made the fastest draw?" Stan Emerson asked, with a puzzled expression on his face.

"Onliest thing is, Buck Elliot's draw was faster," Moe added with a 'gotcha' smile.

The others laughed.

"I sure wish I could 'a seen that," Clyde Jamison said.

"I can't help but have me a feelin' that we just might wind up seein' somethin' like that anyway, if Smythe doesn't back off," George Baker said.

"Here comes Buck now," Sean said.

Because the meeting was planned to include Buck, it didn't actually get underway until he arrived.

"All right," Sean said, "Buck asked me to get everybody

together, because he has somethin' to say. Buck?" Sean said, relinquishing the floor.

"Gentlemen," Buck started, then noticing that Sara Sue was present, he smiled, and started over again.

"I meant to say Lady, and gentlemen."

"You damn well better not leave Sara Sue out," Roan Roberts said. "That is, if you don't want your ears boxed."

The others laughed.

"As most of you have heard, I've been appointed by Governor Tritle to be an Arizona Ranger," Buck continued. "As a matter of fact since I'm the only one who's been appointed by the governor, that makes me chief of all Arizona Rangers."

"What do you mean chief of all Arizona Rangers?" Baker asked, "It's like you said, you're the *only* one."

"I'm the only one now, but before I leave, there will be seven more rangers. As chief of the rangers, I can hire anyone I want." Buck smiled. "I just can't pay them."

"You can't count, either," Sara Sue said, "I see eight of us here."

"All right, Mrs. Tanner, if you want to be included, I'm certainly prepared to count you in."

"Can I ask a question?" Roan Roberts asked.

"Sure, what is it?"

"What's the purpose of making us all Rangers? What is it you're plannin' on us doin'? Because if you're thinkin' that you makin' me a Ranger is goin' to make me want to go over to Eagleshire 'n start arrestin' people, well, you got yourself another think comin' 'cause I ain't a' goin' to do it."

"Let me ask you this, Mr. Roberts. If Smythe sent some of his hands to start stealing your cattle, would you just stand by and watch them do it?"

"Hell, no I wouldn't do it. I'd shoot the sons of bitches."

"Exactly. And you would be justified in doing so. But, if

you were defending your holdings, *and* acting as an Arizona Ranger, an active and duly appointed officer of the law, there would be absolutely no question as to your right to use force."

"Yeah," Roan said. A large smile spread across his face. "Yeah!" he said with more enthusiasm, "I see what you mean."

"Mrs. Tanner," Buck started.

"Oh, for heaven's sake, it's Sara Sue," the gutsy woman said. "If I'm going to be one of you, I don't want to be set aside by how you call my name."

"All right, Sara Sue it is. Sara Sue, and gentleman, raise your hands and repeat after me.

"I, and say your name."

As one, the body of men and one lady followed Buck's instructions.

"Do solemnly swear that I will bear true allegiance to the territory of Arizona, and that I will serve her honestly and faithfully against all her enemies and all violators of the laws of the territory, county, and common sense whatsoever. I will observe and obey the orders of the Governor of the Territory of Arizona, and the orders of the officers appointed over me, so help me God."

The group repeated the oath as read to them by Buck who, like the others, was holding up his hand. At the words, "so help me God," Buck dropped his hand, as did the others.

"When we first started this group I believe there was some discussion as to whether or not the law would be on the side of Nigel Smythe," Buck said. "As of now, that is no longer a consideration. The law is on the side of each one of us."

"I'll be damn, I never thought I would be a lawman," Stan said.

"We need a name," Dub Wilkerson said.

"What do you mean, we need a name?" Baker asked. "We've got a name. We're the Rangers."

"Yes, but we need a name that would make our battalion unique among all the other battalions," Dub insisted.

"Dub, have you gone crazy? There are no other battalions," Moe said as if explaining to someone who had difficulty grasping things.

"But if there were other battalions, we would need a name. And who is to say that, someday, there won't be more Arizona Rangers?"

"I've got a name," Sean Kelly said.

"What is it?"

"The Defenders of Justice Brigade," Sean suggested.

"Yeah," Dub said, "Yeah, I like that. The initials are DOJ like the Department of Justice. I'll bet you Mary Kathleen will like that name too."

"Mary Kathleen? Who's Mary Kathleen?" Baker asked.

"Why, Miss Mary Kathleen Muldoon is going to be my wife," Dub said with a proud smile.

"What? You've gone and got yourself engaged?" Moe Peters asked, "How come you've never introduced her to any of us? Are you ashamed of us? Where'd you meet her? Is she from around here?"

"Damn, you boys sure ask a lot of questions," Dub said.

"Well can you blame us?" Sean asked. "Here you say you're goin' to marry some woman named Mary Kathleen Muldoon, and there ain't a damn one of us, none of your friends, that's ever even met her."

"That's just the point," Dub said.

"What's the point? That none of us have met her?"

"Yes," Dub's smile turned enigmatic, "Because I've never met her either."

. . .

New York:

Mary Kathleen Muldoon stepped down from the Hansom Cab on 42nd Street in front of the huge "L" shaped Grand Central Station which had been built by Cornelius Vanderbilt. This was the first step of her trip west, the money for the trip had been sent to her by a man she had never met, a man she knew nothing about. And yet, she was going to take a ten day train trip not only to meet the man, but to marry him.

What sort of man was he? For one thing she knew he was a trusting soul, though foolish might be more like it. He had sent her enough money to buy the ticket and sustain herself for the long trip from New York to Arizona and she could have quite easily just kept the money. If she had done that there would have been nothing Mr. William W. Wilkerson could do about it.

But she had accepted the money on her promise that she would go west to meet him, and Mary Kathleen was a woman of her word. She would go west, and she would marry him. She justified marrying a man she had never met by remembering that there were arranged weddings back in the "old" country, and how could this be any different?

She was going to a place called Canyon Diablo, and she crossed herself, and said a little prayer asking for protection and guidance.

A short while after she arrived at the station, Mary Kathleen stepped out into the huge car shed to board the first of what would be a series of trains before she finished her journey. She would be changing trains in Chicago, St. Louis, Memphis, Dallas, and Albuquerque before reaching her final destination.

"Think of all those people who went by wagon-train to California," *Mrs. J. Cline Pennington had told her when Mary Kathleen*

announced that she would be going west, by train. "Their trip was arduous, dangerous, and months long. Today you can go by train enjoying the luxury of a railroad car that protects you from rain, snow, beating sun, or bitter cold. Why, you will be able to dine sumptuously on meals served in a dining salon that rivals the world's finest restaurants. You can view the passing scenery while relaxing in an easy chair and you can pass the nights in a comfortable bed with clean sheets."

Although the trip was much faster than going by wagon train, it was nothing like the fantasy Mrs. Pennington had painted for her. Mary Kathleen was in the immigrant car where the seats were crowded and there were no clean sheets because there were no beds. She had to sleep as best she could, while sitting up. On her only visit to the dining car, one glance at the prices on the menu disabused her of any idea that she would be "dining sumptuously". Instead her meals consisted of a biscuit and coffee for breakfast, and a sandwich or a bowl of soup for lunch and dinner, often grabbed very quickly as the train would make a half-hour stop.

It was in St. Louis that she decided she would be more comfortable traveling in men's clothing than the dress she was wearing, so during the night she spent in St. Louis, she bought a pair of trousers, a man's shirt and a jacket. When she boarded a new train the next day, to anyone who gave her only a casual glance, it might have been a young man going west for some adventure.

Adventure, she thought. Yes, that is how she would think of this trip. She was continuing the adventure she had started two years ago when she left Galway, Ireland, as a young woman who had not yet turned nineteen.

. . .

"Mary Kathleen, sure lass, 'n have ye thought this through? 'Tis such a long way to America 'n I've heard that 'tis little love they have for the Irish there," Mary Kathleen's Aunt Mary had told her.

"With pa dead, I've nothing here to sustain me, 'n I'll nay be a burden on my pa's only sister. I have acquired a job in America, 'n 'tis anxious I am to start my new life."

The job in New York was as a maid-servant to Mrs. J. Cline Pennington. Alma Pennington had been a kind employer but when her husband died the old lady moved in with her son and daughter-in-law. There was neither room, nor funds, to continue the extravagance of a personal maid.

And now, for the second time in as many years, Mary Kathleen Muldoon was beginning another chapter in her life with a long and exhausting trip.

Over the last several days of travel, Mary Kathleen had learned best how to position herself in her seat for comfort, and she did that now. She heard the long, lonesome whistle of the train just as she drifted off to sleep.

15

BUSTER TRUAX, DEWEY STEAGLE, AND J.D. NIXON HAD COME into town from Eagleshire Ranch to pick up the mail and an expected shipment that was to arrive by train. It was a task they enjoyed because it got them away from the ranch for a while.

At the moment they were having a beer in the Cow Palace Saloon.

"We'd better get down to the depot 'n pick up that new stove for the cook," Buster said.

Draining the rest of their beer, the three men walked down to the depot to meet the train. The wagon they had brought to town was already there.

The arriving train came to a stop with a hiss and a squeal of breaks before sitting there venting steam and making popping sounds as the bearings and journals cooled. A moment later passengers began stepping down from the train.

"Ha," Buster said, "look at that skinny little feller there. Now just what do you think someone like him is goin' to be a' doin' out here?"

"More 'n likely get 'im a job clerkin' in a store or somethin'," J.D. said. "I sure can't see a little feller like that 'n doin'
nothin' else."

It was hot when Mary Kathleen Muldoon arrived in
Canyon Diablo. Now, some ten days since she had left New
York, the sharp contrast in temperature seemed unreal.
Bracing herself against the heat, she walked from the shade
provided by the roofed-platform, into the bright Arizona
sun.

A Mexican woman was operating a food stand just off the
platform of the depot. The old woman didn't have any teeth
so she kept her mouth closed, and with her hooked nose and
a protruding chin, it looked as if the chin and nose nearly
touched. A swarm of flies buzzed around the steaming
kettles, drawn by the pungent aromas of meat and sauces.
The old woman worked with quick, deft fingers, rolling the
ingredients into something which looked like pie crust. Then
she wrapped the rolls in old newspapers before she handed
them to her customers.

Mary Kathleen was curious about the food, so she walked
over to the old woman.

""N would ye be for tellin' me what it is you are selling?"
she asked.

"Tacos," the old woman said, "very good. You try."

"How much?"

"Five cents."

Mary Kathleen took out a nickel and handed it to the old
woman who, quickly, put together a taco and handed it back
to her.

"Hey, tenderfoot, those things go down a lot better with a
beer," someone called. "Or, don't you have beer where you
come from?"

"Aye, 'n 'tis for sure that Ireland is known for the finest beer," Mary Kathleen said.

"Aye, 'n 'tis for sure that Ireland is known for the finest beer," the man mimicked.

Mary Kathleen was surprised by the bantering tone of the man. She had done nothing to antagonize him. Why was he so belligerent? Glancing over toward the man, she flashed him a look of irritation to let him know she was not pleased with his unwanted attention.

The man was leaning against the front wheel of a wagon. He had his arms folded across his chest and one leg bent at the knee so that his foot was against the wheel. He appeared to be in his twenties, with a dark handlebar mustache and a cowlick of the same color across his forehead. He was dressed in a red checkered shirt and denim trousers with leather chaps. There were two other men similarly dressed who were standing near him, though neither of them had spoken.

The fact that the three men were wearing guns neither disturbed, nor surprised her. She had gotten over the surprise at seeing everyone armed, because the farther west she had come since leaving New York, the more prevalent the sight became. And now it seemed that everyone she saw was armed.

"I don't like that look on your face, tenderfoot. What are you a'lookin' at?" the man asked, standing up straight and letting his arms fall down loosely to his side.

"'Tis apparent to any with eyes to see, that I am looking at an ill-mannered boor," Mary Kathleen said. She looked away from him then, satisfied that she had put him in his place and hoping that if she dropped it, he would go away and leave her alone.

"What'd you call me, boy?" the man blustered. "A boar? Ain't that a hog? You callin' me a dirty pig?"

"Nay," Mary Kathleen said, "That's not what I said."

"The hell it ain't. You insulted me, mister. I heard what you called me. You called me a pig."

"Please," Mary Kathleen said, growing a little frightened. "I don't want any trouble."

"Well, you already got trouble, mister, and plenty of it," the man said. "Nobody calls me a pig and gets away with it."

"Please, 'tis sorry I am if I insulted ye," Mary Kathleen said. She was growing even more frightened. What had she done? How had she gotten into such a situation? All she had done was buy something to eat.

"You packin' a gun, tenderfoot?"

"What? But of course not," Mary Kathleen answered nervously, "Sure, 'n would ye be for tellin' me, why I would want to carry a gun?"

"If you are goin' to go 'roun' callin' folks a pig, then you'd best start packin' a gun to back you up. Some folks might not be as nice as I am. 'N just to show you how nice of a man I can be, I ain't goin' to just shoot you; I'm goin' give you a chance to defend yourself. Dewey, give 'im your gun. I'm goin' to shoot this funny talkin' little son of a bitch right now, but seein' as there are people that'll be watchin' it, I want it to be fair 'n square."

"What?" Mary Kathleen asked, gasping for breath. She dropped her taco and put her hand up to her throat. "What are ye saying?"

"I'm sayin', mister', that I'm goin' to gut shoot you right here 'n leave you for crow bait. But I aim to give you a chance. Give 'im your gun, Dewey, what are you waitin' around for?"

"Buster, this here feller ain't no more 'n a kid. Leave him alone. Hell, he don't even look like he's shavin' yet. Look at that fuzzy cheek."

"Yeah, well how old was Billy the Kid when he

commenced his killin'? Now give 'im your gun, like I told you to."

"No, I ain't a' goin' to do it."

Mary Kathleen felt a sliver of hope that maybe the man's friend could talk him out of it.

"Either give the tenderfoot your gun or use it yourself," Buster said menacingly, "'N I'll tell you right now, it don't make no never mind to me which one you do, 'cause this feller has done got me in a killin' mood, 'n I'd just as soon shoot you as him." He turned to face his friend and moved his hand to let it hover just over the handle of his revolver.

Mary Kathleen couldn't believe what was happening. This fool was bent on killing someone, and it didn't seem to make any difference who it was. He was ready to shoot his own friend if necessary.

"No, no," Steagle said in a frightened voice. He began unbuckling his pistol belt. "I'll give 'im my gun."

The belligerent one smiled, but there was no humor in his smile, "Yeah, I thought you might do that."

"Son, do you really want to fight this pig? Or would you allow me the pleasure of killing him?" a new voice asked. The voice was low and resonant, and the words, though as dramatic as any words Mary Kathleen had ever heard, were spoken in such an off-hand way that one might think he was passing an innocent remark about the weather.

Mary Kathleen looked at this new player upon the stage, and saw that he was tall and blond, with flashing blue eyes that were deep and unexpectedly expressive. Who was this man to speak this casually about shooting someone?

"I . . . I didn't call him a pig," Mary Kathleen said.

"You didn't? Well, on second thought," her rescuer said, speaking just as easily, "I think calling this son of a bitch a pig does a disservice to all the pigs of the world."

Steagle stopped unbuckling his gun belt and he and the

other man who had been a part of the trio moved quickly out of the way, leaving Buster all alone. Even the old taco woman moved back. Only Mary Kathleen, who was new to this country and inexperienced in assessing the raw passions which governed its inhabitants, remained in harm's way.

Buster turned purple with anger. He pointed toward the man who had just challenged him.

"Now look here, Mister, I ain't got no quarrel with you. My quarrel is with this here, fella. But, if you want to butt in, feel free to do so. I reckon I can take care of this feller after I take care of you."

"Why are you so dead set to kill this boy?" Buck said.

"He called me a pig."

"Is that a fact? He called you a pig, did he? Well, in that case, I think you should thank him for elevating your status."

"What makes you think I'd want to do a fool thing like that?"

"Because I'll kill you if you don't."

There was no humor in the man's chuckle, and the smile was sinister. "You're going to kill me are you? Who the hell are you, anyway?"

"I'm the city marshal. You don't need to know any more than that."

"Y . . . y . . . you're the city marshal? You're Buck Elliot? You're the one that kilt Lodeen?"

"Right, on all three accounts," Buck answered. "Now, would you tell me your name? The undertaker might need to know that."

Mary Kathleen was amazed that even though the conversation was of killing, this man who had just identified himself as Buck Elliot still showed no more emotion than he would in ordering a cup of coffee. What sort of men were these who could speak of killing in so casual a manner?

She also saw that there was an immediate change in

Buster's demeanor. Instead of belligerence it was palpable fear. Who was this man standing beside her whose very name could instill such fright?

"No, now, Marshal Elliot, there ain't no need for this to be goin' no further. I wasn't really goin' to shoot 'im. I was just funnin' this little feller, what with him being a tenderfoot 'n all," Buster forced a laugh. "What I was actual doin' was I was just welcomin' him to Arizona. I mean, ain't you never had no fun, hazin' someone?"

"Do you think I'm funning you?" Buck asked.

"What? Uh, no, no I don't, I think you're serious wantin' to shoot me, 'n if you do, it'll be murder, on account of, I ain't a' goin' to draw agin' you."

"I think it would be better for you if you stayed out of my way for the rest of the day," Buck said. "It wouldn't be very smart of you to make me angry again."

"I . . . I ain't goin' to do nothin' to make you mad no more," Buster promised. "But, I work for Mr. Smythe, 'n me 'n my friends here have to pick up a stove 'n take it out to the ranch. So, you might see me again, but it ain't a' goin' to be purposeful."

"All right, I'll keep that in mind. But it would make me feel a lot better if you would apologize to this young man."

"I'm sorry, Mister, I didn't mean nothin' by it."

"'N would ye be for tellin' me why 'tis, that everyone is thinkin' that I am a man? 'Tis a woman, I am."

"What?" Buck and Buster said, simultaneously.

Buck turned for a closer look and was able to see that though dressed as a man, the person standing beside him was indeed a young woman.

"Ma'am," Buster corrected, "I'm sorry ma'am. And Marshal Elliot, I'll apologize to you too. I'm sorry folks didn't understand I was only jokin', I reckon I'll get on over to the freight office to pick up that stove Mr. Smythe ordered."

Buck watched Buster put his pistol away, then he turned toward the young woman.

"Ma'am, I'm sorry that this episode was your welcome to Canyon Diablo. Not everyone is like that ornery cuss. Is there anything I can do for you?"

"Aye, perhaps so. Would ye be knowin' how I might make contact with a gentleman by the name of William W. Wilkerson? 'Tis sure I am that he would have welcomed me if he had known I would be arriving today."

Buck flashed a huge smile. "Well, I'll be. You're talking about Dub, aren't you? You must be Miss Mary Kathleen Muldoon."

Mary Kathleen gasped in surprise. "Aye, that is my name. But would ye be for tellin' me how 'tis that you know that?"

"Dub is a friend of mine," Buck said.

"'N 'tis Dub he is called?" Mary Kathleen asked in confusion.

"Because of the three Ws in his name," Buck explained. "He's been looking forward to your arrival and if you would like, I can get a buckboard and take you out to his ranch."

Mary Kathleen smiled. "Oh, then he really does have a ranch. He is gainfully employed."

"He is considerably more than just gainfully employed, ma'am. Why Dub has a nice ranch, small, but with the possibility of growing into something much more productive."

"'Tis most glad I am to hear such a thing. 'Twas taking a chance I was, by agreeing to such an arrangement. When one does such a thing, one doesn't always know how it will turn out."

"Miss Muldoon, please let me put your mind to rest. Dub is as fine a man as you might ever want to meet," Buck said. "I think you'll be very pleased with what you find." He flashed a big smile. "And I know for a fact that he'll be pleased with what he sees when he meets you."

"'Tis thankin' ye I am. But before we go, I would like to get a room in the hotel, I need a . . . that is, I would like to get cleaned up and dressed." She laughed self-consciously. "I would nay be wanting Mr. Wilkerson to be for mistakin' me for a boy, as did that very rude gentleman."

"You have luggage?" Buck asked.

"Aye."

"All right, let's pick up your luggage then get you checked in to the hotel while I get us a buckboard."

16

"WE SHOULD 'A TOOK 'IM," BUSTER TRUAX SAID. TRUAX WAS driving the wagon. Steagle and Nixon were in the wagon with him.

"You had your chance," Steagle said. "You could 'a shot 'im 'n there wouldn't have been no trouble with the law, seein' as he was bracin' you."

"Yeah, well, he's a killer. I mean, look what he done do Lodeen 'n you know how fast Lodeen was. I wouldn't have stood a chance with him."

"Then what do you mean when you said you should 'a took him?" Nixon asked.

Truax shook his head, "Huh uh, I didn't say nothin' 'bout *me* takin' 'im. What I said was *we* should a' took 'im. There was three of us, only you two didn't seem to have no interest in helpin' out."

"You know what I think, Buster?" Steagle said. "I think that if we'd 'a tried to take a part in it, Elliot would 'a kilt all three of us."

"Yeah, 'n he'd 'a kilt you first," Nixon added.

Truax was quiet for a long moment, then he slapped the reins against the backs of the team of mules.

"We should 'a took 'im," he said again.

When Buck stepped into the hotel half an hour later he didn't notice the woman who was sitting in one of the lobby chairs. He started toward the front desk to check on Miss Muldoon when the woman called out to him.

"Marshal Elliot?"

Turning to the call of his name, Buck was surprised at the startling difference between the young woman who was standing before him, and the tomboy he had met at the depot. This woman had bright red hair, sky-blue eyes, and she was wearing a form-fitting green dress that left absolutely no question as to her gender. She was, in fact, one of the most beautiful women Buck had ever seen.

"Miss Muldoon?"

"Yes."

"Are you ready to go?" Buck asked after he recovered from his surprise.

"Aye, but 'tis nervous I am."

Buck chuckled. "Believe me, Miss Muldoon, you have nothing to be nervous about."

During the trip out to the ranch, Mary Kathleen alleviated her nervousness by telling her story to Buck.

"M' mither died when I was but a wee lass, 'n m' father never took to hisself another wife. He worked in a bar in Galway but one mornin' he just didn't wake up, 'n findin' m'self without family, and in need of employment, I came to America for work.

"'Twas a lucky connection I made in New York, for I was employed by Mr. J. Cline Pennington. 'Twas actually Mrs. Pennington I worked for, 'n as fine a lady I never met before.

But when Mr. Pennington died she had to let me go. Oh, there were tears a'plenty when we parted, but a story in the paper I read was for tellin' how there would be good, honestly employed men in the West who were for wanting wives to come and join them. I read about some of them 'n I chose Mr. Wilkerson."

"I think you'll see that you made a good choice," Buck said. He pointed ahead to where the road was making a rather sharp curve to the left. "This is Mountain Shadow Ranch."

The ranch was well laid out with a neat white house with a red roof and red shutters. There was also a barn, a shed, and a smaller structure nearby. Standing near the barn was a rather rough looking man with unkempt hair and a scraggly beard.

"Is that Mr. Wilkerson?" Mary Kathleen asked. Though she tried, bravely, to keep any disappointment from her voice, Buck could hear it.

"No, that's Beans Evans. He works for Dub," Buck said as he waved to Beans. He drove on by the barn and stopped at the house. Dub, who had seen them drive up, was standing on the front porch. Dub was six feet tall, neatly shaven, with well-trimmed dark hair and brown eyes. "That's Dub," Buck said under his breath as they approached.

"Oh."

Buck smiled at the relief that was evident in her one word reply.

"Howdy, Buck," Dub said, and though he was talking to Buck, he was staring at the pretty red headed woman who was sitting in the seat beside him. "What brings you to Mountain Shadow?"

"You might say I'm making a delivery," Buck said.

"Oh?" Dub had not taken his eyes off Mary Kathleen.

"Dub, I would like for you to meet Miss Mary Kathleen Muldoon. Miss Muldoon, this is Dub Wilkerson."

"Miss Muldoon!" Dub said as he leapt down from the porch and hurried to the buckboard. "Forgive me for not meeting you, but I thought you weren't coming until next week."

"Aye, I left New York sooner than I thought I would. 'Tis hoping, I am, Mr. Wilkerson, that my early arrival isn't an unwelcome intrusion."

"Are you kidding? How could you ever be an unwelcome intrusion? And please don't be calling me Mr. Wilkerson. My name is Dub."

Mary Kathleen smiled, and the smile lit up her face.

"Dub it is, then," she said.

"She has a room at the hotel in town," Buck said, "But I thought you two would want to meet each other as soon as possible."

"You thought right," Dub said, "Oh, Miss Muldoon," he started, but Mary Kathleen interrupted him.

"Here now, Dub, 'n if I'm to address ye so, 'n as we are to be wed, wouldn't ye be for wantin' to call yer bride by her Christian name?"

Dub laughed. "I would at that. Mary Kathleen, if you're not too tired, and, Buck, if you don't mind sticking around a bit longer so you can take her back to town, I'd like her to meet some of our friends and neighbors."

"Sure 'n as they'll be my neighbors as well, I would like to meet them," Mary Kathleen said.

"Good, we'll start with the Kellys. They're the closest."

"Kelly is it?" Mary Kathleen asked with a big smile, "'Twill be good to have Irish neighbors."

Dub hooked a team up to the surrey, and with Buck following, drove Mary Kathleen over to Trailcross Ranch. Even before the surrey and buckboard had come to a halt,

Sean, Nola, and Finn were on the front porch, made curious by the strange arrival. But when Sean saw the pretty young woman sitting in the surrey with Dub, he smiled.

"Well now, would this beautiful young lady be Miss Mary Kathleen Muldoon?"

"It is, and I brought her over to make your acquaintance," Dub said.

"Finn, get your mama," Sean ordered.

After greetings and coffee, Rosaleen and Nola took Mary Kathleen to introduce her to all of the other ladies of the valley.

"Well I'll tell you one thing," Sean said as the three ladies drove away in the surrey, "Mary Kathleen has certainly made a hit with Rosaleen and Nola."

"I have absolutely no doubt but that all the others will take to her as well," Buck said.

"When will the wedding be?" Sean asked.

"I don't know, I haven't asked her to marry me yet," Dub replied. "I'm hoping she'll say yes; then we can set the date."

Buck laughed.

"What is it? Why are you laughing?"

"Dub, do you think Mary Kathleen Muldoon came two thousand, five hundred miles just to see the cactus? Correct me if I'm wrong, but she is a mail order bride, is she not?"

"Yeah," Dub said. He smiled. "I guess she did come to marry me, didn't she?"

With Rosaleen taking the lead, plans were made for the wedding, and the plans included making Dub's house, "fit for a woman to live in."

Sara Sue took over the duties of getting the house ready by hanging curtains, replacing a worn blanket with a newly made patchwork quilt, and adding a colorful tea kettle.

Rosaleen made arrangements with the church, while Edna Emerson baked a cake. But it was Martha Peters who played the biggest role, for she still had her wedding gown which she made available. Nola Kelly was about the same size as Mary Kathleen, so Martha pressed her into service to model the dress for her as she made repairs and adjustments. The result was a wedding dress that was so beautiful that it brought tears to Mary Kathleen's eyes when it was presented to her.

The wedding was held in St. Francis Roman Catholic Church in Canyon Diablo, and every small rancher in the valley was in attendance. In addition to the ranchers, so many of the townspeople were present that there wasn't an empty pew in the entire church.

Dub had asked Moe Peters to be his best man, and Mary Kathleen had asked Nola to be her maid of honor. The organist finished *Pachelbel Canon in D*, then the music switched to *Felix Mendelssohn's Wedding March*, and everyone looked around to see Mary Kathleen being escorted down the aisle by Buck Elliot. Mary Kathleen made such a beautiful picture that all in the church drew a sharp breath in admiration.

Dub had invited Beans Evans to the wedding but Beans begged off. "I ain't very good in fancy places," he said. "Besides which, they's a leak in the roof of the bunk house 'n I need to get it patched."

"All right," Dub agreed.

"But iffen you're goin' to have a weddin' cake, why, you could bring me a piece," Beans suggested with a smile.

"I'll do that," Dub promised.

.   .   .

Beans had just finished putting a patch on the roof when he saw four men approaching. At first he thought it might be someone from the wedding but he recognized one of them as Adam Stillwell, so he knew it wasn't a social call. He climbed down from the roof of the bunkhouse and walked out to meet them.

"What do you men want?" Beans asked.

"How come you ain't at the weddin'?" Stillwell asked.

"'Cause I ain't. What do you want?"

"We've got some business to take care of," Stillwell said.

"What kind of business? Mr. Wilkerson ain't here."

"We know. That's why we're here."

"You ain't makin' no sense," Beans said.

"Well, you don't need to worry none about it 'cause you won't be around no more," Stillwell said. He drew his gun and fired, the bullet striking Beans in the forehead.

"All right boys, like I said, we got some business to take care of, so let's get started."

After the happy reception Dub and Mary Kathleen ran laughing through a shower of rice and climbed into the surrey, to which some of Dub's friends had attached a big sign reading: JUST MARRIED. They drove away with tin cans rattling, and huzzahs and shouts from the town.

"Mary Kathleen," Dub said as they drove away from town, "I swear to you, girl, I'll never do anything to make you regret this major step you have taken to commit yourself to spending the rest of your life with me. And I'll do everything I can to make you start to fall in love with me, so that it'll be a pleasure for you, and not a commitment."

Mary Kathleen took Dub's arm in both her hands.

""N would ye be for tellin' me William W. Wilkerson, why

would ye be for thinkin' I have nay already started to fall in love with ye?"

Dub stopped the surrey, then put his arms around his new bride and kissed her deeply.

"Mary Kathleen, you have made me the happiest man in the world," Dub said.

"'Tis a foine begginin' to the rest o' our lives," Mary Kathleen replied with a big smile.

The smile left Mary Kathleen's face. "Dub, where is that smoke coming from?" She pointed toward a thick, heavy cloud of smoke, boiling into the air.

"What? God, no it's coming from our place!" Dub shouted, and snapping the reins, he urged the horses into a gallop.

Even before they got there, Dub could see that his house and barn had gone up in flames. He also saw, lying face down in the yard half way between the burning house and the burning barn, the body of Beans Evans.

"God in heaven, what has happened?" Mary Kathleen asked, sub-consciously clutching her throat.

17

When Buck drove himself to the shooting location the next day he was met at the crafty wagon by the screenwriter.

"You aren't going to like the scene today," Ryan Gilmore said as he added copious amounts of cream and sugar to his coffee.

Buck chuckled as he took his own cup of black coffee. "How will this be any different from yesterday?"

"I'll let you be the judge of that."

The shooting location was a train depot and the lighting and sound technicians were getting everything ready. Several of the actors and actresses were standing around most of them, Ryan pointed out, bit actors who were here just to provide faces in the background. A smiling Clive Malone came toward them, accompanied by a beautiful young woman. Seeing the way she was dressed, Buck assumed she would be portraying a saloon girl.

"Buck," Clive said, "I'd like you to meet Miss Pauline Townsend."

Buck smiled. "Miss Townsend, I've seen you in pictures before. It's a pleasure meeting you."

"Oh, my, you're still a very handsome man, Mr. Elliot," Pauline said with a flirtatious smile. "I can see why you were such a ladies' man in your youth."

"I beg your pardon?" Buck said, confused by the woman's comment. "Ladies' man?"

"I read the whole script," Pauline said, effusively.

"Places!" Guy Lashlee called.

"We'd better do what the director says," Clive said as he ushered Pauline away. "Buck, perhaps we can have lunch today."

Pauline Townsend stood on the depot platform and three of the actors got into position just across the platform from her.

"Picture is up," the Assistant Director announced, "Everyone settle please.

"Action."

ROWDY NUMBER ONE

Well, ain't you a purty thang though. Come over here darlin' and give me a kiss.

MARY KATHLEEN

My name is Mary Kathleen Muldoon. Would your name be Dub Wilkerson?

ROWDY NUMBER ONE (laughing)

No, I ain't that cattle rustler. I ride for the biggest ranch in the whole state. Now, come over here 'n give me a kiss, or I'll come over there 'n get it.

MARY KATHLEEN (*looking around in fear*)

Oh please, can't someone help me? I'm a mail order bride and I'm here to meet my husband.

BUCK

My name is Buck Elliot, ma'am, and I'm here to help you.

ROWDY NUMBER ONE

Draw your guns boys, let's teach this varmint a lesson!

All three rowdies draw their guns but Buck draws his two guns faster. After an exchange of gun fire the three rowdies go down. Buck puts his left hand gun in the holster, twirls his right hand gun on his finger then holds the barrel up to his lips to blow the smoke away.

MARY KATHLEEN

Oh, you have saved me.
        Mary Kathleen puts her arms around Buck's neck and kisses him.

BUCK

Here now, didn't you say you're here as a mail order bride?

MARY KATHLEEN

Aye, but I'm not married yet, so 'tis no crime in kissing the man who is my hero.
    Mary Kathleen kisses Buck again. Finally Buck pulls away from the kiss.

BUCK

Who have you come to marry?

MARY KATHLEEN

I am to be wed to Dub Wilkerson. Isn't that a funny name?

BUCK

I think it is a very good name. Dub is a friend of mine. I'll take you to him.

MARY KATHLEEN

Oh, you are such a handsome man. Sure 'n 'tis too bad you are not Dub.

. . .

"Cut!" Guy Lashlee called.

"Damn, Johnny, I thought you were going to fall to the left," the actor who had portrayed rowdy number one said, as the three got to their feet. "I had to twist around to keep from fallin' on you."

"Yeah, well, I'm glad you missed me."

It took four more takes before the director was satisfied.

"All right," Lashlee called, "break for lunch! Day actors, if you're in the next scene, don't miss your call, because if you do, you'll be replaced."

The catering service provided a hot lunch for staff, crew, and actors. The tables were set by precedence with the lead actors and senior production staff getting the premium tables. Buck wasn't sure where in the hierarchy of the *Legend of a Gunfighter* Production that the technical consultant actually fit. But his question was immaterial because he was invited to share the head table with Clive Malone, Alcy Harris, Guy Lashlee, and Pauline Townsend. Ryan Gilmore was at the table as well, but Buck didn't know if he was there by right of being the screenwriter, or whether he, too, had been invited by Clive.

"Tell me. Mr. Elliot, what did you think of the scene we shot this morning?" Harris asked.

"That's not at all how it happened," Buck said.

"But we took that scene directly from the book," Harris said, "Are you saying you didn't have a confrontation at the depot when Miss Mary Kathleen Muldoon arrived in Canyon Diablo?"

"I had a confrontation, yes," Buck said, "but it didn't end with me killing three men, and I certainly didn't kiss Mary Kathleen."

"You can never have too much action in an action movie," Harris said.

Clive picked up Pauline's hand. "And I ask you, how can

you shoot a scene with Pauline Townsend, the most beautiful woman in Hollywood, and not kiss her?"

"Pauline Townsend. Is that your real name?" Buck asked.

Pauline giggled. "That's my screen name, do you like it? My real name is Polly Tuckwaller."

"Buck, one thing you have to understand about screenplays is because of the constraints of time and story continuity, some actual events are going to be combined," Lashlee said.

"All right," Buck said, without taking his observation any further.

"But you did come to the aid of Mary Kathleen Muldoon, didn't you?" Pauline asked.

Buck smiled, and nodded. "Yes, I did do that."

"I'm glad you did. I can't tell you how pleased I am to portray her, I mean, a young woman who gives up everything and comes west to marry a man she's never met. What courage she displayed."

"Yes, I'd say she showed a good deal of courage, not only by coming west to marry Dub, but to have left Ireland in the first place."

"And was she a beautiful woman?" Pauline asked.

Buck chuckled. "Yes, as it so happens, Mary Kathleen was a very beautiful woman. But, Miss Townsend, you've portrayed Calamity Jane and Bell Star, and believe me, they were so ugly they'd make a freight train take two miles of dirt road. So any woman you would portray is a beautiful woman, just because you are portraying her."

Pauline laughed, then leaned forward to offer Buck a generous view of her cleavage. "My, how gallant of you to say such a thing."

One of the technicians came over then, and he leaned over to whisper something to Harris.

"Are you sure?" Harris asked.

"Yes, sir," the technician replied.

"All right, no more shootings on location today. We'll have to shoot on set this afternoon, so back to the studio, everyone."

After the meal was finished, Buck walked back out to the Plymouth that the studio had supplied for him to drive.

"The Plymouth has floating power, you know," the production assistant had said when Buck picked up the car.

"What's floating power?"

"I don't know," the PA replied, sheepishly, "But it's in all the newspaper and magazine ads so it must be something very good."

When he turned off West Pico he was greeted by the gate guard at Starburst Studios.

"Hello, Mr. Elliot, how are you doing today?"

"Oh, about as well as can be expected, thank you, Mr. Usher."

"You know, there's actors 'n studio people that's been here for years 'n they ain't never took the time to even learn my name," Usher said. "I appreciate you doing that, Mr. Elliot. Here." Usher handed a license plate-sized card to buck.

"What's this?" Buck asked taking the card.

Usher smiled. "It's a Class A parking permit. Stick it up in your windshield, 'n it'll let you park anywhere on the studio lot that ain't already marked with somebody else's name."

"Why, I appreciate that, Mr. Usher, thank you," Buck said with a little salute as he drove onto the Starburst Motion Picture Studios lot.

Buck had just gotten out of his car when he heard the low, growling rumble of Clive Malone's open top Cord driving up, with Pauline Townsend riding beside him. He stopped in a place that was marked with his name.

"Oh, Clive you shouldn't have driven so fast," Pauline complained. She ran her hand through her hair. "The hairdresser is going to be so upset with you when I tell him this mess is your fault."

"You're the one that kept saying go faster," Clive said.

"Oh, I did, didn't I?" Pauline replied with a little laugh. "It was so much fun, but it'll take me forever to get ready for my next scene."

"Don't worry about it, you aren't in the next scene," Clive said, "I am."

"Ha! And what scene are you not in?"

"If you want to be a star, you have to have time on screen," Clive said, "and my contract guarantees that I'll have a lot of it, no matter what picture I do."

It took over an hour before they were ready to shoot and just before photography began, Guy Lashlee gave Buck a shooting script. Clive Malone walked into the middle of the street in the "town set" then nodded toward the director.

Once all the preliminary directions were given, and photography started, Buck followed along on the script as it was played out before him:

EXT. STREET - DAY
Elliot is standing in the middle of the street. Several
passersby stop to look at him. A teenage girl lets out a
delighted shriek.

LODEEN has ridden his horse into the middle of the street and now looks around to see what all the fuss is about. When he makes out Elliot standing alone, his expression changes.

LODEEN

Elliot, folks tell me that you are king of the roost in these parts. Well, you ain't goin' to be after today. After today I'm goin' to be known as the man that kilt Buck Elliot, then I'll be king of the roost.

BUCK

You are all talk, Lodeen. You are a little man with a big mouth.

LODEEN

Die, Elliot, die!

Lodeen spurs his horse and gallops toward Buck shooting.
The bullets kick up the dust in front and back of Buck who
now raises his pistol slowly. A bullet tears through Buck's hat and it goes flying. Lodeen is almost upon him before Buck fires. Lodeen is knocked off the horse and hits the street dead.

"Cut!" Lashlee called.

"That didn't feel right to me. Guy," Clive said, "I'd like another take."

"Another take?" the actor who was playing the role of

Lodeen said. "All right, we can do another take, but I've got an idea. This time, Clive Malone falls off the horse."

There was a scattering of nervous laughter as Clive glared at the actor.

"All right, let's reset," Lashlee called, "We'll do another take."

1 8

Although the big house, the barn, and the shed were burned, for some reason the small cabin that had been the residence of Beans Evans, was not. And it was here that Dub and Mary Kathleen spent the first night of their married life. It was not the typical wedding night that bride and groom normally have with the nervousness, the hesitancy, and yet the eager exploration of each other. Rather this night was one of anger and sorrow on Dub's part, and apprehension and confusion on the part of Mary Kathleen.

I intend to find the sons of bitches who did this, Dub thought grimly.

What have I let myself in for? Mary Kathleen wondered.

"Mary Kathleen," Dub said when they were lying together in bed, with the lantern extinguished so that they were in total darkness, "I know that we're supposed to, I mean, that I should be . . . uh, well, I know what it's supposed to be like on

137

our wedding night. But . . ." Dub let his thought hang, uncompleted.

Mary Kathleen reached down and took Dub's hand in her own, "I know," she said, and she squeezed his hand, "I know," she repeated.

And with that acknowledgement and understanding, their love was born.

The next morning they were awakened by the sound of singing.

"I'll take you home again Kathleen
Across the ocean wild and wide
To where your heart has ever been
Since first you were my blushing bride
The roses all have left your cheek
I watch them fade away and die,"

"What is that?" Mary Kathleen asked, sitting up as the song came streaming through the window.

Your voice is sadden when you speak
And tears bedim your loving eyes
Oh, would I will take you back Kathleen
To where your heart will feel no pain
And when the fields are fresh and green
I will take you to your home again

Dub hopped out of bed and padded over to look through the window.

Sean Kelly was singing, but he wasn't alone.

"Mary Kathleen!" he said excitedly, "Mary Kathleen, it's our neighbors. They've come with wagons and lumber!"

Dressing quickly, Dub and Mary Kathleen hurried outside where, already building material was being unloaded.

"Dub, my friend, we'll have this house and your barn up in no time," Sean Kelly promised.

Rosaleen, Nola, Sara Sue and the other ladies were also present and as the men began unloading the lumber, nails, and tools; the women unloaded food, and started cooking breakfast.

"Welcome to the Mogollon Rim, Mary Kathleen Wilkerson," Sara Sue said, "but it's a sorry welcome, I have to say, finding your home burnt to the ground."

"'Tis sad I am for the poor dear man, Mr. Evans," Mary Kathleen said. She looked over toward the men who were already cleaning away the burnt debris of what had once been a fine house. "But there could be no warmer welcome than is being shown here today."

It was mid-morning by the time Buck arrived and the blackened remains of the original house had already been cleared and construction started.

Buck greeted everyone.

"Grab a hammer, Buck," Sean called.

Buck was about to do so when he got a feeling in the pit of his stomach. There was no scientific explanation for these "feelings" that he experienced from time to time, but more often than not, they bore fruit. And the feeling he got now was that he should check on the homes of the volunteers who were here to help Dub rebuild his house.

"You men go on without me," Buck said. "I think it might

be a pretty good idea to check on your places while all of you are here."

"Yes," Sean said, "yes, I think you're right. You go ahead, Buck, we'll get the house up without you."

Buck had checked two of the ranches without finding anything, and he was about to leave Moe Peters' Sundown Ranch when he saw three riders approaching. Remaining mounted, he moved around behind the barn, knowing that he couldn't be seen by the riders as they approached. He recognized two of three: men he knew as Bud Clayton and Icky Sanders. He knew them only because he had seen them in the Mogollon Saloon. And from that casual encounter with them, he also knew that they were riders for Nigel Smythe. But, as had been pointed out to him, they weren't actual cowboys. They were part of Smythe's "special" riders.

"Where's Lem at? How come he ain't with us?" Sanders asked.

"He dropped off back a ways to keep watch," Clayton said.

"What's he need to keep watch for? Ever' one of them dumb sons of bitches is over to the Wilkerson place helpin' 'im to rebuild his house."

"Yeah," Riley Walker said with a laugh. "How do you think they're goin' to like it when they come back 'n find they got 'em another 'n that's a' goin' to need to be rebuilt?"

"I think they're goin' to be a mite upset," Clayton said, and all three laughed.

"Damn, wouldn't it be good iffen we was to have us some sticks of dynamite we could just chunk in through the winders, instead of lit torches," Sanders asked.

"No, hell no," Clayton insisted, "That'd make a noise to

wake the dead. This way they won't have no idea what we're 'a doin' 'til they come back 'n find their house all burnt down just like the other 'n is."

"Yeah, but they's more 'n likely goin' to have that 'n done in another couple of days or so. Then they'll commence a' buildin' on this 'n. So what's the purpose of us a' doing this?" Walker asked.

Sanders chuckled. "It's a lot easier burnin' 'em down than it is buildin' 'em back. We could just keep on a' doin' this 'til ever' thing settles down, 'n the pilgrims will get tired of it 'n ride off some'ers else. 'N whenever they do that, all this land will belong to Smythe."

"Lordee, by the time Smythe's finished he's a' goin' to wind up with more land than the entire state of Rhode Island."

"How do you know, Clayton? Have you ever been to Rhode Island?"

"No, but I somebody tol' me about it once, 'n I know it ain't a very big state."

It would be easy, Buck thought, to just start shooting. From this angle and range he could cut down at least two of the three before they even knew they were in danger. But Buck wasn't the kind of man who would dry-gulch his quarry. Instead, he decided to confront them.

"After we get the fire goin', we goin' to cut out any of his cattle?" Buck heard one of the men ask.

"We didn't take no cows when we done the Wilkerson place."

"That's 'cause we thought they'd be comin' back real soon. But we could drive off the ones that's right here, real easy."

"Ha! When you think about it, I went into this business in

the first place 'cause I didn't want to punch cows no more, 'n what am I doin'? I'm punchin' cows," Sanders said.

The other two laughed, then Walker replied. "Yeah, but Smythe wants all these little ranchers run off, 'n our cut is a dollar a head for ever' one of these cows we move. You know any cowboys that's a' makin' that kind of money by punchin' cows?"

"No, I don't reckon I do."

They were close enough now that Buck could hear them quite clearly so he urged his horse around the corner of the barn, then rode out in front to challenge them. There, no more than twenty yards away, he saw the three riders getting ready to light their torches.

"Why don't you fellas just hold it right there?" he called.

"What the hell? Where'd you come from?" Clayton hissed, startled by Buck's sudden appearance.

"Where I came from doesn't matter," Buck said. "Drop that torch, shuck your guns and raise your hands. I'm puttin' you boys under arrest."

"You can't arrest us," Sanders insisted, "You're a town marshal, you ain't got no authority out here."

"Yeah, I do," Buck said with a righteous grin. "I'm an Arizona Ranger; I have authority anywhere in the entire territory."

Suddenly there was an angry buzz, then the "thocking" sound of a bullet tearing into flesh. A fountain of blood squirted up from the neck of Buck's horse and the animal went down on its front knees, then collapsed onto its right side. Buck barely avoided being pinned under the horse. He also dropped his pistol on the way down and now as he lay behind the horse, the pistol was just out of reach of his grasping fingers.

"What the hell? Who's that shootin'?" Sanders shouted,

pulling hard on the reins of his horse which while not hit, was spooked by the sight of seeing Buck's horse go down.

"It was Lem done the shootin'!" Clayton shouted back. "Look at Elliot! He's pinned down behind his horse. Here's our chance to kill the son of a bitch!" He raised his gun and fired at Buck.

Clayton's bullet dug into Buck's saddle and sent up a little puff of dust, but did no further damage.

"Shit!" Clayton said, "I can't get to him from this angle."

"Come on!" Sanders called, "let's get the hell out of here while the gettin' is good!"

"Not until I put a bullet in that bastard!" Clayton insisted. "He's worth a thousand dollars, remember?" He slapped his legs against the side of his horse and moved around to get a better shot at Buck.

Buck made one more desperate grab for his pistol but it was still out of reach. His rifle, however, was in the saddle sheath on the side of the horse which was on the ground, and Buck could see about six inches of the stock sticking out. He jerked it from the sheath and jacked a shell into the chamber just as Clayton came around to get into position to shoot him.

"Goodbye," Bud Clayton said, mockingly, as he raised his pistol and took careful aim. The smile left his face as he saw the end of Buck's rifle raise up and spit a finger of flame. The .44-40 bullet from Buck's rifle hit Clayton just under the chin, then exited the back of his head along with a pink spray of blood and bone as he tumbled from his horse.

"He got Bud!" Walker said.

"That's his own damn fault. Let's get the hell out of here!" Sanders shouted.

At that moment Lem Varner rode up.

"Where are you goin'? Why are you runnin'?" Varner asked. "I got 'im didn't I?"

"You only got his horse," Sanders said. "He's still alive 'n he's done kilt Bud."

Sanders continued to gallop away and Walker and Varner followed, the three men riding away hard now, not even bothering to look back to see what happened to Clayton.

After the riders were gone Buck looked down at his dead horse. He felt a sense of sadness because he had had Scout for over ten years, and he'd been a good and smart horse. At least he died quickly.

Buck knelt on one knee and closed the horse's eyes.

"Goodbye, Scout," Buck said quietly. "We've come a lot of miles together."

Buck managed to capture Clayton's horse, which had trotted away during the shooting but afterward, wandered back to begin cropping grass. Mounting the horse, Buck rode back to where Clayton's body lay sprawled in death. After switching out the saddles, he picked the rustler up and draped the outlaw's body across the horse. Then he mounted behind the body and rode off.

Nobody from Eagleshire on Sherlons Fork Ranch came to claim Clayton's body, or even to acknowledge him. As a result he was buried without ceremony in the Potter's Field part of the Canyon Diablo Cemetery.

By contrast, Beans Evans had a preacher read over him, and his burial was attended by all who had come to help rebuild Dub Wilkerson's house. The name they put on his grave marker was Beans Evans, even though they weren't sure that Beans Evans was his real name. Someone said he had been with Custer at Washita, though he had left the army before the Battle at the Little Big Horn. Some suggested that it was by a dishonorable discharge; others said that he may have deserted.

"I don't care about his past," Dub once said emphatically. "It's the present that I care about and Beans Evans, or whatever his name is, is a damn good hand."

Beans wasn't buried in the town cemetery, but rather on Mountain Shadow Ranch, under a spreading cottonwood tree, and less than a hundred yards from the new house that was under construction.

BUCK WAS IN THE COURTHOUSE STUDYING THE PROPERTY LINES of the ranches: Trailcross, Mountain Shadow, Baker Ranch, Bar 20, Sundown, Circle J, Tumbling R, and the T Bar X. There were also half a dozen other ranches of similar size to the ones he was studying, among them: Thirty-four Corners, Pin Hook, Ten Pines, Double Duce, Quickstrike, and the Rocking M. All those ranches were on one of the three creeks that provided water to the valley, and all six of the ranches were covered by cross hatches.

"Why are these ranches cross hatched?" Buck asked the courthouse clerk.

"Oh, don't you see this heavy line extended from Eagleshire on Sherlons Fork?" the clerk asked, pointing out the line that encompassed the cross hatched ranches. "Those ranches don't exist anymore. Smythe bought 'em out, 'n now they're all part of Eagleshire on Sherlons Fork," The clerk chuckled. "This 'on Sherlons Fork' thing is how the English sometimes name their estates and such, I'm told. But Mr. Smythe may wind up changing the name of his ranch since, by buying these other ranches, Eagleshire is now on Sherlons Fork, Laroux Fork and Cottonwood Creek."

"Tell me, did any of these ranches have a fire that may have persuaded the owners to sell out to Smythe?"

"Yes, as a matter of fact, Thirty Four Corners and the Rocking M both had fires—bad fires that took out the houses and the barns. That could've been the reason they sold out. I know some of 'em were just real grateful to Mr. Smythe for helping them out when that happened."

"He *helped* them out, you say?" Buck emphasized the word "helped" to show that he didn't believe it.

"Yes, sir, I don't know what would have happened to Mr. Byrd and Mr. Matthews if they hadn't been able to sell out. I mean both families lost everything in the fire, but when Mr. Smythe bought 'em out, they wound up with enough money to start over somewhere else."

As Buck studied the map a little longer, he saw something he could use. With what he learned from the map, he developed a plan to help the remaining ranchers, and he knew exactly how he could implement the plan.

When he left the courthouse Buck encountered Sheriff Jones on the front steps.

"Marshal, good, I was told you were here."

"You're looking for me?"

"Yes, I'd like you to come to the undertaker's office with me."

"Another Mexican girl?"

"Yes."

"As you can see," Ponder said a few moments later, pointing to the body of a young Mexican woman, "like the other two, an earring has been ripped from her left ear."

"I don't know who's doing this, but if the son of a bitch

ain't stopped, there's not goin' to be a Mexican whore left," Jones said.

"Maybe that's his intention," Ponder suggested. "Maybe it's some do-gooder who feels he has a message from God to rid the world of evil, and he's doing that by killing whores."

"Or, maybe it's someone who wants us to think that," Buck said.

"Elliot," Sheriff Jones said, "I know that me 'n you ain't exactly got off on the right foot, I mean I side with Mr. Smythe 'cause I'm convinced that some of them ranchers are stealin' his cattle, 'n I think he's good for the businesses in this here town. And you've come down on the side of the small ranchers. But on somethin' like this, I'd like to see us work together. I don't know who that Mexican son of a bitch is that's doin' all the killin', but I want him found and stopped."

"I agree. We need to find out who it is and stop him," Buck said. He stuck out his hand and Jones took it.

"Good," Jones said with an approving nod of his head.

"Are you serious?" Parker asked Sheriff Jones a short while later. "Are you really sidin' up with Elliot? How can you do that when you know he's agin' Smythe?"

"We're only teamin' up for this one thing," Jones said, shaking his head. "I don't care who you are. It ain't right all them women gettin' kilt."

"Hell, Sheriff, why are you wastin' your time with that? You know damn well it's some Mexican that's prob'ly pissed off on account of he don't like it that his whores is a' lyin' with Americans."

"You visit 'em pretty often, don't you, Parker?"

"I wouldn't exactly say it's all that often," Parker said. "I go there when I feel the need, 'n why not? Them whores is a lot cheaper than the Americans that's on this side of the track."

"You don't have to go makin' no excuses to me," Sheriff Jones said, holding up his hand. "I've been known to get a little myself once in awhile. I was just thinkin' that maybe while you're down that way, you might keep your eyes open 'n see what you can find out. I mean, see if there's anythin' suspicious goin' on."

"Yeah," Parker said with a conspiratorial grin. "Yeah, it wouldn't be like I was goin' down there just for a poke or anythin'. I'd actual be investigatin', wouldn't I?"

"That's my point," Jones said.

"All right, Sheriff, if you say so. Maybe I'll go down there right away. As part of the investigation, you understand."

Jones smiled, and nodded, "Right, as part of the investigation."

Fifteen minutes after his conversation with Sheriff Jones, Lanny Parker stepped up to the bar in Bustamante's Cantina and ordered tequila.

"Say, Bustamante, I'm investigatin' the killin' of all the Mexican whores that's been goin' on. Do you have any idea who might be a' doin' it?"

"No, *Senor*," Bustamante replied as he poured Parker's drink.

"What do you think about the Anglos who come in here?"

"I think it is business, Senor."

"It don't bother you none to see a Anglo with a Mexican whore?"

"No, *Senor*."

"Well, they's some son of a bitch that lives down here that it bothers a lot on account of he's killin' all the whores because of it. So if you hear anythin', I want you to let me know about it."

"Si. Senor, but . . ." Bustamante halted in mid-sentence.

"But what?" Parker said as he tossed the drink down.

"If it is someone who does not like the Americans being with the *putas*, why does he kill the *puta* instead of the American?"

"Don't go tryin' to figure it out," Parker said. "You ain't smart enough for it. Leave the figurin' out part to me."

"Si. Senor Deputy."

MOUNTAIN SHADOW RANCH

"You want us to put all of our cattle together?" George Baker asked, responding to a suggestion Buck had made at a meeting he had called.

"Why not? It'll work," Buck said. "All the cattle are branded so once it's time for the gather there won't be any question about which cow belongs to which ranch. And with one large herd to guard, instead of several smaller ones, we'll be better prepared to fend off rustlers."

"You mean against Smythe's men," Dub said.

Buck nodded. "Yes, like I said, against rustlers."

"There's only one thing wrong with that," Moe Peters said. "If we're all gathered in one bunch, what's to keep them bastards from burnin' our houses like they burned Dub's house?"

"I've got that figured out as well," Buck said. "I've studied the map of the valley, and there are three peaks where we can post someone to keep a lookout. Every possible approach to any of the ranches is covered by those peaks and if one of our lookouts sees someone heading toward one of the ranches, he can send us a signal, and we can intercept them."

"Send us a signal, how?"

"By heliograph."

"By what?" Pete Connors asked.

"It's something the army uses," Buck explained. "They use a mirror to send a flash and it can be seen from miles away. It's like a telegraph."

"Yeah, but there don't none of us know nothin' about telegraphin'. Howard McGill said.

Buck laughed. "You don't have to send a book, just a message, and we can work that out real easy. There are eight ranches, so we'll have three lookouts posted. If you give us three flashes, that means someone is coming. Connor, you'll be in position to see the approach to the Bar Twenty, Sundown, and Mountain Shadow. If it's the Bar Twenty, you'll follow the three flashes with one flash, if it's Sundown, with two flashes and if it's Mountain Shadow, with three flashes.

"Ken, you'll be looking after your pa's ranch as well as the T Bar X and the Baker Ranch. It'll be just like I told Connor. Three flashes, then one flash for the Tumbling R, two for the T Bar X, and three for the Baker Ranch.

"I want to be a lookout," Finn Kelly said. "There's only Trailcross and the Circle J left, 'N Trailcross is Pa's ranch, so it's mine, too. I think you ought to use me."

"Sean, I think he can handle it," Buck said, "and it would free up another man to handle the herd."

Sean agreed, and young Finn Kelly's services were put into effect, his instructions the same as had been given to the others.

"Finn, can you shoot?"

"Yes, sir," Finn said, "I can shoot a squirrel out of a tree slick as a whistle."

"I want you to carry a rifle with you, but it is only for defense. Don't shoot at someone just because you see them. If you see them, do exactly as I said, and send us a signal by mirror flash. Do you understand?"

"Yes, sir, I understand."

"Good. All right now, as to the rest of you, as soon as we get a message that any of the ranches are in danger we'll respond to engage them."

"Yeah!" Dub said. "I hope they try again, and I hope it's the same sons of bitches that burnt out my place."

"What are you complainin' about? You got a new house and barn out of it, didn't you?" Moe teased.

"Yeah," Dub said with a smile. "Now that you mention it, I did at that."

"What about the women?" Sara Sue asked.

"What about 'em?" Moe replied.

"If the rest of us is all together, herdin' our cattle, that's going to leave the women and children back in the houses, all alone."

Buck nodded. "They aren't going to be all alone. Sean and I have already talked about that. We're going to bring all the women and children here to stay at Sean's house. It's large enough to accommodate everyone if the women are willing to double up. And we can make pallets on the floor for the kids."

"Ha! My kids will get a big kick out of that," Clyde Jamison said. "They'll think it's one big party."

Eagleshire on Sherlons Fork:

"They've made a gather," Buster Truax said. "They've rounded up all their cows 'n brung 'em all over to Trailcross."

"Hmm, I must confess, that is very smart of them," Smythe said, "There is strength in numbers."

"Yeah," Stillwell said. "But if all of 'em is at Trailcross watchin' the cows, who's watchin' the other ranches?"

"Excellent observation, my good man, a most excellent observation," Smythe replied, "Do you suppose we might be able to take advantage of their miscalculation?"

"Yes, sir, you just leave that up to me. I'll be wantin' to take some men with me," Stillwell said.

"Take all the men you need, but, leave Corbett behind."

"Why should I leave him behind? Frank's the best man we got," Stillwell said.

"Let's just say that I don't want to be exposed while you and the others are attending to business."

"All right, for what I got planned, I don't reckon we'll be needin' him anyway. With who I'll be takin' I figure we'll be able to handle anything they throw at us."

It was Nola Kelly who saw the flashing mirror from Ken Roberts. Nola had been put in position to monitor all the lookout posts, and she watched the entire mirror sequence until she was able to determine, by the flash code, that there were men proceeding toward the Tumbling R Ranch.

She sent a mirror flash back toward Ken, one flash, a pause, two flashes, a pause, then one flash to let him know that the message had been received and understood. Then she mounted her horse and hurried to find Buck.

Buck looked up as Nola approached. "What are you doing here, Nola? Have you seen anything from our lookouts?" he asked.

"Yes, sir, Ken sent a message that they're heading for their ranch," Nola said, excitedly. "Mr. Elliot, please don't let them burn the Tumbling R. The Roberts are such good people."

"And my sister is sweet on Ken," Timmy said, teasing Nola.

"Good job, Nola. And don't you worry about the Tumbling R," Buck said. "I'll put some men together to protect the ranch."

"Since they're heading for my place, I'll go with you," Roan said.

"Me too," Earl Roberts added.

"All right, but I'll need two more. Howard, Pete, why don't you two come along as well? Sean, you and the others keep an eye open here. And be particularly alert for any attempt to cause a stampede. They might try that to keep us busy, so that we wouldn't notice them approaching one of the ranches."

"I'll do some scouting around," Moe said.

Buck nodded then he, Roan, Earl, Howard, and Pete started toward the endangered ranch.

21

GRAND CENTRAL AIRPORT – GLENDALE, CALIFORNIA - 1931

Buck stood at the window of the terminal and watched the tri-motor Fokker F 10 land, roll out to the end of the runway, then turn onto one of the taxi-ways in order to come to the terminal. The Fokker F 10 resembled the Tri-motor Ford that had brought Buck to California in that it was a high wing aircraft, and it had three engines, one hanging off each wing and one in the nose. But there the similarity ended. The Tri-motor Ford was of all metal construction, thus earning it the name, "Tin Goose". The Fokker, on the other hand, was of wood and fabric construc-tion. Two months earlier it had received bad publicity because one wing had failed in flight, killing all eight aboard. One of the passengers was Knute Rockne, the Notre Dame football coach.

As the Fokker taxied up onto the parking apron, a man holding two orange wands aloft stepped out to wave the aircraft toward him. His right hand pointed to the airplane's left wheel, and with his left hand held high, he made a circle. The result was a perfect pivot to the airplane's left; then the ground-guide crossed the wands, which was the signal to the pilot to kill all three engines.

Six passengers stepped out of the plane, and then Buck saw a tall man with a receding hairline, a narrow face, a prominent nose, and even more prominent ears, exit the airplane. This was the author, Ernest Haycox, and Buck smiled in pleasure at seeing him. It was Buck's hope that with Ernest's help he might have a little more input in what would go into the making of the movie.

"Ernest, my friend!" Buck called out as Haycox stepped through the door and into the terminal building.

A big smile spread across Haycox's face as well, and he started toward Buck with his right hand extended.

"Buck, it's good to see you again," he said, shaking hands enthusiastically.

"I'm glad you could come," Buck said. "Would you like to get a bite to eat? I've found a pretty good place on Wilshire Boulevard. That is, if you don't mind eating in a hat."

"I was hoping you'd suggest that," Haycox said, "I'm starving to death. When you say, eating in a hat, I take it you're talking about the Brown Derby?"

"You know the place?"

"I've eaten there a few times, and I know they serve a pretty good steak," Haycox said, "and right now I think I could eat the whole hind quarter of a steer."

Buck led Haycox to the Plymouth, helped him put his suitcase in the back seat, then climbed behind the steering wheel.

"I'm told real famous people go there to eat," Buck said a few minutes later as they drove toward the restaurant. He chuckled. "And seeing as you are one of the most famous people I know, I guess that means we're going to the right place."

Haycox laughed. "Buck, I only *write* the books. There have been at least a dozen books written *about* you."

"Yes, and none of them are true except the one you wrote."

"When an exaggeration is printed, it becomes legend, and once it becomes legend, it is immutable fact."

"I hope that same reasoning doesn't hold true when something is put on film," Buck said. "Ernest, there's nothing about this motion picture that resembles either your book, or the truth."

"Yes, you said there was a problem," Haycox said.

———

As Buck and Ernest were heading toward the Brown Derby, Clive Malone was in Alcy Harris's office at the headquarters of Sunburst Pictures.

"Did you know that Buck Elliot sent for Ernest Haycox?" Clive asked.

"No, I hadn't heard that," Harris replied.

"I don't know why he sent for him, but it can't be for any good reason, I'm pretty sure of that," Clive said.

"Well now, hold on there, don't go off half-cocked. After all, when Haycox was writing the book, he and Buck Elliot worked together, so I'm sure they became pretty good friends. Maybe that's why Haycox is coming."

"You mean the way Buck Elliot and I are working together and have become good friends?" Clive asked.

Harris's laugh was a sarcastic cackle. "Hell, Clive, you don't have any friends. I thought you knew that."

"I don't need friends. I have fans, millions of them." Clive pointed a finger at Harris. "And that's something you need to remember in case Elliot and Haycox come around trying to get you to make any changes to this movie."

"Clive, Ernest Haycox's book was a national best seller, and Buck Elliot is an icon of the American West, like Wyatt Earp, or Wild Bill Hickok, or even General Custer. I'm afraid that if we get too far away from the real story we may get a negative reaction that would be bad, not only for the picture, but for your screen career as well. I know you've hired your own writer to change the script to be more Clive Malone, and less of Buck Elliot, but you might want to think about not getting it so far away that the original story isn't even recognized."

Clive smirked. "Not to worry, Mr. Harris. Within two months after this picture is released I will have made Buck Elliot more famous than he ever was before. Why I expect that you'll receive one of those new Academy Awards for being best picture, and I'll get one as best actor. Warner Baxter and George Arliss will have nothing on me."

"I *would* like for Starburst Motion Picture Studios to win the best picture award—that I admit. Carl Laemmle at Universal has been insufferable, and I'd love to take him down a notch or two," Harris said.

"We can do it, Alcy," Clive said, taking liberties by using the first name of the studio head. "You just keep Elliot, Haycox, and Gilmore off my back. I know motion pictures as well as anyone in this business, and I say that if I'm left alone to do the picture that I want to do, it will be the best picture Starburst has ever produced."

Harris nodded, then slapped his hand on the desk, "Shoot the picture the way you want, Clive. I'll deal with Buck Elliot and Ernest Haycox."

"You do that and I'll bring an Oscar in for both of us," Clive said with a self-assured smile.

Harris watched the arrogant young actor leave his office;

then he turned in his swivel chair and looked at the garden just outside his office. Had he just made a deal that would bring an Academy Award to the company, or had he just sealed its doom?

At that moment Buck was parking his car on Wilshire about half a block from the restaurant. "The Brown Derby Restaurant is just . . ." he started to say, but Haycox interrupted him with a chuckle.

"You don't have to point it out, Buck. It's the only hat on the block."

"I suppose it is," Buck said, laughing with him.

There were several movie stars in the restaurant, including Marlene Dietrich, Lew Ayres, Norma Shearer, and Douglas Fairbanks Jr. Because all were busy in their own world, none of them noticed when Buck and Haycox entered.

Shortly after they were seated a waiter brought each of them a menu for their perusal.

"Now, this is what I want," Ernest said, and he read aloud, "Char-grilled filet of beef with glazed squash and toasted Cipollini onion."

"Sounds good to me," Buck said, putting his menu down without reading it.

A short while later their orders, with the steaks still sizzling, were put before them and the two men began eating with great relish.

"I have never tasted anything this good," Ernest said.

"That's because you never ate buffalo hump cooked by an Indian woman who knows how to do it," Buck replied.

"Buck, you told me on the phone that you were upset by the way Sunburst is doing the picture. What are they doing, specifically, that you don't like?"

Buck chuckled. "There's no way I can answer that."

"That's a strange response. Why can't you answer?"

"It would have been easier to answer if you had asked what, specifically, do I like about what they're doing, and I could've answered, nothing. Although I suppose I could say the biggest problem is Clive Malone."

"Ah yes. America's *Favorite* Cowboy," Ernest said, mocking the promotional tag Sunburst Pictures had applied to their leading star. "I've heard that he's somewhat of a prima donna and can be most difficult to work with. I can talk to him, I suppose, but I'm absolutely certain that I won't have any influence with him."

"That's right, you won't, but it isn't just you. Honor, logic, and reason also have no meaning as far as Clive Malone is concerned. No, sir, I asked you to come here because I want you to meet Ryan Gilmore."

"The screenwriter?" Ernest wrinkled his brow. "I've met him. And if you're waiting for me to talk to him about how he wrote the screenplay, I have to tell you, I don't know that it would be very productive. I guess it is proprietary. We each feel the story is our personal possession."

"That's not the problem," Buck said. "I've read Ryan's script, and with just a few exceptions, it's staying fairly close to your book."

"If Gilmore's screenplay is close to the book, and I know that you signed off on the book, what's the problem?"

"Ryan's script is fine. It's what they are calling the shooting script that I'm having trouble with. The shooting script is nothing like the book, it is nothing like Ryan's script, and it is damn sure nothing like anything I ever did."

"Let me guess, it's all Clive Malone, being Clive Malone."

"You got it." Buck chuckled. "You know how on the radio shows they sometimes say, 'this is a true story; only the names have been changed to protect the innocent?' Well, if this movie makes it to the theaters the way it's being shot, the very first thing they should say is 'These are real names. Only the story has been changed, for God knows what reason.' "

Ernest laughed. "All right, I think I have an idea of what you might be dealing with. And you're right; perhaps I should meet with Gilmore, and a good lawyer."

"A lawyer?"

"I want him to look over the contract I signed with Star-burst when they bought the film rights to the book. It may be that he'll be able to find a little leverage, somewhere."

"I hope so."

"Hmm," Ernest said, just noticing someone else in the restaurant. "It just might be that there's someone in here, right now, who can help."

"Someone in here, now?"

"Yes. Do you see that man over there, the one with glasses and smoking a pipe?" Haycox asked.

"I see him."

"I'm not ready to try and recruit his help yet, but he's someone I'd like you to meet."

Haycox steered Buck through the tables until they reached the one with the man he had pointed out. When they got there, the man looked up, and seeing Ernest, smiled in recognition.

"Ernest, what brings you to Hollywood?"

"Starburst Motion Picture Studios is producing a movie from one of my books," Haycox said.

"Oh, yes. *Legend of a Gunfighter*, isn't it? I knew Harris was doing that. I tried to get Fox to acquire the property because I'd love to have directed that picture. From what I've heard, this Buck Elliot fellow is a genuine Western hero, the kind that we can only put on film."

Haycox nodded his head. "Yes, I would say Buck Elliot is a genuine hero. And John, this gentleman is the very hero we're talking about." He pointed to Buck. "Buck, this is John Ford, who is, in my opinion, the best director in Hollywood. If you haven't seen *The Black Watch*, you need to."

"I have seen it, and I enjoyed it very much," Buck said. "Mr. Ford, it's a pleasure meeting you."

22

BUCK LEARNED THAT THE SHOOTING FOR THE DAY WOULD BE AT the 2,700 acre "Western Location" that the Starburst Studios maintained in the Agoura Hills near Malibu Creek. When Buck and Haycox arrived, the cameras were already set up, and there were several actors in costume milling around as they waited for photography to begin.

"Ernest!" Ryan said animatedly when he saw the writer exit Buck's car.

"Hello, Ryan," Haycox said, returning the screen writer's greeting with equal enthusiasm.

"What are we shooting today?" Buck asked.

"We're shooting the scene where you defend the Tumbling R Ranch," Ryan said.

"Well, that's a pretty straight forward scene. Ernest covered it accurately in the book, and I must say you did it justice in the screenplay."

"You haven't read the screenplay," Ryan said, as he rolled his eyes.

"Yes, I have. I've read the whole thing."

Ryan shook his head. "No, what you read was the production script. The shooting script has been significantly altered."

Buck turned to Haycox. "I guess you won't have to wait too long to see what I'm talking about."

"Where's Clive Malone?" Haycox asked.

"Now that's a good question," Ryan said. "We're supposed to start shooting in ten minutes, but our *star* isn't here yet." Ryan put a negative influence on the word star.

"Here comes Clive!" someone called and looking up the road, Buck saw a huge, swirling cloud of dust following the fast moving sports car. Clive slammed on the brakes then whipped the car around so that everyone was covered with the dust.

When Clive stepped out of the car he was wearing his signature white outfit, this time with a wide black band around the bottom half of his shirt. He was wearing a gun belt with two holsters, and the pistols were nickel-plated with ivory handles.

"All right, people, our star has arrived," Guy Lashlee said. "Let's get set up."

"We can't, Guy," the AD said.

"What do you mean we can't? We've got a schedule to keep."

"I'm sorry, but the dust from Clive's arrival has gotten into the cameras. It's goin' to take at least an hour to get them all cleaned."

"All right, all right," Guy said, clearly agitated by the delay. "Cast and crew, stand down while the cameras are being cleaned."

Clive walked over to join Buck and the two writers who were still standing by the Plymouth.

"I'm Clive Malone," he said gregariously as he extended his hand.

"Ernest Haycox."

"Are you looking for a part in the movie?" Clive asked.

Buck laughed. "There wouldn't be a movie without him. He wrote the book. Didn't you recognize the name?"

"Oh, well, no, I didn't, but then there's no way I would recognize it. I didn't read the book."

"Clive, can you come over here for a few minutes?" Guy called.

"Excuse me," Clive said as he started toward the director.

"He told us he didn't read the book," Ryan said quietly. "Now there's a statement of the obvious for you. Next the son of a bitch will tell us that he always wears white."

"You wore white a lot, did you, Buck?" Haycox asked with a little chuckle.

"Only if I couldn't find it in pink," Buck replied, and the other two laughed.

"Quiet on the set," Guy called when they were ready to shoot.

At a signal, Clive Malone mounted a palomino horse. Some distance away, there were eight riders, one of them dressed all in black. They mounted their horses at the same signal.

"Here," Ryan said, handing some pages to Buck and Haycox, "You might want to follow along with this."

"Action!" Guy Lashlee called.

Buck followed the scene on the shooting script.

EXT. - DAY Buck Elliot rides at a gallop to arrive at the ranch before Stillwell and his men.

INTERCUTTING Stillwell and seven men are riding cross country, their horses straining up craggy hills and sliding down dusty slopes. Buck Elliot is heading for the Tumbling R Ranch to cut

Stillwell's men off and he closes ground quickly over choppy terrain. Stillwell's men come through some trees along the bank of a stream and splash across to the other side. SHOTS ring out. They look at each other in surprise. Buck is right in front of them.

OUTLAW NUMBER ONE

What is this? Stillwell, you said no one would be here!

Stillwell's men whip their horses around and head flat out across the open space toward a cluster of boulders. They are vulnerable and exposed as shots PING around them. They are not going to make it.

Buck jumps from his horse onto the top of a boulder and lies prone, bracing his Winchester for an accurate shot.

BUCK
(aloud to himself)

Stillwell, you've learned what it's like to run into Buck Elliot.

INTERCUT – Stilwell and his men exchange shots. As each of the seven outlaws are each man reacts to the shooting by dropping his guns then standing and throwing his hands up in the air for dramatic effect as he is hit. Soon, all are dead except for Buck and Stillwell.

STILLWELL

It's just you and me now, Elliot. Shall we see who's the best?

BUCK

Where do you want it, Stillwell? In the heart, or between the eyes?

INTERCUT CU OF FACES Buck shows determination and confidence. Stillwell shows fear and licks his lips nervously.

With pistols in their holsters, Buck and Stillwell walk toward each other. Stillwell makes a grab for his gun but Buck is faster. Buck blazes away with both pistols.

SFX – blood erupts from Stillwell's chest.

STILLWELL

You got me, I thought I was better.

BUCK

Well, you were wrong, weren't you?

EXTREME CLOSE UP Buck lifts the pistols, one at a time, and blows smoke from the ends of the barrels.

. . .

"Cut!" Guy Lashlee called.

"What the hell?" Haycox asked.

He pointed toward Clive, and the actor playing Stillwell, the two men standing together and laughing at some shared comment which was a secret between them because of the distance.

"Is that supposed to be a scene from the book, *Legend of a Gunfighter?*"

"Not exactly. It's the scene where Clive Malone stands alone to kill all the bad guys and saves the ranch," Ryan said, derisively.

"You mean Buck Elliot," Haycox said.

"No, I mean Clive Malone. Our famous, high-paid movie star has made this his own story. So far the facts of Buck Elliot's life have had little to do with it, and as the shooting progresses, I'm afraid they will be even less," Ryan said.

"Ryan, I know you," Haycox said. "How could you have written such a script?"

"I couldn't, and I didn't."

"Ryan's telling the truth," Buck said. "When principle photography began, and I found out what scenes they would be shooting the next day, I'd read them the night before. Then, when they actually started shooting, I would think that perhaps I'd read the wrong scenes."

"Only he hadn't read the wrong scenes," Ryan interjected. "What he read were the scenes I wrote, but they weren't the scenes that were being shot."

The scene required several takes before Lashlee was satisfied with it, and as a result it was the only scene shot during the entire day. That evening Buck, Haycox, and Ryan ate together in the dining room of the Hotel Normandie.

"Tell me, Ryan," Haycox said as he cut off a piece of his

salmon, "how did the shooting script get to be such a mess? I know your work; you've done some excellent writing, both in original scripts and adapting novels to the screen. Why would the shooting script be such a departure from the one you wrote?"

"Look no further than the man in white," Ryan said. "Because of his earning power for Starburst productions, it would be an understatement to say that he has tremendous influence on any production that the studio undertakes."

"I swear if I had known they were going to deviate this far from my book, I never would have sold the rights to Starburst."

"I agreed to be a consultant on the production because I thought that by being here I could help them tell the truth," Buck said, "but I can see now that my being here has been nothing but a huge waste of time. Tomorrow, I'm going to tell Harris that I'm withdrawing my services."

"I don't blame you," Haycox said. "I'll be leaving tomorrow, too."

"No, wait," Ryan said. "I know Hollywood, and I know a few ways we might be able to play this. Don't leave yet. I'm sure that if the three of us make a united front we can get the changes we want."

"All right," Buck said with an affirming nod. "I've never been one to run away from a fight, but I have to admit, I've never really been in this kind of a fight before. I'm willing to let you take the lead. What about it, Ernest? Are you willing to stick around for a few more days?"

"I'll stay." Haycox smiled. "And I know how to take care of the problem. Next time there's a shooting scene, we could just put real bullets in the guns of the actors who are shooting at Clive."

Buck and Ryan laughed.

. . .

As Buck lay in bed that night, he thought of the scene that had been shot today. He didn't think it was possible for it to be any further from the truth. He had not stood off Stillwell and his men by himself. He had had four good men with him. Of the four who were with him, Roan and Earl Roberts, Howard McGill and Pete Connors, only Earl was still alive. Earl lived here in Los Angeles and had made a substantial amount of money from the real estate business. He hoped Earl would not see this movie.

23

MOGOLLON RIM – 1885

Earl Roberts had led Buck and the others from Trailcross to the Tumbling R, because he knew a short cut that would get them to the ranch before the approaching riders. Part of the route took them through an arroyo that was so narrow that it required them to ride in single file. They had to duck under the limbs of trees, thus helping to conceal their approach.

After a ride of about half an hour they emerged from the abyss and saw the homestead of the Tumbling R just ahead.

"Thank God, they haven't been here yet," Roan said.

"Let's get in position to greet them," Buck suggested.

Roan and Earl climbed up into the loft of the barn, while Pete and Howard found a depression that was large enough to conceal them from the approaching riders.

Buck didn't pick one particular place because he wanted to keep himself mobile. He chose a tree and two rocks, the three sites actually forming a triangle. The tree was the point of the triangle, and the two rocks formed the base. The tree was the closest to the approach the oncoming raiders would take, and Buck took his position behind it.

Less than a half mile distant from where Buck and the others were waiting, Stillwell and the men he had chosen for this mission were coming up the road, confident that they would find an abandoned ranch.

"Hey, Stillwell, before we burn the place down, can we have a look around 'n see if there's anything we might want?" Dewey Steagle asked.

"Like what?" Stillwell replied.

"Well, they may have some money hid. Lots of folks keep money hid in their house. Most ever' house has some things that's valuable in 'em, 'n it'd be a shame to burn this here 'n down without at least takin' a look."

"Yeah," one of the other riders said. "We ought to at least look around. They might have a cooked ham, or maybe even a pie or cake or somethin'."

"A piece of pie would be just real good now," Steagle said.

"We ain't goin' to be wastin' no time lookin' around," Stillwell replied gruffly. "We come here to burn the place down 'n that's what we're goin' to do."

"It just don't seem to me like it's right to burn the place without at least lookin' to see if they got 'ny money put away somewheres," Steagle said.

"There it is," Stillwell said. "Quit your palaverin' 'n get the torches ready."

Two of the men removed prepared torches that had been lashed to the back of their saddles, then held them out so they could be lit.

"I'll fire 'em up," Steagle said,

From his position behind the tree Buck raised his rifle, took careful aim and waiting until the match was lit, fired.

Steagle was about to light the torch being held by Harold Guthrie, when he felt the wind of a bullet passing between the two men. It didn't just pass between them; it extinguished the lit match.

"What the hell?" Guthrie shouted in surprise and fear.

Buck's shot was a signal to the others, and from the loft Earl and Roan opened fire as Buck moved from behind the tree to one of the rocks that was closer to the house.

Pete and Howard began shooting as well, their fire covering Buck's move. The would-be arsonists also found cover and for the next few minutes the valley roared with gunfire as flashes of orange erupted from the bullets striking the rocks. Lead whistled through the air and whined off stone. One by one those who had come to burn the ranch went down under the withering gunfire until only two were left, and they threw down their guns and raised their hands.

"Don't shoot! We give up! Don't shoot no more!" one of the men yelled.

"Hold your fire!" Buck called out to the others.

Buck stepped out from where he had taken cover and, holding his rifle at the ready, motioned for the two men to come toward him.

"Who are you?" Buck asked.

"Uh, I'm Deek McGee, 'n this here's Lazzie Logan."

"Who are you riding for?"

"Don't tell 'im nothin', McGee," Logan said.

"We ain't ridin' for nobody," McGee replied.

"Did Smythe send you here to burn down Roan Roberts' house?" Buck asked.

"Who says we was goin' to burn down a house? We was just out for a ride, is all."

"What are we goin' to do with 'em, Buck?" Roan asked, having climbed down from the barn.

"I'm going to take them into town, put them in jail, and charge them with arson," Buck said.

Roan and Earl were both with Buck and they aroused quite a bit of attention as they rode into town. Buck was behind McGee and Logan, both of whom had their hands tied to their saddle horns. Roan and Earl were leading three horses each, and all six horses had a body lying belly down over the saddle.

"Lookie there, that's Adam Stillwell laid over that horse!" someone shouted, pointing to one of the bodies.

"Yeah, 'n that's Dewey Steagle."

"Hey, Elliot, did you kill all them fellers?" another shouted.

Two of Smythe's riders, Mike Mollett and Muley Calhoun were in the Cow Palace Saloon when they heard the commotion, and they stepped out front with the others to see what was going on.

"What the hell? That's McGee 'n Logan that's tied onto to their saddles there," one of them said.

"'N there's Steagle 'n Stillwell," Mollett added, "All of 'em is dead."

"Yeah, well, I don't care none about Stillwell, I never liked that son of a bitch nohow," Calhoun said. "Me 'n Steagle got along good, though. Who's the others, can you make 'em out?"

"Guthrie's one of 'em. Can't make out the other 'ns."

"Think we ought to tell Smythe?"

"What do you think?"

· · ·

"Roan, you and Earl take the bodies on down to Ponder's. I'll get these two put in jail," Buck said, as he stopped at the sheriff's office.

Roan nodded, then he and Earl led the procession on down to the undertaker's place, the macabre parade witnessed by the morbidly curious who were standing on either side of the street.

"What's this?" Sheriff Jones asked stepping outside, as Buck was dismounting in front of his office. "Why are these men here?"

"Arson," Buck replied.

"We didn't burn nothin'," McGee said.

"The bodies I saw going by," Sheriff Jones said, "weren't they Smythe's men too?"

Buck chuckled. "Yes, and thanks for confirming it. I couldn't get either one of these two to admit that they worked for Smythe."

"Smythe's not goin' to like this," the sheriff said.

"I don't expect he will. Let's get 'em in jail," Buck said.

"I've got no reason to hold 'em. There ain't no charges against 'em."

"I just told you, I'm charging them with arson, and I'll be holding them until the trial," Buck said.

"Are ya, now? And whose jail are you goin' to be holdin' 'em in?" Jones asked. "This here's a county jail."

"It's also the city jail, and I'm the city marshal."

"You were out of the city marshal's jurisdiction when you brought 'em in."

"I arrested them as an Arizona Ranger with jurisdiction over the whole territory. Now that I have them in town, I'm turning them over to the city marshal to hold them in jail until the trial."

"But you are the ranger and the marshal," Sheriff Jones said, not quite following Buck's logic.

"That I am," Buck said.

"How many dead?" Smythe asked.

"They was six of 'em layin' belly down over the saddle when they brung 'em into town," Mollett said.

"And one of 'em was Stillwell," Calhoun added.

"Deek McGee and Lazzie Logan is both in jail," Mollett said.

"Go back to town and visit McGee and Logan and tell them to say nothing. Tell them I will take care of things," Smythe said.

"They're in jail. How are we goin' to visit 'em if they're in jail?" Calhoun asked.

"Tell Sheriff Jones that I am requesting permission for you to visit with them."

———

"They ain't my prisoners, they're Elliot's prisoners, but seein' as how they're in my jail, I don't see why you can't visit 'em," Sheriff Jones said when Calhoun and Mollett told him of Smythe's request. "But before you go back there, take your guns off and leave 'em with me."

The two men did as Sheriff Jones asked, then stepped into the back of the jail where McGee and Logan were sharing the same cell.

"Well, you boys got yourself catched, did you?" Mollett asked with a little chuckle.

"Yeah," Logan said, "Someone must a' told 'em we was comin' 'cause they was there waitin' for us. We didn't hardly have no chance at all."

"What are you two boys doin' here?" McGee asked.

"Smythe sent us," Calhoun said.

"So he knows we're here, huh? Is he goin' to get us out?"

"Yeah, he said don't say nothin' to nobody 'bout what you was doin' 'n he'll take care of it."

"How's he goin' to take care of it?" Logan asked. "It warn't the sheriff that arrested us; it was Buck Elliot 'n you know damn well he ain't goin' to pay no attention to Smythe."

"Yeah, well, you just keep quiet like Smythe says, and more 'n likely ever' thing'll work out all right."

———

When Nigel Smythe stepped down from the train in Flagstaff, he knew exactly who he was going to see. Harcourt Chamberlin III was a lawyer who had come from Philadelphia one year earlier, and in that year he had helped Smythe increase the size of his ranch by several thousand acres, including the acquisition of water rights.

Chamberlin's office was a neat, one story brick building on San Francisco Street, and because Smythe had done considerable business with Chamberlin, the lawyer's greeter, sometimes called a receptionist, recognized him.

"Mr. Smythe, it's good to see you again," she said.

"Good afternoon, Miss Woodward. Is Mr. Chamberlin in?"

"Yes, just a moment, and I'll announce you."

Miss Woodward knocked lightly and let herself into a back office. A moment later, Chamberlin stepped out to greet Smythe.

"Nigel, what brings you to Flagstaff? Chamberlin asked, extending his hand. "More land to acquire?"

"Not this time," Smythe said. "Two of my men are going to be tried for a rather serious crime, and I want you to defend them."

"Step into my office."

"I shall make some tea," Miss Woodward offered.

"That would be refreshing," Smythe said.

A moment later when both were seated, Chamberlin asked a few questions.

"What are they accused of? Are they guilty? And whatever it was they were doing, were they doing it on your instructions?"

"They are accused of attempted arson, and . . ."

"Wait. Attempted arson? You mean they didn't get the job done?"

"No, they were stopped before they could do it."

"Who stopped them?"

"A man named Buck Elliot. He and some of the smaller ranchers ambushed my men as they were about to burn down one of the houses."

"Any shooting?"

"Oh, heavens yes. Six of my men were killed."

"Six of your men were killed, and no arson was committed?"

"Yes."

There was a knock on the door and Miss Woodward came in carrying two steaming cups of tea.

"Sorry to interrupt, but here's your tea."

"Thank you, Dottie," Chamberlin said. He waited until she left before he spoke again.

"Did your men kill anyone?"

"No."

Chamberlin smiled, and took a sip of tea before he spoke again.

"Don't worry, this will be an easy case to make."

24

HOLLYWOOD – 1931

FADE IN

Interior Courtroom Day

A US Flag stands against the front wall, Camera pans over the galley which is full of spectators then moves to jury and pauses on INDIVIDUAL JURORS. All have intense expressions and hang on every word that is being spoken. JUDGE T. GORDON FITZHUGH is on the bench. BUCK ELLIOT is on the witness stand, being questioned by the prosecutor, MANLEY HAMPTON.

CU Buck Elliot, shows expression of confidence and determination.

Move to two shot Elliot and Hampton.

HAMPTON

Mr. Elliot, would you tell the court, please, what happened on the morning of the 15th, Instant?

BUCK

I had come to the Tumbling R Ranch to make certain that no one would attempt to harm it.

HAMPTON

And did someone attempt to harm it?

BUCK

Yes, they did.

Camera moves to defense table. The two defendants McGEE and LOGAN are wearing jeans and denim shirts. The lawyer HARCOURT CHAMBERLIN III is wearing a suit and a monocle. They are studying Buck.

BUCK (continued)

These two men and six others came with torches and matches with the intention of burning down the home of my friend Roan Roberts.

HAMPTON
And were they successful?

BUCK

They were not, for I extinguished the match by shooting out the flame before the torches could be lit. Then I challenged them to stop what they were doing or face the certainty of hot lead. They chose to fill their hands, and in the shootout that followed, I killed six of them and captured these two, who refused to fight, but threw up their hands in surrender, proving themselves to be nothing but cowards.

HAMPTON

But how were you able to do that? You were outnumbered, eight to one.

BUCK

I wasn't outnumbered. I had two pistols with six shells each. That made the odds twelve to eight in my favor.

CU on Buck's face to see triumphant smile.

HAMPTON

Your witness counselor.
   CHAMBERLIN Stands and removes his monocle, polishes it, then places it back in his eye before speaking

CHAMBERLIN

Mr. Elliot, you murdered six men who were doing nothing but taking a ride through the countryside. When did you decide to kill them?

BUCK

When they decided to try and kill me.

"Cut!" Guy Lashlee called.

"Guy, let's do this scene again," Clive said, "only this time when I answer Chamberlin's question, I think it would have more impact if I would walk over to the jury box and point to them, putting my finger in a few faces."

"You're in the witness chair, Clive," Guy replied. "That's not something any witness would do."

"Yes, but I'm not any witness, I'm Clive Malone. And it's something my fans would want me to do."

"All right," Guy agreed, "let's get set up for another take."

Buck, Ryan, and Ernest Haycox left the studio before the scene could be reshot.

"You know there was no jury in that trial," Buck said, "It was a bench trial."

"I have to confess that I put the jury in," Ryan said. "A court room scene has more impact if it has a jury. But none of what you just heard was my dialogue. That was vintage Clive Malone."

"And I certainly did not stand off eight men all by myself," Buck said. "There were four of us."

"Yes, and except for adding the jury, I wrote the ranch scene and the courtroom scene exactly as it was depicted in Ernest's book. But even if he *is* portraying you, it is still Clive Malone."

"Ryan, have you spoken to Harris about this?" Ernest asked.

"Many times, but I told you Harris is over a barrel. Other studios have been trying to woo Malone away from Starburst and Harris will do anything it takes to hang onto him."

"What if another studio were to take the picture away from Starburst?" Ernest asked.

"What studio?"

"I know that John Ford over at Fox wanted the picture," Ernest said. "He made me an offer, but Starburst made a higher offer, so I sold the rights to Alcy Harris. I should have thought about more than just money. Ford might still want it."

"What good does it do that he might still want it?" Ryan asked. "The deal has been struck and Starburst has the picture."

"For many years, I've made my living by the printed word," Ernest said, "and I'm a man who believes in the power of those words."

"I don't see where you're going," Ryan said.

"The Hollywood Reporter," Ernest replied with a conspiratorial smile.

"Yes, you and Buck could go there and protest the way the picture is being made," Ryan said. "That's a good idea."

Ernest shook his head. "No, I don't want Buck involved in the protest, at least not yet. For the time being, I think it would be better to keep him on the inside because we may need him later. In fact, I'm certain that we'll need him later. But for now, I can begin by being a writer who's upset by the way the studio is adapting my book. Initially it won't have a significant impact, but I do have a rather substantial base of readers, and if they perceive that I'm upset, then they, too, will be upset."

"Yes, your fans could have some influence, and I agree, it

might be better to keep Buck affiliated with the picture for now," Ryan said.

The next day, *The Hollywood Reporter* ran the story of Ernest Haycox's disillusionment with Starburst Motion Picture Studios.

Well Known Writer Calls for Boycott of Legend of a Gunfighter the Starburst Film Adaption of His Book of the Same Title

By

Jasper Darnell

Ernest Haycox is well known for his many short stories and novellas. He is the author of several bestselling books, among them, Free Grass, a Western novel, and Legend of a Gunfighter, a nonfiction account of the life of Buck Elliot, an authentic icon of the West.

It is the latter of the two books, however, that has brought Ernest Haycox from that private domain in which a writer toils, into the public arena. Ernest recently sold the movie rights of Legend of a Gunfighter to Starburst Motion Picture Studios, and therein lays the difficulty.

"I sold the book to Starburst with the understanding that the production would faithfully follow the authentic life of Buck Elliot as I have portrayed it in my book. But nothing could be further from the truth," Haycox said.

Mr. Haycox has visited the production on set, and it is his belief that the film is much more a vehicle for the aggrandizement of Starburst's most popular actor, Clive Malone, than it is the portrayal of a true icon of the American West.

When asked if he had any recourse in addressing his problems, he admitted that more than likely, he did not. "For now, I can only but ask that my readers petition Starburst to adhere more closely to the book. Barring Starburst's favorable

response to the vox populi, I would ask that the picture be
boycotted.

"Boycotted?" Alcy Harris protested so loudly that spittle flew from his lips. He held up the copy of *The Hollywood Reporter* to show to Buck and Ryan. "Have you two read this article?"

"I've read it," Buck said.

"So did I," Ryan added.

"Fifteen thousand dollars!" Harris said. "That's how much I paid Haycox for movie rights. That's an enormous amount of money, and this is how he repays us? By calling for a boycott?"

"He's upset by the way his book is being produced," Buck said, "and quite frankly, Mr. Harris, so am I."

"What are you upset about?"

"Practically everything. Take the scene at the Tumbling R ranch where Clive Malone supposedly killed six men and captured the remaining two. It was nothing like that at all."

"Oh, pish posh, Buck," Harris said with a dismissive wave of his hand. "I know you've lived a life of conflict and physical effort, so it's not surprising that you would have no concept of the world of the artist.

"As artists, we must deal with worlds of our own making on a daily basis, worlds that are half in the known universe and half in the unknown universe."

"I am quite familiar with poetic license," Ryan said, "Indeed I have departed from the truth myself, for impact. As I pointed out to Buck I wrote a jury into the courtroom scene even though I knew it was a bench trial, because I thought having a jury would add dramatic impact.

"But Clive Malone's testimony from the witness stand is such a departure from my script, and the truth, that we can make no valid claim that this picture is based upon actual events."

"Ryan, you should know better than anyone," Harris said, "that when fiction makes a better story than fact, you go with fiction."

"If you're going to make a Western film, then why don't you do that?" Buck asked. "Why pretend that it's a story about my life when obviously it is not?"

"Because, dear boy, bio pics about popular figures do good box office. And the more popular the portrayed character is, the more people come to see it."

"Unless they are being urged to boycott by someone who's as popular as the man the movie's about," Buck said.

CANYON DIABLO, ARIZONA TERRITORY - MOGOLLON RIM – 1885

The first thing Harcourt Chamberlin III did was demand a speedy trial, and his request was granted, the trial scheduled to be held within one week after McGee and Logan were arrested. By now everyone in town was aware that the prisoners were Eagleshire riders, and they also knew that Smythe wouldn't let them be indicted without a fight.

The trial was the discussion in every saloon in town.

"What Smythe done was, he brung in one o' them real high-powered lawyers, that same feller that gets him all that land that he sued for a little while back. I don't actual recollect his name," one of the saloon patrons said.

"Chamberpot," another said.

"No it ain't, it's Chamberlin," another corrected. "I heered he come out here from Philadelphee."

"Whose goin' to do the prosecutin'?"

"I ain't a' heered that yet."

. . .

Manley Hampton's law office was a small room that he rented at the back of Al Peacock's dry goods store. It was said that Hampton, who was in his early sixties, had been a good lawyer as a younger man, back in Virginia. But that was several years ago. Nobody knew what happened to him, or why he left Virginia, but since coming to Arizona, he could be found in a saloon more often than in a court room.

Hampton read the court order through whiskey-clouded eyes.

Know all by these presents that by appointment of Circuit Judge T. Gordon Fitzhugh, Manley Hampton will act as prosecutor in the case of Territory of Arizona vs the defendants:

Deek McGee

Lazzie Logan

The Charge is Arson

"I can't give you no information, on account of I don't know nothin' about it," Sheriff Jones said when Hampton asked him.

"And just how am I supposed to try this case if you know nothing about it?"

"You'll need to talk to our City Marshal," Sheriff Jones said.

"Would you like a cup of coffee?" Buck offered when Hampton came into his office to tell him that he would be prosecuting the case.

"Yes, thank you."

Buck picked up the coffeepot from the small stove and started to pour.

"Only half a cup, please," Hampton said.

"All right."

Hampton removed a silver flask from his inside jacket pocket and filled the rest of his cup with whiskey. Buck noticed it, but withheld any comment.

"Tell me what happened," Hampton said.

Buck explained how the small ranchers had joined all their herds together, and then posted lookouts to protect the empty houses. He went on to tell about the gunfight at the Tumbling R which resulted in the death of six men, and the arrest of McGee and Logan.

During the entire dissertation, Hampton continued to "sweeten" his coffee with whisky, until the flask was emptied.

"Do you need me to write anything out for you?" Buck asked when he finished telling what happened.

"No, this is enough, thank you."

"What about Roan? You'll want to talk to him too, won't you?"

"Who is Roan?"

"Roan Roberts. I told you, it was his house we were defending."

"Yes, I'll talk to him as well," Hampton promised. "I need to go, now."

When Hampton left, Buck stood at the front window of his office and watched the lawyer cross the street, then go into the Mogollon Saloon.

"From what I've been able to find out, he was quite a man once," Tristan James Clay said. Clay, who had come to talk to

Buck about the trial, was responding to Buck's question about Hampton. "He had planned to run for congress from the state of Virginia, and then the Civil War broke out. He was a Captain and a company commander in Armistead's Division of Pickett's Brigade at Gettysburg. During Pickett's charge, Hampton lost all but three of the men in his company, including his own brother.

"After the war was over, he went home to find that his family estate was gone, and his wife had taken up with a Yankee carpetbagger. He never got over it, and to this day, he suffers from what the doctors call 'nervous disease' because of what he went through during the war. The story is, he got drunk and came West, and he's been drunk ever' since."

"Thanks, I guess I have a better understanding of him, now."

The story ran in the *Brimstone* on the day before the trial was to be held.

Arson Trial to be Held

On the 15th instant, which is the day after this publication shall appear upon the streets of Canyon Diablo, a trial will be held in the county courthouse to determine the guilt or innocence of Deek McGee and Lazzie Logan.

McGee and Logan are riders for Nigel Smythe, who this paper has learned has secured the services of Harcourt Chamberlin III, a lawyer of considerable renown, to act for their defense. Mr. Chamberlin will have his work cut out for him as there are several witnesses who are prepared to testify in court and under oath, that they observed the attempted arson.

Buster Truax and J.D. Nixon had come into town to attend the trial, and when they went into the Cow Palace Saloon for breakfast, they saw that Frank Corbett was already there.

"Damn, Corbett, what'd you do, spend the night in town?" Nixon asked.

"More 'n likely with one o' them Mexican whores," Truax said.

"It ain't none o' your business where I was last night," Corbett replied, his voice nearly a growl.

"Yeah, well, it don't make me no never mind where you was at," Truax said. "I was just makin' conversation is all. Are you goin' to the trial? Or are you goin' to be sore at me for askin' you that, too?"

"Yeah, I'll be goin' to the trail," Corbett replied. "Ain't ever' body?"

"You think this fancy lawyer Smythe's got hired can get them two boys off?" Nixon asked.

"They say he's real good," Truax said.

Because of the intense interest in the case, people began gathering outside the courtroom, even before it was open. Many had already been here for at least two hours.

Because it was still early in the morning, a few enterprising vendors were taking advantage of the crowd. One was selling hot coffee and doughnuts, while another was selling sausage biscuits.

The townspeople, as well as several of the ranchers and ranch hands who were part of the crowd, welcomed the vendors, who provided them with the breakfast they had given up in order to attend the trial.

Buck, who expected to testify, was having breakfast in the Dutch Skillet Cafe. He wasn't eating alone; Roan Roberts who was also scheduled to testify was with him, as were Roan's son, Earl, and Dub and Mary Kathleen Wilkerson.

"I'm convinced that these were the same polecats that burned Mountain Shadow," Dub said, "and I want to see 'em get what's comin' to 'em."

"It looks like there's going to be quite a crowd," Buck said, draining the last of his coffee. "Earl and Roan and I are witnesses, so our seats are reserved, but if you two are going to get a seat, I expect we'd better get over there now."

Although the residents of the barrio were well aware that a trial was to be held this morning, few of them paid any attention to it because it dealt with the gringos and had no bearing on their lives. Canyon Diablo was almost two separate towns: the gringo, or Anglo area, which was on the north side of the railroad tracks, and the barrio, or Mexican area, which was south of the tracks.

Juan Bustamante, who owned the cantina, was the wealthiest, and the most influential resident of the barrio. He lived with his wife and three children in an adobe house next door to the cantina. Four young women, who worked in the cantina, had rooms over the top of the bar. There were actually seven rooms on the second floor, and there had been seven young women working for him. Now, only four girls remained. Three of the girls had been killed by what the Mexican residents were calling *el monstruo que mata a las putas,* or 'the monster who kills whores.' Bustamante had been unable to recruit any new girl because all were afraid of the *monstruo.*

The prevailing thought was that it was one of their own, someone from within the barrio who was killing the girls. Bustamante wasn't so sure of that.

The four remaining girls, Imelda, Jacinta, Elvita and Renata were always frightened now.

"Who will be next?" Jacinta asked.

"We will never be alone," Imelda suggested, "If we go somewhere, we will make certain that there are at least two of us."

"But how can that be when we are working?" Renata asked. "If we have a man in our bed, we must be alone."

"No one has been killed in her bed," Imelda said.

That had been the plan, and so far the four women had stuck to the plan. Wherever one went, another was always with her.

It was Jacinta's time to cook breakfast, and she was making huevos rancheros.

It had been a busy night for the young women who, because their number had been reduced, were forced to entertain even more men.

"Last night all the men were Americana," Jacinta said.

"Si, but they pay the most," Elvita said, taking money out of her pocket, and putting it on the table. "Jacinta, that looks so good! I am so hungry."

"When are you not hungry, Elvita?" Imelda asked. "I think if you continue to eat as you do, you will one day be as fat as Senora Hernandez, and no man will want to come to your bed."

"By then I will be old and wrinkled and no man will want to come to my bed anyway," Elvita replied, and the other two laughed.

"Where is Renata?" Jacinta asked.

"Ha. The lazy Renata is sleeping in this morning," Elvita said.

"Her breakfast is getting cold," Jacinta said.

"I will get her," Elvita offered.

After Elvita left, Jacinta began putting the eggs and tortillas on the four plates. She had just dished out the last one when the scream from upstairs made Jacinta and Imelda's blood run cold.

26

In the few minutes before the trial was to begin, Smythe and Chamberlin were standing together in a corner, away from everyone else. Chamberlin was an impressive looking man with perfectly coiffed silver hair, a silver moustache, thin lips and a strong chin. A Phi Beta Kappa key hung from a gold chain that stretched across his silken vest.

Buck couldn't help but contrast the dignified looking defense counsel, with the man who had been appointed as prosecutor. Manley Hampton looked exactly like what he was: a man given to drink. And the further into the bottle he sank, the less attention he paid to personal hygiene. This morning his suit was wrinkled and his shoes were scuffed.

And now, in the few minutes before the trial was to begin, he was slumped behind the prosecutor's table looking straight ahead. At first Buck thought he might be napping, but Hampton's eyes were open, and he was looking straight ahead in a blank stare. Hampton had a cup of coffee sitting on the table in front of him, and Buck knew without asking, that the cup contained more whiskey than coffee, if indeed it contained any coffee at all.

Buck also noticed something else.

"Mr. Hampton, I don't see the torch we gave you," Buck said, "Wouldn't you like to use it as evidence?"

Hampton shook his head. "It won't hold up in court."

"What? What do you mean it won't hold up in court?"

"Chain of evidence," Hampton said. "We have no way of accounting for the possession and location of the torch with an officer of the court, between the time of the alleged crime and now."

"Sure we do. It has been in my possession, and I'm an officer of the court," Buck said in an exasperated tone of voice.

"Where is it now?"

"It's with Sean Kelly."

"Is Mr. Kelly an officer of the court?"

"He' one of my deputies."

"Does he hold a commission from the governor, or from a judge?"

"No."

"Then he isn't an officer of the court and the torch, as evidence, is invalidated," Hampton said.

"I'm not a lawyer, but it seems to me, that not having that torch as evidence to support our claim might hurt our case."

"Shh. Here's the bailiff," Hampton said.

Frustrated, Buck returned to the bench that had been reserved for the witnesses, and took his seat beside Roan Roberts.

Deputy Parker had drawn the duty of being bailiff, and after coming through one of the back doors, he stepped up to the front of the courtroom.

"This here trial is about to start with the judge bein' T. Gordon Fitzhugh. Ever' body stand up!" Parker shouted and the gallery stood as the judge came into the court. Judge

Fitzhugh, who was a tall, skinny man with dark hair and a dark Van Dyke beard, took his seat behind the bench.

Chamberlin had requested a bench trial so there would be no jury present.

"Bailiff, would you read the purpose of this hearing, please?" Judge Fitzhugh asked.

"These here two men, Deek McGee 'n Lazzie Logan, good boys both of 'em, is bein' charged with settin' fire to the Roberts place, which they didn't do, on account of the Roberts place ain't been burned down."

"Thank you, Bailiff, but I will ask you to keep your opinions to yourself," the judge said. He turned toward the defense table where Chamberlin and the two defendants were sitting.

"Would the two defendants please stand."

At Chamberlin's urging both men stood.

"The defense counsel has made the petition that this be a bench trial. How say you. Mister . . ." the judge looked down to get a name, "Logan." He was looking directly at McGee as he spoke.

"I ain't Logan, he is."

The judge looked at Logan.

"What's that mean?" Logan asked.

"Do you agree that I should hear the case, without a jury?"

Puzzled, Logan looked at Chamberlin who nodded in the affirmative.

"Yeah, that's what we want," Logan said.

"Yes, Your Honor," Chamberlin whispered, and corrected himself.

When asked, McGee's response was the same.

The judge looked over at Hampton.

"Mr. Prosecutor, make your case."

Hampton didn't react to the judge's charge.

"Mr. Hampton?" Judge Fitzhugh said in a louder voice.

"Oh, uh, sorry, Your Honor," Hampton replied. He was a short, bald, overweight man with a liquor-induced, blotchy red face, a rather bulbous nose, and rimless glasses that enlarged his gray eyes. He stood up, but didn't step away from his table.

"Your Honor, Buck Elliot, who has presented himself to me as an Arizona Ranger, has lodged a charge of attempted arson against McGee and Logan. There are witnesses to support that claim, and I shall call them as I attempt to make that charge," Hampton sat back down.

"Is that the extent of your opening remarks, sir?" the judge asked, surprised by the brevity.

"Yes, Your Honor," Hampton replied.

"Damn," Buck said quietly to Roan Roberts, "He doesn't sound all that confident, does he?"

"Mr. Chamberlin, your opening remarks, sir?"

Chamberlin cleared his throat then stood, and unlike Hampton, strolled to the front of the gallery. Also, unlike Hampton who had mumbled his words, Chamberlin elucidated clearly and with sufficient volume to be heard by everyone in the courtroom.

"Your Honor, I know that prosecution intends to question a few witnesses. As to the veracity of those witnesses, we shall determine that, when we subject them to cross during the course of this hearing. But because even witnesses cannot gauge intent, in addition to the testimony of witnesses, attempted arson charges generally require additional factors. These may include a defendant having a prior felony conviction, attempting arson during commission of another felony, or attempting arson with the specific intent to injure or kill another person.

"I would also point out, Your Honor, that there is an administrative error in the bill of indictment. The charge is for attempted arson, but there are three possible charges, specifically willful and malicious arson, reckless arson, and aggravated arson. The 'attempt' in the bill of indictment, does not refer to any of those specific charges. In addition, these charges require proof of some physical act, such as an actual attempt to ignite the fire upon the building to be burned.

"Defense suggests, Your Honor, that not a single one of these requirements for conviction of attempted arson has been met, and because these charges are not supported by any of those requirements, I am going to request, at this time that there be a bench dismissal."

When Chamberlin sat down, McGee and Logan smiled at each other.

"I thank you, Mr. Chamberlin, but we will continue with the trial," Judge Fitzhugh said. "Mr. Prosecutor, you may present your case."

The first Witness to be sworn in was Roan Roberts.

"Mr. Roberts, this attempted arson took place at your home, did it not?"

"Yes, sir."

"I've been told that all the smaller ranchers have made a gather, and that your herds are together now, is that true?"

"It's true."

"If all the herds have been combined, how is it that you were at your home instead of with the herd?"

"I was there 'cause we seen 'em comin', 'n they was headed right for my house. We knew damn well they was goin' to burn my house just like they done to Dub Wilkerson's house so . . ."

"Objection! Your Honor I object to the comment that my clients burned Mr. Wilkerson's house. That is a statement not supported by evidence, nor was such an allegation included in the indictment which precipitated this trial."

"Objection sustained."

"Well I know damn well them sons of bitches is the ones that burnt Dub's house and . . ."

Judge Fitzhugh began a loud banging of the hammer, "I have sustained the objection, and you are out of order. If you say one more word on this subject, I will put you in jail for contempt of court. Mr. Prosecutor, please control your witness."

"Yes, Your Honor," Hampton replied. "Mr. Roberts, please, just respond to the questions I ask."

There were no more outbursts from Roan, and his testimony was followed by Buck. Both men testified that they had seen Steagle attempt to light a torch. Earl, Howard, and Pete also gave the same testimony.

Chamberlin withheld all cross examination until the last witness had testified. Then he recalled Roan back to the stand.

"Mr. Roberts, how badly was your house damaged in this arson attempt?" Chamberlin asked.

"What?"

"When Mr. McGee and Mr. Logan set fire to your house, how much of it was burned?"

"Well, there wasn't none of it burned."

"Oh? Maybe I have misunderstood the charge. I thought the charge was that McGee and Logan held a torch against your house in an attempt to burn it down."

"No, they didn't do nothin' like that."

"In fact it is true, is it not, that neither Mr. McGee nor Mr. Logan ever even held a torch, or a match?"

"No sir them two didn't, but they was both of 'em there all right. It was a couple of the others that held the two torches."

"Did Harold Guthrie hold a torch?" Chamberlin asked.

"Yes, sir, now, that he did."

"And was he able to set fire to your house?"

"No, sir."

"Why not?"

"On account of his torch was never actual lit. He was holdin' it out to be lit, you see, 'n Steagle, he was holdin' the match to do it with, onliest thing is, he never got the job done on account of Buck Elliot shot out the match."

"How do you know Mr. Elliot shot out the match?"

"Because I saw 'im do it."

"Were you close enough to actually see this? Where were you when this happened?"

"I was plenty close enough; I was in the barn, no more 'n fifty yards away."

"And you saw the actual bullet extinguish the flame?"

"Yes. Well, I mean, you can't hardly see the actual bullet itself, you understand. There can't nobody really see the bullet on account of it bein' too small 'n goin' too fast. But what I seen was, I seen Buck shoot, 'n then I seen the match go out."

"So you admit that you didn't actually see the bullet extinguish the flame."

"No, that ain't right. I just told you that I did see it."

"No, Mr. Roberts, what you said was, you did not see the actual bullet extinguish the flame."

"Well, no, not if you put it that a' way."

"Mr. Roberts, is it not possible that Mr. Steagle had second thoughts and blew out the match of his own volition?"

"Yes, sir, that's what he done all right, 'cause I seen 'im do it. I seen ole Dewey blow out that match," McGee called out from his seat at the defense table.

Again, Judge Fitzhugh banged his gavel and called for order.

"Now what he just said," Roan said, pointing to McGee, "I mean him sayin' that Steagle blew out the match, that ain't true 'cause, that ain't the way it happened a' tall. I'm tellin' you that Buck Elliot shot the match out."

"Mr. Roberts, this court has the awesome responsibility of determining whether or not these two accused men are innocent or guilty. And because that responsibility is so awesome, safeguards have been built into the system. One of those safeguards is the presumption of innocence until proven guilty, and the other is the requirement that judge and jury must be convinced beyond a shadow of a doubt. And since you cannot state, positively, that the bullet extinguished that match, your claim has no bearing on this case."

"But I saw Buck shoot," Roberts said.

"Oh, I'm sure you did. Tell me, Mr. Roberts, the shot that you claim extinguished the match, was that the first shot fired?"

"Yes, sir."

"And what happened after that?"

"Oh, all hell broke loose after that. Ever' one commenced a' shootin'."

"So you admit that Mr. McGee, Mr. Logan, and the six others who were with them that day were just riding up with purpose unknown, when Buck Elliot opened fire, beginning the shooting that would ultimately take six lives."

"What? No! I mean, yes, he shot first but it . . ."

"That will be all, no further questions. Your honor, defense calls Mr. Nigel Smythe to the stand, please."

"What are you callin' him for? He wasn't even there," Roan asked.

"Witness has been dismissed. Please take your seat," the judge said.

Smythe was even more elegantly dressed than Chamberlin. Like Chamberlin, Smythe was wearing a three piece suit, but in place of the Phi Beta Kappa key, Smythe was wearing a medal, the Order of the Bath. He was sworn in.

"Mr. Smythe, you are a member of the English Peerage, are you not?" Chamberlin began.

"I am, yes."

"And what is your title?"

"I am a Viscount."

"You had to give up the title when you came to the United States, is that correct?"

"I still hold the title in England, but can't use it here. However, it is a privilege I gladly gave up in order to live in this wonderful country of America."

"You may have given up the title, but you still adhere to the tradition of honor and honesty that is inherent with the title. Is that correct?"

"Indeed it is, Sir."

"Good, then I'm going to ask you, Mr. Smythe, did you send a group of men over to the Tumbling R Ranch?"

"I did sir."

"Did you send them over to burn down Mr. Roberts' house?"

"No, not at all, quite the contrary, in fact," Smythe said, resolutely.

"Then why did you send them?"

"Word reached me that all the smaller ranchers had made a gather and had unified their herds. I was aware that a short time ago some villainous vandals burned Mountain Shadow down, so I knew that the small ranchers would be on edge about such a thing. It is because I was somewhat worried about the welfare of my neighbors that I sent some men over as a good will gesture. It was my intention that they watch over Mr. Roberts' ranch to make certain those same villains didn't burn Mr. Roberts property."

"And how was this good will gesture received?"

"Oh, I'm afraid it wasn't received well at all. They were given absolutely no opportunity to explain their reason for being there, because as soon as Mr. Stillwell and the others arrived, Buck Elliot, and several men who were waiting in ambuscade, began firing on my men.

"If you ask me, the charges were filed against the wrong party. If there be any charges pursued as a result of this tragic event, they should be filed against Buck Elliot, and those who were with him on that fateful day. And if the charge not be murder, then it should certainly be for manslaughter, because they killed six of my men."

"Your witness, Mr. Hampton," Chamberlin said.

"As he is not a material witness, I suggest that his entire testimony has no bearing," Hampton said. "Therefore I will not cross examine him."

"Mr. Chamberlin, will you be putting Mr. McGee or Mr. Logan on the stand?" Judge Fitzhugh asked.

"No, Your Honor, I will not," Chamberlin replied.

"Wait a minute!" Roan shouted. "How are we goin' to prosecute them two sons of bitches, if we don't even get to ask 'em anything?"

"Order in the court!" Judge Fitzhugh shouted, as he banged his gavel.

"The defendants don't have to testify," Hampton explained to Roan.

"Closing, Mr. Chamberlin?" the Judge said.

Chamberlin stood, and though there was no jury, he faced the gallery, more than half of whom either worked for Smythe, or were dependent upon the rancher's business for their livelihood.

Chamberlin shook his head and made a clucking sound, then he turned toward the judge.

"Your Honor, I don't know how this charge even got this far. What we should be deciding here is the guilt of these . . . *ranchers.*" Chamberlin made a scoffing sound. "They claim that there was an attempt to light a torch, but no torch has been introduced as evidence. And without evidence of the existence of the torch, we can dispose quickly, of the charge of attempted arson.

"By the admission of Mr. Roberts, Mr. Elliot, and every surviving person who was present at this unfortunate incident, not one building was burned, not one building was scarred. And yet six men died, shot down by these men," Chamberlin pointed to Buck and Roan.

"I will grant that the arrival of eight riders from Eagleshire on the Sherlons to provide aid might have been ill-timed, and perhaps there should have been some earlier coordination. But that does not excuse Buck Elliot for being the one who fired the first shot, as was testified by Mr. Roberts. I submit to you, Your Honor, that this so-called Ranger, and those with him, overreacted and six innocent men died, men whose names I'm going to read now because they deserve the decency of being remembered," Chamberlin picked up a piece of paper and began to read: "Adam Stillwell, Dewey Steagle, C. F. Wallace, Merlin Cline, Thad Lawson, and Harold Guthrie."

Chamberlin put the paper back down, "Mr. McGee and Mr. Logan are innocent, Your Honor. If there is any guilt to be decided here today, it should be a finding of murder, or at the very least, manslaughter. Defense rests."

"Mr. Prosecutor?"

Hampton stood to address the judge, "Your Honor, Mountain Shadow—house, barn and out-buildings—had been burned to the ground, the hired hand murdered. Buck Elliot, an Arizona Ranger by appointment of the Governor of the Territory of Arizona, Mr. Roberts and the others with them, had every reason to believe that McGee, Logan, and the other six armed men who approached with a torch, were doing so with the intent to burn the Tumbling R. The only intent of Buck Elliot, Roan Roberts, Earl Roberts, Howard

McGill and Pete Connors, was to protect that property. And the very fact that McGee, Logan and the others arrived carrying a torch validates that belief. Your Honor, I see no possible conclusion to this trial, other than the finding of guilty as charged for Lazzie Logan and Deek McGee. Prosecution rests."

"That's it? That's your whole case?" Buck asked, as Hampton sat down.

"I can only argue with the evidence I have," Hampton said. "You brought me a very weak case, Ranger Elliot."

The judge rapped his gavel on the bench, then cleared his throat, "I see no need for a recess before I make my judgment. I find the defendants not guilty."

More than half the gallery broke into applause. Judge Fitzhugh rapped his hammer a few times, but when it had no effect, he simply stood, and left the court.

27

HOLLYWOOD. CALIFORNIA – 1932

"That's the way the trial actually happened," Buck said after sharing the story with Ernest, Ryan, and Jasper Darnell, the journalist for *The Hollywood Reporter.*

"That's exactly how I wrote it in the book," Ernest said.

"And, except for the fact that I added a jury for dramatic effect, that's how I wrote it in the screenplay," Ryan added.

Jasper Darnell, who was having coffee with Buck and the two writers, took a sip from his cup, then put it down before he responded.

"I can write my next article just like that, if you want me to," Darnell said.

"But?" Ernest asked.

"Ah yes," Darnell replied, "there's an implied 'but' to my statement isn't there?"

"But what?" Buck asked.

"If I write the story now, this close behind the one I just wrote about Mr. Haycox's disapproval of the screenplay, it will seem like it's little more than sour grapes and petty disappointment because Ernest Haycox isn't being given enough credit in the development of the film."

"That's not right," Ernest said.

"Oh, I'm sure that's not right, but that will be the perception, and Ryan can tell you that in Hollywood, perception is everything."

"What about me?" Buck asked. "I don't want credit. I just want the truth to be told."

"Oh, I'm afraid you're the most vulnerable of all," Darnell said. "This is a story about your life, and any complaints that you may put out, will be perceived as if you're disappointed that you're not being shown as a big enough hero."

"But that's not true. My complaint is just the opposite. Why the way Clive Malone is portraying me, you'd think I could walk on water."

Darnell chuckled. "Remember what I said. Perception is everything. Besides, Clive Malone isn't portraying you, he's portraying himself."

"You do understand then," Ryan said.

"Oh, dear boy, I understand perfectly. But I am not your solution."

"Then who, or what, is the solution?" Buck asked. "To tell you the truth, I'm prepared to do just about anything it takes to get this picture stopped."

"I'm afraid I can't answer that for you," Darnell said. He smiled. "But I promise you this. Whatever you come up with, I'll report on it favorably."

John Ford opened the door to his large, but not overly lavish home, on Wilshire Boulevard.

"Come in, gentlemen, come in," Ford said.

"Thank you for seeing us on such short notice, John," Ernest said.

"You're always welcome, Ernest, even if we couldn't get together on the screen rights for your latest book."

"Yes, well, that's why we're here," Ernest said. "You already know Ryan, and you've met Buck Elliot."

Ford smiled and nodded. "Would this visit have anything to do with how displeased you are with the way Alcy Harris is doing your book?"

"You know about that?"

"Hollywood is a small town. News travels."

"Yes, that's exactly why we're here," Ernest said. "John, you're the best director in Hollywood, and you know this business better than anyone."

Ford chuckled. "If you're trying to pick an argument with me, that won't work, because I agree with you."

The others laughed.

"Good, so now since we all agree, maybe you can come up with something to help us," Ernest said.

Ford shook his head. "I'm afraid I have no influence with Alcy Harris, and even less influence with Clive Malone."

"Yes, but to be honest with you, it's not as much as having you exercise any influence with them, as it is having you help me take the rights away from Starburst Motion Picture Studios so I can sell them to you."

Ford held out his hand. "Now Ernest, you may remember that I did make you an offer for the film rights. And you turned it down, because Starburst made a better offer."

"They made a bigger offer that is true. But as it has turned out, it was a long way from being a *better* offer," Ernest said. "And I was an absolute fool for not seeing that."

"You know that I can't match what Harris paid you."

"What if I told you that if you could figure out a way to get the picture away from Starburst, I would let you have the rights for zero advance, and take only a percentage of the net."

"Net, not gross?"

"Yes."

"Damn, you must really want to get the rights away from Starburst."

"It is absolutely the worst deal I have ever negotiated."

"What about you, Mr. Elliot? Clive Malone is the hottest Western star in Hollywood now, and one could make a case for saying that he is the most successful star in Hollywood, period. Don't you feel honored to be portrayed by him?"

"I am afraid, Mr. Ford, that Clive Malone is portraying Clive Malone," Buck replied.

Ford laughed out loud. "Very good, Mr. Elliot, very good. I can see how you survived as many difficult situations as you did. You are a man of discernment and discrimination, and you're able to get right to the heart of the issue.

"But you, Ryan, you are a first tier screen writer with Starburst. And you are here with Ernest and Mr. Elliot?"

"Yes, Buck's history, Ernest's fine book, and my screenplay are being destroyed by Clive Malone. Somehow we need to stop it."

"How strongly committed are you to this?" Ford asked.

"I wouldn't be here, if I wasn't committed," Ryan replied.

"Are you committed enough to quit Starburst and come to work for Fox Studios, and announce your reason for quitting?"

Ryan smiled. "You mean you'd hire me?"

"Yes, I'm certain that with my recommendation, William Fox would hire you."

"I'll do it."

"Good. Now all we need is to get *The Hollywood Reporter* to do the story on their front page," Ford said.

"That's not a problem," Ernest said. "We already have one of their reporters on our side."

Ryan Gilmore Quits Starburst to Join Fox Movie Studios
By
Jasper Darnell

Citing his differences with the production of Legend of a

Gunfighter, noted screenwriter Ryan Gilmore has announced that he is taking the unprecedented action of leaving a company in the middle of the production of one of his screenplays.

"I join with Ernest Haycox, whose bestselling book Legend of a Gunfighter was adapted by me as a screenplay, in expressing my displeasure with the production," Gilmore told this reporter.

"Starburst Motion Picture Studios has been so unduly influenced by Clive Malone that a wonderful story about one of America's most celebrated Western heroes has been so distorted that there is little of my screenplay, even less of Ernest Haycox's book, and none of the nobility of Buck Elliot's remarkable life remaining.

"I have urged Alcy Harris - (editor's note: Head of Starburst Motion Picture Studios) to address the abandonment of the original story, but he has either refused, or is unable to do so."

Gilmore goes on to say that he is thankful to Mr. William Fox of Fox Movie Studios for offering him the opportunity to continue with his screenwriting career.

Trailcross Ranch – Mogollon Rim – 1885

"I can't believe they didn't find McGee and Logan guilty,"

Sean Kelly complained when, after the trial, all were back at Trailcross Ranch.

"Why were you surprised, Sean?" Dub asked. "We've run across Judge T. Gordon Fitzhugh before, remember? He decided four water and two property disputes in Smythe's favor."

"Yeah, that's the same judge, isn't it?" Sean replied.

"It is, and it wasn't very likely that he was going to be any different in this case," Dub said.

"I see what you mean."

"Yes, and it didn't help any that we had a weak prosecutor," Roan said. He chuckled. "I believe we could have made a stronger case if I'd been the prosecutor."

"What do we do now?" Moe Peters asked. "Are we just going to let Smythe run over us?"

"He's not going to be able to do that," Buck said. "Maybe we didn't get this case decided the way we wanted, but we did show Smythe that he won't be able to act against us without getting stung. I don't think it's very likely that he'll be making any other attempts to burn any of the ranches, but I do think we should still keep our lookouts posted. We'll set up a rotating schedule so nobody will have to be on watch for too long."

The men were holding their discussion under a pinyon pine tree, and they looked up to see Mary Kathleen coming from the house toward the men.

"Would ye gentlemen be for wanting to take your dinner now? For 'tis a fine meal that the ladies are putting before ye," Mary Kathleen said as she approached them.

"I'm the luckiest man in the world," Dub said quietly, beaming as he looked at his beautiful young wife.

"That you are. Dub, that you are," Buck agreed.

. . .

Back in town and at that very moment, Sheriff Jones was sitting with his feet propped up on his desk. He was feeling pretty good about things now. Buck Elliot, with his governor's commission as an Arizona Ranger, had been getting a little too uppity, but he had been cut down a notch or two by the trial this morning.

And as a bonus, though he knew it was something he shouldn't be glad about, six more of Smythe's men had been killed, including Adam Stillwell. With Stillwell and Lodeen both dead, that left Smythe with just one actual gunfighter, Frank Corbett. And although Sheriff Jones was generally allied with Smythe, he had been getting a little worried about the army Smythe was building.

There were some in town who accused Jones of taking money from Smythe, and although Smythe had offered to put the sheriff on his payroll, Jones had declined. He had allied himself with Smythe, because he genuinely believed that Smythe was good for business in the entire area. But he didn't approve of some of the things Smythe did, and though he suspected that Smythe was responsible for the murder of Isaac Mitchell and his wife, he couldn't prove it any more than he could prove it was Smythe's men who burned down Dub Wilkerson's place.

As Sheriff Jones sat behind his desk contemplating Smythe's business impact on the area and wondering if he might not have hitched his wagon to the wrong team, Juan Bustamante came into his office.

"Hello, Juan, what are you doing over here in gringo land?" Jones greeted.

"There has been another, Senor Sheriff," Bustamante said.

"Another?" Jones wasn't sure what Bustamante meant.

"It was Renata."

"Renata? Wait, are you telling me that another one of your girls has been killed?"

"Si, Senor. We found her in her bed this morning."

"Was her, uh," Sheriff Jones raised his hand to his face.

Bustamante looked puzzled for a moment.

"Earring," Jones said, and he put his left hand to his ear lobe and made the motion of jerking it downward. "Was it gone?"

"*Si arete tirado de su oreja,*" he said in Spanish, then he tried to translate it so that the sheriff would understand, "Her," he pointed to his own ear, "pulled off."

"And you say you found her in bed?"

"Si."

"Who was her last customer?"

"It was a gringo."

"An American? Do you know who it was?"

"Si, I know."

"Well who was it, man?" Jones asked anxiously. He would like to solve this case, and show up Buck Elliot.

"I . . . I am afraid to say."

"Afraid? Look man, if this is the same person, you've lost four women who work for you. Don't you want the killin' to stop?"

Bustamante paused for a long moment, then he spoke quickly. "*Fue el ayudante.*"

"*Fue el ayudante?*" Sheriff Jones replied, repeating the words phonetically.

"Si."

"I don't understand. What does that mean?"

"I can say no more, Senor," Bustamante said, as he hurried out the door.

"*Fue el ayudante,*" Sheriff Jones repeated. He wanted to remember exactly how to say the words so he could find someone who would translate them into English.

As Sheriff Jones contemplated what Bustamante had said, he decided that Parker might be able to translate the phrase for him. Parker spoke Spanish better than most Americans that Jones knew. His deputy was away from the office right now, but he was pretty sure he would find Parker in one of the saloons.

Sheriff Jones began his search in the Mogollon Saloon, and as soon as he stepped through the bat wing doors he was greeted by Maud Walker.

"Well now," the pretty young woman said, "what brings you here in the middle of the day, Sheriff? I thought you'd be sheriffing."

"I'm lookin' for my deputy. Has he been in here?"

"Yes, he's here. He's back there with Manley Hampton," Maud said, pointing to the deputy who was sitting with the lawyer at a table next to the piano.

Jones went back to join them. "Mr. Hampton, Lanny."

"Have you come to commiserate with me, or excoriate me?" Hampton asked.

"I don't have no idea in hell what either one of them two

words you said even means," Jones said.

"Surely, Sheriff, you are aware that I lost a case that should have been won by a first year law student."

"Hell, it don't bother me none that you lost that case. If you'd a won, McGee and Logan would be back in my jail, and Smythe would be going at me. And I'd just as soon not have him to deal with."

"Ah yes, Nigel Smythe, the Iago of the Mogollon Rim," Hampton said.

"Who?"

"Iago was a villain created by Shakespeare. And like His Lordship, Viscount Nigel Smythe, Iago controlled everyone around him." Hampton set off his pronouncement by drinking the rest of his whiskey.

"You have something you need me for, Sheriff?" Parker asked.

"Yeah, Lanny, it happened again last night."

"What happened again?" Parker asked.

"Another one of the Mexican whores got herself kilt."

"Damn, another one? Who told you?"

"Bustamante. He came to see me hisself."

"All this time we've been thinking it's some Mexican been doin' the killin', but Bustamante tells me it's an American."

"An American? The hell you say. Anyway, how would Bustamante know that?" Parker asked.

"He not only knows it was an American, he knows who it was."

"What? No, there's no way he could possibly know," Parker said. "Did he tell you who he thinks it is?"

"Yes, he told me. That's why I want to talk to you."

"What do you mean you want to talk to me?" Parker asked, obviously agitated by the question, "What is it you're a'wantin' to talk to me about?"

"When I asked Bustamante who it was, he didn't give me a name."

"I thought you said he know'd who it was."

"He does, but he didn't give me a name."

"Then why is it you're wantin' to talk to me?"

"On account of you speak Mexican about as good as anyone I know. 'N when I asked Bustamante who it was that done the killin', all he said was *Fue el ayudante*."

"*Fue el ayudante?*"

"Yes. Do you know what that means?"

Parker shook his head. "I tell you the truth, Sheriff, I don't have no idea what that means."

"Damn, I need to find out. I'd sure like to know who it is that's doin' all this," Jones said. "Whatever that means, it's tied in with whoever it is that's kilt all them whores in some way, 'n if I could find somebody to tell me, I could figure out who's doin' the killin'."

"Why are you a' worryin' 'bout this anyhow?" Parker asked. "I mean, there ain't nobody a' gettin' kilt but Mexican whores. I thought you said this was Elliot's problem 'n we wasn't goin' to concern ourselves about it none," Parker said.

"Yes, but that was before I knew there was an American involved," Jones said. "Besides, I'd like to find out 'fore Elliot does. I'd show 'im we don't need his kind around here."

"Hell, Elliot ain't goin' to be worryin' none about it, that's for sure," Parker said, "All he cares about is them damn ranchers."

"You may be right."

"But I tell you what, I'll ask around 'n see what I can find out," Parker offered, getting up from the table.

"Thanks, Lanny. You need me to say that phrase for you again? Maybe you can get some of your friends on the other side of the tracks to tell you what it means."

"Yeah, let me hear it again."

"Fue el ayudante."

Parker repeated it, "I got it. I'll see what I can find out."

"Thanks."

"I'd better go as well," Hampton said, getting up to leave.

Sheriff Jones remained behind sitting at the table all alone. Having bought a beer he figured he may as well finish it and had just taken a swallow when the bartender, Ben McDaniels, approached him.

"I just thought you might like to know who else is here," Ben said. "He's in the back room, him 'n that fancy lawyer he hired."

"You're talking about Smythe?"

"His Lordship himself," Ben said, speaking the words in a way that showed his disapproval of the wealthy rancher.

Sheriff Jones didn't respond to the bartender's sarcasm. Instead he walked to the back of the saloon and knocked on the door that led to the private room.

"Come in."

Jones pulled the door open and stepped just inside. The private room of the saloon was fixed as place where a small group could hold meetings. It was where C.E. Felker of the Cattleman's Bank sometimes held board meetings which would include Nigel Smythe. But now the only two men in the room were Smythe and Chamberlin.

"Sheriff, come in, come in," Smythe invited. "Have a glass of wine." Smythe pointed toward the half empty bottle by way of invitation.

"Thanks," Jones replied, grabbing a glass before he sat down.

"Harcourt, this is our sheriff, Emile Jones. And Sheriff, you saw Harcourt Chamberlin the third in court. He is the most brilliant barrister in the entire territory of Arizona to be sure, but I would not limit his standing to Arizona alone. No sir, I am quite certain he is one of the best in the country. But I don't have to tell you that, you saw his brilliance for yourself."

"Yes, sir, you was about as slick as any lawyer I've ever seen," Jones said.

"I am keeping Mr. Chamberlin company, until his train leaves this afternoon. And, not that your company is unwelcome, but I feel you might have some reason for coming to see me."

"Yes, sir, I do. You know all them Mexican women that's bein' kilt? Well, sir, there's been another 'n that was kilt last night."

"Another one? What a ghastly business this is. How many does that make now? Three?"

"Four."

"Sheriff I would advise you to do what you can to get to the bottom of this as quickly as you can. The town's business and ultimately my own business, can be hurt by such a thing."

"Yes, sir, I agree with you. But seein' as Buck Elliot is the town marshal, seems to me like this would be more his problem than my own. Only the thing is, me 'n him don't get along all that well, 'n I know damn well you got no truck with him."

"That may be so, but it would be best for all concerned if you could find out who is doing all this. Besides if you solve the case, it could only enhance your standing, don't you think?"

"Yes, sir, that's pretty much what I was thinkin' too."

"Do you have any suspects?"

"No sir, not really, because at first I wasn't none too concerned about it, seein' as we figured it was a Mexican that was doin' all the killin'. But now I was told the killer was American."

"An American, you say?"

Jones nodded. "That's what I'm thinkin' now."

"*A las putas Mexicanas las matan?*" Chamberlin asked, speaking for the first time.

"What?" Sheriff Jones asked.

"I asked if the Mexican women who are being killed are whores."

"Yeah, all four of 'em. Wait a minute, you speak Spanish?"

"One cannot have a flourishing business in Arizona without being able to speak the language of almost half the population. Yes, I speak Spanish."

"What does *fue el ayudante* mean?"

Chamberlin laughed. "Is this some sort of test, Sheriff? To test my ability to speak Spanish?"

"Damn it, this is important. What does it mean?" Sheriff Jones demanded in a harsh voice.

"It means 'it was the assistant.' " Chamberlin replied, puzzled by the harshness of Sheriff Jones request.

"It was the assistant," Jones said. He cupped his elbow in one hand and with the other hand, pinched the bridge of his nose. "It was the assistant," he repeated. "What the hell does that mean?"

"I was about to ask you the same question, Sheriff. And I don't appreciate the way you spoke to Mr. Chamberlin," Smythe said.

"I'm sorry, Mr. Chamberlin, but a Mexican said that to me. The person that's killin' all them whores was the assistant."

"Assistant what?" Smythe asked.

Sheriff Jones shook his head. "If I knew, then I'd know who the killer is."

"The man didn't give you any more than that?" Chamberlin asked.

"No, sir, that's all he said. Just them words."

"That seems rather odd," Smythe said. "If the person who told you this, knows that the killer is some sort of assistant, then I've no doubt but that he knows who the killer is. Why didn't he tell you more?"

"He didn't tell me no more on account of 'cause he said he's a' scared," Jones said.

Corbett, Truax, and Nixon were in the saloon when Maud Walker stepped over to their table.

"Ben wants to know if any of you want anything else to drink?" she asked with a bright smile.

"Yeah, I'll have some tequila," Corbett said.

"Ha!" Truax said. "You spend so much time in the barrio that you've commenced to drinkin' Mexican."

"I like tequila," Corbett said.

"What about you boys?" Maud asked.

Truax and Nixon both ordered beer.

"Oh, did you hear that the sheriff might know who's killing all those poor Mexican girls?" Maud asked.

"What?" Corbett asked, looking up sharply. "They've caught the killer?"

"Not yet, but Ben says it's an American that's been killing 'em. And Bustamante knows who it is, but he's too afraid to give the name."

"Bustamante knows, huh? Well, I'll be damn," Nixon said. "Ain't that a kick in the head? He knowed, but he let 'em die anyway."

When Juan Bustamante stepped into his storeroom to get a few more bottles of liquor, he had no idea there was someone in the room waiting for him. He didn't see his unexpected visitor even after he stepped through the door, and was totally unaware of a foreign presence until he started to open a new case of tequila.

His first awareness of another presence was the sharp pain he felt on his throat as a knife cut so deeply that not only was the carotid artery opened up, but his windpipe was sliced through, preventing him from calling out. The last conscious awareness of his life was that he had just been killed.

Deputy Parker stepped into the cantina.

"Si, Senor Deputy?" the bartender asked.

"I'll have a tequila," Parker replied.

"Si, Senor."

Parker took the drink then turned to look at the three bar girls, Imelda, Jacinta, and Elvita.

"I've been told they was another *puta* that was kilt last night," Parker said.

"Si, Senor Deputy," Imelda said, speaking for all three of them.

"Where was she found?"

"In her bed, Senor Deputy."

"Damn, in her bed?" Parker chuckled. "Imagine that, a whore gettin' kilt in her own bed. Well, sir, the sheriff, he wanted me to investigate this, so I need to take a look at the bed. One of you want to take me up there so I can see where it was that this happened?"

The three women looked at each other with expressions of fear on their faces.

"Look, what the hell do you have to be afraid of?" Parker asked, "I'm an officer of the law, just doin' my duty."

None of the three women replied.

"All right, never mind, I'll get Bustamante to take me up."

· · ·

When Sheriff Jones returned to his office he was surprised to see Hampton sitting there, waiting for him.

"Hampton, what are you doing here?"

"I know the definition of the phrase you were looking for," Hampton said.

"Yes, well, thanks, but I already got the definition. It means, 'It was the assistant.' Is that right?"

"Yes."

"Well, thanks anyway. Wait a minute. If you knowed what it meant, why didn't you tell me when I asked?"

"I didn't want to say it in front of Parker," Hampton said.

"You didn't want to say it in front of Parker? What do you mean? Why not?"

"Parker is your deputy."

"So? Ever' body knows that."

"In Spanish, a deputy sheriff is *ayudante del sheriff*, or assistant to the sheriff. You said Bustamante was afraid to tell you. I think he was just afraid to come right out and tell you, because I think Deputy Parker is the one who has been murdering all those Mexican women."

"That isn't possible," Sheriff Jones said.

Hampton was quiet for a long moment, then he stood. "You're probably right," he said quietly. "I'm sure it was just my imagination getting the best of me. Well, I did give you the translation of that phrase, so use it as you wish." He started toward the door.

Sheriff Jones watched him leave and thought about what the lawyer had just told him. Could the killer actually be his deputy?

Jones knew that Parker spent a lot of time in the barrio, and that Parker understood a lot of Spanish words. How was it that Parker couldn't tell him what this phrase meant, when both Chamberlin and Hampton knew it immediately?

On a notion, Jones sat down at Parker's desk and began

rifling through the drawers. In the bottom drawer on the left hand side of the desk, he found a tobacco pouch. Removing the pouch, he laid it on top of Parker's desk, then pulled the cord.

Jones gasped, because inside the pouch he found four gold earrings.

"Damn, Lanny, what the hell have you done?" Jones asked the question aloud, but in a quiet, and awe-struck voice.

Jones stayed behind the desk just staring in disgust at what he had discovered. How the hell could Parker have done anything like this?

At that moment the door to the sheriff's office opened and Parker stepped inside. "Sheriff, I talked to some of the Mexicans 'n they don't none of 'em know any . . . " Seeing Sheriff Jones staring at something on his desk, Parker stopped in mid-sentence.

Sheriff Jones held up the pouch. "You know what's in this bag? Earrings. The ones you jerked offen the ears of them whores. Parker, how could you do . . .?" That was as far as Sheriff Jones got with his question before Parker drew his gun and pulled the trigger. Parker's bullet took out one of Jones' eyes, but Jones would never miss that eye. The same bullet that took out his eye also killed him.

29

"I knew about the murder of the Mexican prostitutes," Ryan said, "not only from Ernest's book, but also from reading the contemporary newspaper accounts. It made quite a splash."

"At the time, it rivaled the Henry Brown incident," Ernest said.

"Henry Brown?" Ryan asked.

"Oh yes, Henry Newton Brown," Buck said, shaking his head. "His was a tragic story. At one time, it was said that he rode with Billy the Kid, then he turned his life around and became a hell of a good marshal up in Caldwell, Kansas."

"What was so tragic about that?" Ryan asked. "Was he killed?"

"He was," Buck said, "but not the way you think. He went to a neighboring town and tried to rob a bank."

"And that's where he died?"

"It was," Ernest said. "You know, Buck, I've been thinking I should write a book about his life."

"You should do it," Ryan said. "I'd write the screenplay, and it could be your next movie."

"It'd be a good story," Ernest said. "I could call it *The Town Marshal*. Actually, there are a lot of similarities between old Henry and our boy, Lanny Parker. Both of them were lawmen who betrayed the trust the people had given them. By the way, how come you didn't put the Parker business in your screenplay?"

"A simple reason—time constraints," Ryan said. "I had to get everything in, in 120 pages, and I thought what Parker did was not germane to Buck's life."

"If we can get Starburst to stop production, maybe you can write another script and put the Parker–prostitute story line in the new screenplay." Buck suggested.

"Do you have any idea how we might do that?" Ernest asked. "Get Starburst to stop production, I mean."

"Jacob Parnelli," Ryan replied with a smile.

"Jacob Parnelli?"

"Parnelli has a law office on Sunset Boulevard, and he specializes in entertainment law," Ryan said. "I've done some business with him before. Let's go see him."

The Parnelli Law Office was in suite 715, and after checking in with the receptionist, Ryan, Ernest, and Buck took a seat in the waiting room.

"Coffee?" Ryan asked, stepping over toward a counter where there was a large coffee maker.

"Yes, please," both Ernest and Buck replied.

As Ryan held cups under the little spigot, Buck picked up a brochure from the table beside the sofa.

WHAT CAN THE PARNELLI LAW OFFICE DO FOR YOU?

We are dedicated to serving all talent (actors, artists, singers, writers, dancers, directors, producers, editors, engineers, executives), and entertainment companies (film studios, recording facilities, record labels, management companies, agencies, publishing companies, film studios, distributors) with all of their personal, career, business and law needs.

Buck looked through the brochure and had just finished when the receptionist came over to them with a pleasant smile to announce that Mr. Parnelli would see them.

Parnelli was a rather short man with thinning dark hair that he wore combed over a thinning spot on the top of his head. He had come to work in a suit, but now the jacket was draped over the back of his chair, his shirt collar was unbuttoned and his tie loosened. His eyes were brown.

"Ryan," Parnelli said, extending his hand, "what brings you to see me, today?"

"Jacob, I'd like to introduce you to a couple of friends of mine," Ryan said. "This is Ernest Haycox, and this is Buck Elliot."

"Haycox," Parnelli said, "You're a novelist, aren't you?"

"I write some fiction, but I also write non-fiction," Ernest replied.

"And Buck Elliot, I've heard of you as well," Parnelli said. "I had the pleasure of representing Wyatt Earp a few years back. He had a high opinion of you—said you were one of the better known gunfighters of the Old West. And a damn good one, too."

"I'm not sure I agree with him," Buck said, "but it was mighty nice of Wyatt to say that. In those days, most everybody knew about everybody else, even if we weren't that close."

"Speaking of knowing about everybody, Ryan, I saw in *The Hollywood Reporter* that you left Starburst. Is that why you're here to see me? Are they raking you over the coals?"

"We're here to talk about Starburst," Ryan said, "but it's not because I quit. As a matter of fact, I expect they were about as glad to get rid of me as I was to leave."

"Is that so? Then what's the problem?"

"It's the production. They're supposed to be producing my screenplay, but if they were shooting the telephone book it would be closer."

Parnelli held out his hand, "Whoa, hold it Ryan. You've been in this business long enough to know that once you do the production script, they can pretty much do anything they want with the shooting script."

"I know that, but I'm not the one who's going to file the complaint. It will be these two gentlemen," Ryan said. "The script is based upon Ernest's book, *Legend of a Gunfighter*, which is the authentic history of Buck Elliot. The operative term here, Jacob, is 'authentic'. There is absolutely nothing authentic about this . . . this abomination they're shooting."

"Mr. Parnelli," Ernest started, but Parnelli interrupted him.

"Please, it's Jacob. And exactly, what is it you want me to do?"

"I want out of the contract with Starburst, and I want production of the film stopped," Ernest said.

"Well now, that's quite an order. May I ask the reason for such a request?"

"It's as Ryan said, they aren't using his screenplay, they aren't using the story that I wrote, and they for sure aren't telling the true story of Buck Elliot."

"Actually, they don't have to stop the shooting," Ryan said. "All three of us are in agreement on that score. They can continue with the picture they are shooting, since it has so little to do with the book or with the incidents from Buck's life. We just want them to change the title, and not use Buck's name with regard to the role that Clive Malone is playing."

"That's still asking a hell of lot," Jacob said.

Ryan smiled. "That's why we came to the most brilliant entertainment lawyer in Hollywood."

"Well, I'll give you credit for discernment," Jacob replied, his smile as large as Ryan's. "But you were a staff writer, so that means you don't have standing in this case, but Ernest, just might. Did you happen to bring a copy of your contract with Starburst?"

"I did," Ernest said, presenting the document. Jacob began to read the contract aloud.

"Paragraph one, services. Producer hereby retains the film rights to the book *Legend of a Gunfighter*, hereinafter called the property, from Ernest Haycox, hereinafter called the writer in relation to the production of a proposed motion picture to be called *Legend of a Gunfighter*, hereinafter referred to as the Production, on the terms and conditions set out below. Literary materials and all other products of the writer are referred to collectively in this agreement as the "Work". The Services shall include the preparation and delivery of the following: Ten copies of the published book, *Legend of a Gunfighter*, which is an accounting of the life and times of Buck Elliot, an authentic person of American history and the Old West.

"Paragraph two, use of work: Producer may, in his sole discretion, use or not use the Work or any part thereof, and may make any changes in, deletions from or additions to the Work."

Jacob stopped reading, then looked up at the three men and shook his head, "Gentlemen, I'm afraid they've got us right here," he said, "This part, 'may use or not use the work or any part of, and make any changes in, deletions from or additions to the work." Jacob shook his head. "Studio lawyers have been around the film industry for as long as there has been such a thing, and they have perfected performance and property contracts so that they are pretty much iron-clad. I see no way we can get around that."

"I've read this contract over several times," Ryan said, "and I believe I've found a loophole for us."

"And where would that loophole be, because I certainly don't see it."

"I'd rather not tell you yet," Ryan said. "I want you to keep reading, and if you see the same loophole that I do, then I'll think it's a legitimate approach."

"All right," Jacob said. He continued to read: "Performance Standard: All of the Services shall be rendered promptly, professionally and efficiently and in accordance with the instructions of, and under the control of, Producer.

"Warranties, representations, indemnities: Writer warrants and represents that all of the Work shall be wholly original, except as to matters within the public domain and except as to material inserted by Writer pursuant to specific instructions provided by Producer.

"None of the Work shall infringe upon or violate the rights of privacy or publicity of, or constitute defamation against, or violate any common law or any other rights of, any person, firm or corporation . . ." Jacob stopped reading, then looked up with a huge smile.

"Defamation!" he said loudly, "We can say that the script, as being produced, is defaming the character of Buck Elliot!"

Ryan returned the smile. "It's true what they say, Jacob, great minds do think alike."

"The lawsuit is going to have to come from Buck," Jacob said. "He's absolutely the only one who has standing in this case."

"There's only one problem with that," Ryan said.

"What's that?"

"Now that I've left the production, Buck's the only one who's still inside. It seems to me that it would be a good thing to leave him there. If Buck sues the production for defamation of character, they're going to get him off the set as fast as they can."

"You're right. Okay, Buck, you stay with them while I gather as much information as I can put together. Then when I'm ready we'll file the lawsuit."

30

EAGLESHIRE ON SHERLONS FORK RANCH – 1885

"Yeah, well, wait here while I see if the boss wants to talk to you," Frank Corbett said in response to Lanny Parker's request for an audience with Smythe.

"Tell him it's important," Parker said.

"He'll decide if'n it's important," Corbett replied.

As Parker waited to meet with Smythe, he stepped over to look at a full suit of armor that stood against the wall. He had never seen such a thing, and he wasn't sure what it was. It looked a little like a statue, but if it was a statue, why didn't it have a face?

"Parker?" Corbett said a moment later, "Mr. Smythe says come on in."

Smythe was sitting behind his desk with his hands clasped in front of him.

"Mr. Corbett says that you have something important to tell me," Smythe said.

"Yes, sir, I do."

"Tell me, my good man, if it really is important, why is it that Sheriff Jones sent you, instead of coming himself?"

"That's what's the important thing," Parker said. "Sheriff Jones can't come see you no more on account of he's dead."

At that piece of information Smythe dropped his façade of detachment and leaned forward, his expression changing from indifference to intense interest.

"What's that you say? Sheriff Jones is dead?"

"Yes, sir, 'n bein' as I was his deputy, that makes me the sheriff now, so I reckon me 'n you will be doin' business just like you 'n him was." Parker smiled.

"What are the circumstances of his demise?"

"What?" Parker replied, not understanding the question.

"How did Sheriff Jones die?"

"Oh, he was kilt," Parker said.

"Was he murdered? And if so, have you someone in custody, or at least a suspect?"

"Oh, you mean who is it that kilt him? Well, maybe you ain't heard, but they's been someone killin' a lot of the Mexican whores."

"I am aware of that. The sheriff and I spoke of it just recently."

"Yeah, well the thing is, me 'n the sheriff figured that most likely it's some Mexican that's a' doin' it. 'N what I'm thinkin' is, Sheriff Jones, he figured out who it was, 'n when the Mexican that's a' doin' it found out that the sheriff know'd who he was, that's when he come to the jail house 'n kilt the sheriff, on account of that's the way I found 'im."

"Are you sure it was a Mexican? Because I thought Sheriff Jones believed it might have been an American," Smythe said.

"Yeah, he did think it for a little while, but then we figured out that it had to be some Mexican, 'n it's more 'n likely the same Mexican that kilt him."

"That is quite unsettling," Smythe said.

"Yeah, I guess so. But what I come out here for, is to tell you that I'm the sheriff now so whatever it is that you 'n the sheriff was doin' why now you can do it with me."

"Under the circumstances I suppose you are right," Smythe said, "You are the sheriff, and we will be working together."

"So, how much was you payin' Emile?"

"Emile? You called your superior by his Christian name?"

"His what?"

"Were you in the habit of addressing Sheriff Jones by his first name?"

"Oh, no, not while he was livin' I didn't. Only he ain't alive no more so I don't reckon it matters none. Anyhow, how much is it you was a' payin' 'im for workin' for you?"

"Why, whatever are you talking about, Mr. Parker? I wasn't paying him anything," Smythe replied, omitting the information that he had offered to pay the sheriff for his services, only to have the offer turned down. "Sheriff Jones' only remuneration was in the knowledge that helping me was the right thing to do. I assume you and I will have the same arrangement."

"Look here, are you tellin' me you wasn't givin' Jones nothin' at all?" Parker asked incredulously.

"Yes, Mr. Parker, that is exactly what I'm saying." Smythe smiled knowingly. "I take it that you would prefer a different arrangement from the one I had with the late sheriff."

"What?"

"You would like to be paid."

Parker smiled broadly. "Yeah, I wanna be paid."

"What is your salary now, Deputy Parker?"

"Well, bein' as I was the deputy, I was makin' eighty dollars a month. But the sheriff now, he was makin' a hunnert 'n twenty dollars a month so I reckon soon as I get swore in as the sheriff, I'll be makin' that much."

"Suppose I match that," Smythe said. "You will continue to draw your one hundred twenty dollars pay for working for the county, and I will pay you an additional one hundred twenty dollars a month for your, let us say, loyalty, to me. Are you agreeable to that?"

"Yes, sir! Uh, what do you want me to do?"

"Nothing at the moment. I will let you know when I need you, and I will expect your immediate and unquestioned loyalty."

"Yes, sir. When do I get my money?"

"I suppose I can give you an advance now," Smythe said and getting up he walked over to the wall where he moved a picture to one side, revealing a safe behind. After twirling the knob a few times, he opened the safe.

Parker was watching him very closely, and when the safe door was opened, he saw several stacks of bills inside. He gasped, because he had never seen so much money.

"Wow! How much money is in there?" Parker asked in awe.

"That is none of your concern," Smythe replied as he counted out several bills before closing the door to the safe. "Your only concern is the one hundred twenty dollars we have agreed upon."

Smythe laid the bills in Parker's hands.

———

From the Canyon Diablo Brimstone:

Sheriff Jones Found Murdered

Emile Jones, who has for the last three years been the sheriff of Yavapai County, was found murdered in his office by his deputy, Lanny Parker. It is Parker's belief that the sheriff was killed by the same man who has so brutally murdered four Mexican prostitutes in the last two months.

On the same day that Sheriff Jones' body was found, the body of Juan Bustamante was also discovered. This is believed to be related because it is known that Juan Bustamante visited the sheriff shortly before both were killed. It is reasonable to assume that the visit was to give the sheriff some information on the perpetrator of the horrendous murders of the prostitutes.

Judge Fitzhugh has since sworn in Lanny Parker as the sheriff, a position he will hold until the next election.

Trailcross Ranch

There were more than six thousand head of Hereford cattle gathered at Trailcross Ranch. There was enough grass to feed them, and because the grazing field was on the Laroux Fork, they didn't lack for water.

There was very much a tactual awareness of that large a gather of cattle, and the air resonated with the bawling and the rumble of their activity. It was an impressive sight, so many cows so close together, so that it looked like one very large brown undulating tapestry. But perhaps the most prominent sensory input was the smell, pungent and practically overpowering at first notice, though it was a scent to which the men quickly adjusted, so much so, that it became a comfortable part of their environment.

Buck was at Trailcross ranch with Sean, Dub, Roan and the other ranchers. At the moment, the men were discussing their options.

"Since we can't do business with Teasdale's holding pens, I've made arrangements with Tony Heckemeyer to take our cows to Winslow," Sean said. "He's got twice as many pens as the ones in Canyon Diablo, and he'll be able to take our whole herd at the same time."

"But we'll have to trail our cows to Winslow," George Baker said.

"It's only forty miles. Hell, we can make a drive like that in two days, easy," Sean said. "Why, I remember a trail drive that me 'n Buck made that was over a thousand miles. Right, Buck?"

"That's right, I remember. And when we weren't plowing through a thunderstorm or a blizzard, we were fighting to find enough water to survive," Buck said.

"How long will we have to keep our cows penned up in Winslow?" Moe Peters asked. "Because if you think about it, every day they have to stay there will mean just that much more money it'll cost us."

"That won't be our problem," Sean replied. "There's a fella in Winslow who says he'll buy the whole herd from us. That means the storin' 'em, 'n arrangin' for cars to ship 'em out will be on him."

"Hey," Roan said, pointing to an approaching rider, "ain't that the deputy sheriff?"

"He ain't a deputy no more," Stan Emerson said. "It weren't two days after Sheriff Jones got shot, Parker managed to get hisself swore in as the new sheriff."

"Yeah, well he was the deputy, so I guess it's fittin' that he'd be the new sheriff," Moe said.

"I wonder what he wants," Roan asked.

"Whatever it is, it can't be good," Sean said.

Parker rode on up to the small group of men who had gathered to watch his approach. He didn't dismount.

"Who is it that's the head o' this bunch?" Parker asked.

"We don't have a head," Sean answered. "Each one of us is a owner, and we all got about the same number of cows in this gather. As far as I'm concerned, that means we're all equal."

"You seem to be the one that's doin' all the talkin' though," Parker said.

"What is it you want, Parker?" Buck asked, bluntly.

"Yeah, well, here's the thing," Parker said. "I've got me what they call a court order here. And this here court order is signed by the judge, 'n it says you can't keep all these cows bunched up here like this no more. You got to," he paused, looking for the word, "disperse. That means you can't keep 'em all in one place."

"What do you mean we can't keep these cows here? This is my land, my grass, and my water. And the owners of the cows that aren't my own, are here as my guests."

"Yeah, it might be your land and your grass, but it ain't your water," Parker said. "You see the law says that any water as what may come a flowin' through your land can't be . . .," Parker stopped and again consulted the piece of paper he had just produced, "impeded," he concluded.

"Impeded? What does that mean?" Moe asked.

"That means we can't cut off the water for any of the downstream ranches," Buck explained.

"Yeah, that," Parker said, triumphantly.

"Look here, Deputy, my ranch is the only one that's downstream from here," Clyde Jamison said. "And I get plenty of water."

"I ain't the deputy no more," Parker said, pointedly. "I'm the sheriff."

"All right, so you're the sheriff. But my point is, I'm the only ranch that's downstream from here, 'n I don't mind that all these cows is drinkin' the water, seen' as some o' them cows as is doin' all the drinkin' is mine."

"That don't matter none. What this here judge's order says is that you got yourselves one week to get these here cows all broke up again, or ever' damn one of 'em will be confiscated. Here it is, read it for yourself," Parker said holding the paper out. Buck reached for it.

CIRCUIT COURT YAVAPAI COUNTY TERRITORY OF ARIZONA

CASE NO. CO3

PLAINTIFF – NIGEL SMYTHE

DEFENDANTS – SEAN KELLY, WILLIAM WILKERSON, MOE PETERS, GEORGE BAKER, STAN EMERSON, CLYDE JAMISON, ROAN ROBERTS, AND SARA SUE TANNER

SUMMARY JUDGEMENT

This matter comes before the Court on plaintiff's motion for summary judgment. Plaintiff argues that in accordance with GLO and U.S. Grazing Service the natural flow of Laroux Fork Creek is being impeded by an excessive gather of cattle owned by the defendants. Such gather constitutes a violation to the regulation governing rights to lands affected by the flow of water, such as lakes, streams, or rivers, and the right to use the land as well as to the jurisdiction of the sovereignty where land upon which the waters flow is situated.

Plaintiff further argues that by the improper impediment of the natural flow of Laroux Fork Creek that all livestock, both domestic and wild that are not a part of the current gather of cattle by the Defendants, are being illegally denied access to water.

CONCLUSION

Having reviewed plaintiff's motion for summary judgment, the Court hereby ORDERS:

The Plaintiff's motion for summary judgement is approved and the gather of cattle will be dispersed according to ownership and returned to the lands of the individual defendants.

This case is CLOSED. The Court will enter plaintiff's proposed permanent injunction upon entry of this Order.

The Clerk shall direct a copy of this Order to all counsel of record.

DATED this fifth day of September in the Year of our Lord 1885.

T Gordon Fitzhugh

Circuit Judge Yavapai County Arizona Territory

"How long do we have before this order is enforced?" Sean asked.

"The judge said you've got to do this within a week," Parker replied.

"Parker?" Buck said.

"That would be Sheriff Parker," Parker replied.

"Parker," Buck said again, pointedly omitting the title, "how are you going to enforce this order?"

"What do you mean, how am I going to enforce it? Why, if these here cows ain't been moved out within a week, I'm goin' to come take 'em."

"By yourself?"

"Uh, no, I, uh, I'll have me some help by then."

"Where are you going to get help? I won't let you use anyone from Eagleshire, because as Smythe is actively trying to run these men out of business, I don't think it would be fair."

"What do you mean, you ain't goin' to let me use any of Smythe's men? I'm the sheriff."

"And I'm an officer of the Arizona Territory, which means I have authority over you."

"Yeah? Well, we'll see about that," Parker said as with an angry snort he jerked his horse around and rode off.

"Ha! You told him!" Sean said. "He sure didn't like hearing that you have authority over him."

"That's true, ain't it, Buck? You do have authority over the sheriff, don't you?" George Baker asked.

"Yes."

"But what about the court order?" Dub asked. "Do you have authority over that?"

"No, I don't."

"Damn! What are we going to do about that?" Roan asked.

31

STARBURST MOTION PICTURE STUDIO - 1931

INT. MAGOLLON SALOON - DAY
  Buck, Dub Wilkerson, and Mary Kathleen are sitting
  at a table. Nearby are THREE ROUGH LOOKING MEN.
Buck's table is approached by MAUD, a bar girl.

MAUD (to Mary Kathleen)

You're a good lookin' woman, honey. Are you looking to be one of the working girls here?

DUB
This here is my wife.

MAUD
Dub, you mean this is the mail order bride you sent off for?

DUB
Yeah

MAUD
Oh, my, didn't you get yourself a pretty one though?

MARY KATHLEEN

Dub, you allow such creatures as this to address you by your Christian name?

MAUD

Now, honey, don't you get all upset with Dub. There ain't that many women out here and men do get lonely, you know.

Giggling. Maud walks away from the table.

Buck has noticed something out in the street and carrying his beer he gets up from the table, and walks to the front entrance, looking out over the batwing doors.

EXT. STREET DAY
   Buck sees a buckboard moving by. His attention is drawn to the front seat of the buckboard. A BEAUTIFUL YOUNG WOMAN is sitting beside A MAN WHO MIGHT BE HER FATHER. Buck is interested enough in the pretty girl that he barely registers a new arrival at the saloon's hitching post. The newcomer takes his saddle-bags and a Henry .44 rifle from his horse and comes up into the saloon.

. . .

INT. SALOON - DAY

The newcomer is An OLDER MAN with white hair and a scruffy looking white beard. His clothes are well-worn. He is not wearing a pistol belt and has no weapon other than the rifle. Going into the saloon he steps up to the bar, but nobody comes to take his order. The three rough looking men stare at the older man. Buck, returning to his table, notes their attitude and glances over at the old man at the bar.

BARTENDER

What do you want?

OLD MAN

I haven't had a beer or slept in a bed in a month of Sundays. Give me a beer.

The old man has leaned his rifle against the bar and he wraps both hands around the beer mug. Maud approaches the old man.

MAUD
(in a teasing voice)

How long has it been since you shared a drink with a woman?

OLD MAN

Too long, honey. Why don't you join me?

. . .

The three rough looking men exchange looks as the old man puts the money down for a drink for the bar girl. When the bartender places a drink glass in front of the bar girl, the old man picks his beer mug up and holds it out toward the girl in a long moment of pleasant anticipation.

ONE OF THE THREE ROUGH LOOKING MEN

Hey, you! Ain't you too old for a young woman like that?

OLD MAN
Sonny, you don't never get too old to enjoy a drink with

a pretty woman.

ROUGH LOOKING MAN
That's my woman, I don't want you havin' no drink with her.

MAUD
Don't be silly, Arnold, It's my job to drink with the customers.

ROUGH MAN

Yeah? Well if you have a drink with this old man, I aim to shoot 'im.

The other two Rough Men quietly rise and separate, moving toward the opposite ends of the bar.

Buck has been watching the interplay and now he stands and moves away from the table where he had been sitting with Dub and Mary Kathleen. He holds his hands near his guns.

BUCK

I think you boys need to get on out of here now and leave this gentleman alone.

ROUGH MAN

You buyin' in?

BUCK

I am.

ROUGH MAN

Shoot 'im boys!

The three men draw but are shocked to see how quickly Buck draws both guns shoots, first the rough man who has been doing all the talking, then he spins, and shoots the other two who are standing at each end of the bar.

OLD MAN

Mister, I've seen a lot of things in my life, but I ain't never seen no one draw a gun and shoot as fast as what you just done. I thank you for comin' to my aid like you done.

Buck twirls both guns around his fingers, blows smoke from the barrels, then puts the guns back in the holsters.

BUCK

It seemed to me like it was the right thing to do.

"Cut!" Guy shouted, "Good scene, people, this one is going into the can."

Buck had been sitting behind a folding table that was out of the way of both the set and the cameras. He was drumming his fingers in irritation as a smiling Clive approached him.

"What did you think of the scene?" Clive asked.

"It was exciting enough, I suppose," Buck replied, "But I don't recall anything like that ever happening."

"It doesn't matter that it never happened," Clive said, "You said yourself, it was an exciting scene."

"And that's all that's necessary? Truth doesn't matter as long as the scene is exciting?"

"Buck, you have to understand that the motion picture industry is an entertainment industry. If you want to learn history, read a book."

"I agree with you there," Buck said. "This movie should be more entertainment than history, so why are you using my name?"

"Because we're making a movie from the book *Legend of a*

Gunfighter, and the book is about you," Clive said, as if he were explaining something to a child.

"The book is about me, yes, but the movie isn't."

Clive sighed in exasperation. "Buck, I shouldn't have to explain this to you. *Legend of a Gunfighter* was on the national best seller list for forty-six weeks. Nearly everyone in America has heard of it. And because of that, the studio paid Ernest Haycox good money for the right to use his book and title, and your name I might add, as a means of promoting the movie we're making. But all we really need is the book title and your name."

"My name isn't for sale."

Clive smiled. "You think not? You've already sold it. Look, Buck, don't get all upset about this. Hell, if this movie flops, I'm the one who'll be hurt, not you. A box office failure could cost me my career. It won't make any difference to you."

"That's where you're wrong. Clive," Buck said. "For me, it's a matter of honor."

Clive grinned. "Yeah, I've heard that all you old Western guys were big on honor."

"Clive, we're setting up for the next shot," Guy shouted.

"I'll be right there," Clive called back.

Buck had had about enough for the day, so before the bell rang to close everything down for the next scene, he left the set.

Buck was supposed to meet with Ernest and Ryan in the hotel lobby at four o'clock, but because he left the set early he knew that they wouldn't be there yet. Six years ago he had come to Los Angeles to visit Dub and Mary Kathleen. Dub had died last year, but he was pretty sure that Mary Kathleen was still here, so he took a chance that the telephone number he had was still good and made a call.

"Hello?" It was Mary Kathleen's voice.

"Mary Kathleen, this is Buck Elliot."

"Oh, Buck, 'twas hoping I was that ye would be for calling me while you were in town."

"You knew that I was in Los Angeles? How did you know that?"

"Your name was in the paper because 'tis a movie they are making about you."

"They are making a movie, that's true. But the only thing about me they've gotten right so far has been my name."

"Buck, could you be for stopping by for supper tonight? 'Tis a good Irish stew I'll be making."

"I well remember your Irish stew, Mary Kathleen. Thanks for the invite and yes, I'll be there."

"Seven o'clock?" Mary Kathleen said.

"Seven o'clock."

As Buck waited in the lobby of the Hotel Normandie to meet Ernest and Ryan, he saw a young hotel employee using a push broom on the tile floor. His name was Julian Throckmorton. He had told Buck that he was from Sikeston, Missouri, and that he had come to Hollywood to break into the movie business.

"Hello, Julian, how are things going for you?" Buck asked. He had met the young man shortly after he arrived at the hotel.

"My name is Tim now, Mr. Elliot," the young man replied with a broad smile. "Tim Curtis. That's the name MGM wants me to use."

"Oh, well, things must be going well for you."

"Yes, sir! Well, sort of. I've got a part in a movie, but I don't have any speaking lines, and I won't get any screen credit for it. I am 'Man at the Table' but back home ever' one will get a good look at me. And I don't think they would've asked me to change my name, if they didn't plan on usin' me at some time in the future."

"I think you must be right," Buck said. "If all they wanted

you to do was sit at a table, why I'm sure the name Julian Throckmorton would have been just fine."

"Yes, sir, that's exactly what I'm thinking," Julian said.

The young, would-be actor continued with his work as Buck saw Ernest and Ryan come into the lobby. He stood to meet them and they were both smiling as they approached.

"We had a good meeting with Jacob," Ernest said, "but he thinks the idea of you suing me, and my suing Starburst isn't going to work. The lawsuit is going to have to come from you for defamation of character."

"I thought it might come down to that," Buck said.

"It will mean we no longer have anyone inside," Ryan said.

Buck chuckled. "To tell you the truth, Ryan, I'd just as soon not be 'inside' anymore. I've had about as much of that arrogant son of a bitch as I can stand."

"You aren't alone. Half the people who work at Starburst feel the same way about Clive," Ryan said.

"What sort of odds is Jacob giving us that this lawsuit will work?" Buck asked.

"He's pretty sure that we can bring enough pressure against Starburst to drop the project, or at least, give up the idea of saying that it's a story about you," Ryan said.

"What about the title?" Buck asked. *"Legend of a Gunfighter* is about me. So will they have to change the title?

"Not unless they want to," Ernest said. "You can't copyright a title."

"You can't?"

"Nope. I could write a book called *The Sun Also Rises*, and Ernest Hemingway couldn't do anything about it. Only thing is, because that book is so well known, no publisher would use the title a second time. So if they want to keep the title, there's nothing we can do to stop them."

"They aren't going to give up without a fight though," Ryan said. He laughed, "Funny thing is, at first Clive Malone was against portraying you. But I think now he sees it as a way of making himself a legitimate actor, rather than a matinee idol."

"When does this lawsuit get started?" Buck asked.

"Mr. Parnelli will let us know. He's going to talk to Alcy Harris first," Ryan said. "He thinks he might be able to work something out, but that's because he doesn't know how much power Clive Malone has with the studio. Harris can make no deal without Clive Malone's approval."

"Which means you're going to wind up suing the studio," Ernest said.

"Like I said, I'm willing. Whatever it takes."

Later that evening Buck stopped the Plymouth in front of the small house on San Gabriel Street in South Gate, a Los Angeles suburb that was twenty-two miles from his hotel. As he was getting out of the car, a young woman came down the sidewalk to meet him. She looked remarkably like the young Irish woman who had stepped down from the train in Canyon Diablo, forty-six years ago.

"Hello, Mr. Elliot, I'm Sue Ellen. Granma asked me to meet you."

"Yes, I know who you are, but you've certainly grown since the last time I saw you. How old are you now?"

"I'm sixteen," Sue Ellen said proudly.

"The last time I saw you, you were about ten."

"I remember before grandpa died, he said I looked like Granma used to look."

"You do, and what a beautiful young woman your grand-mother was."

The house was filled with the aroma of simmering Irish stew, and Mary Kathleen greeted Buck with a hug as soon as he entered.

"Buck, sure 'n 'tis a treat for these tired old eyes to be seeing you again. Sue Ellen's own sweet m'ither will be for joinin' us for supper as soon as she gets off work."

Sue Ellen's father had been Dub and Mary Kathleen's son, Ian. During the Great War, Ian became a flyer in the 94th U.S. Aero Squadron, better known as the Hat in the Ring Squadron. He flew with such men as Raoul Lufbery, Doug Campbell, Reed Chambers, Ham Coolidge, and America's greatest ace, Eddie Rickenbacker. Ian was shot down and killed in France and his widow, Tina Mae, never remarried but lived with her in-laws while she worked to raise Sue Ellen.

"I've a wee bit o' whiskey I can serve," Mary Kathleen offered. "'Tis against the law, that's for sure, but what kind of Irish house would I be keepin' if I did'na have whiskey for m' guests."

"Thank you, Mary Kathleen, a shot of whiskey would be much appreciated."

Mary Kathleen moved a big vase that exposed the door to a wall cabinet, then she took out a bottle and poured a small glass for each of them.

"'Tis a mystery to me how a country as foine as the United States would ever pass a law making criminals of people who want only a wee drop o' the creature," Mary Kathleen said as she tossed down the drink.

"Tell me about Dub," Buck said. "What happened? How did he die?"

"He died a happy man," Mary Kathleen said. "He had played a game of cards with some o' his friends 'n came home a winner. He went to sleep that night with a smile on his face." Mary Kathleen's own smile vanished and she got a much more subdued look about her. "He didn't wake up the next mornin'."

"Mary Kathleen, he wasn't happy just because he won a game of poker. He was happy because he had you."

"'Twas the smartest move I ever made when I answered that ad 'n went West to marry a man I had never laid eyes on," Mary Kathleen said. "'Twas a happy marriage 'n for sure 'twas made in heaven."

Tina Mae worked as an agent for Earl Roberts' real estate firm, and she arrived about half an hour before supper. Buck was able to see where Sue Ellen got her looks, for not only had Mary Kathleen been a beautiful woman in her youth, Tina Mae was quite pretty.

"Mr. Elliot, I told Earl you would be our guest for supper tonight, and he sends his regards to you," Tina Mae said.

"It's good to hear from him," Buck said, "Has he heard from Ken?"

"Oh, yes. Ken and Nola have merged Trailcross and the Tumbling R, and they're quite the ranchers now. Of course, they have two sons, and a son-in-law to help."

"I'll have to get back to see them sometime, soon," Buck said.

"It's time for supper," Mary Kathleen announced, interrupting the conversation.

"Ma, Granma says Mr. Elliot is going to be in a movie," Sue Ellen said over supper.

"I'm not *in* the movie—the movie is supposed to be *about* me. Only, it isn't," he added.

When Mary Kathleen questioned him, he explained the problem.

"We're trying to get a court order to stop the production," Buck said.

"'N would ye be for talkin' about the same kind of court order that that *gombeen* Britisher got his lackey of a judge to issue against the wee cattlemen of the Mogollon Rim, now?"

Buck chuckled, "You would be talking about Smythe?"

ROBERT VAUGHAN

"Sure now, 'n who else would I be for talkin' about if not that *shoibag*?"

"Ma Wilkerson, who in the world are you talking about?" Tina Mae asked.

"I'm talking about Nigel Smythe," Mary Kathleen said, "He was as evil a man as England ever produced. He tried to shut down Mountain Shadow, 'n all the other wee ranchers in the valley.

"Your ranch in Arizona? Yes, Ian was born there and he used to talk about it. He always said that when he returned from the war he wanted to go back there."

"He 'n Dub often talked about going back, but of course, we didn't own the ranch any longer."

"Oh, please don't tell me you lost it in that court order you were talking about."

"'Tis happy I am to tell you that we didna' lose the ranch, 'n the reason we didna' lose it is sitting at this self same table with us, sharing our food." With a big smile, she pointed to Buck.

"You saved grandpa and granma's ranch?" Sue Ellen asked.

"I wasn't alone," Buck said. "Your grandfather," Buck looked at Tina Mae, "and your boss, Earl, and every other small rancher fought off Smythe and all his men."

"But 'twas you that brought down Sheriff Parker," Mary Kathleen said.

"A sheriff? You fought with a sheriff?" Sue Ellen asked. "But wouldn't that be fighting against the law?"

Mary Kathleen laughed. "You don't understand, darlin'. Parker was the law, yes, but Buck was the law his ownself, 'n Sheriff Parker was as evil a man as ever drew a breath."

33

CANYON DIABLO, ARIZONA TERRITORY – 1885

"Are you sure you want me to try to get Judge Fitzhugh's court order set aside?" Manley Hampton asked. "After all, I didn't do so well when I prosecuted Deek McGee and Lazzie Logan."

"Yes," Buck said. As he sat in a chair across the desk from Hampton, he glanced around at his surroundings. Bookshelves filled one wall, and while there were several legal tomes as one might expect, there were also several other books, including works by Shakespeare, Mark Twain, Edgar Allan Poe, Charles Dickens, and Henry David Thoreau.

"I must say that I'm flattered that you would come to me considering, well, let us just say the ignominy of my station."

"I know you are an alcoholic, Mr. Hampton, but I have known others with the same affliction. Some have been able to overcome it and some have been defeated by it." Buck smiled. "But I also know that you're one of the smartest men I've ever met, and I can't help but have the feeling that you might be one who can beat the problem. So yes, if you're willing to try, the small ranchers of the Mogollon Rim would like to hire you to represent them in this case."

Hampton drew open the bottom left hand drawer of his desk and pulled out a bottle of whiskey that was three quarters of the way full. He looked at it for a moment, then walked over to the window, raised it, stuck his hand out and emptied the bottle.

"I'm not so foolish as to think that just pouring out this bottle is going to solve my problem," Hampton said, "but as the Chinese philosopher, Lao-tzu once said, the journey of a thousand miles must begin with a single step."

Buck laughed out loud. "Now, do you see there? That's why I'm sure you can do the job for us. Who else would know such a thing?"

"I first heard of the sayings of Lao-tzu from Ralph Waldo Emerson. I met that august gentleman during one of his lecture tours."

Hampton dropped the empty whiskey bottle into the waste basket, rubbed his hands together, and smiled at Buck. "Now, tell me, Mr. Elliot, do you have a copy of the court order with you?"

"I do."

Hampton held out his hand. "Let me take a look at it."

Buck gave the lawyer the document.

"Give me about an hour, and I'll see if I can come up with some way to construct the challenge."

Buck left Hampton to his study and walked down the street to the Mogollon Saloon. When he stepped inside he saw Sheriff Parker arguing with Ben McDaniels.

"I'm the sheriff now," Parker was saying, "and it seems to

me like if you don't want no trouble with the law, you'd be willing to give me a free drink ever' now 'n then."

"I've never had trouble with the law before, and I don't know why I'd be having any trouble now," Ben replied.

"Oh, now that I'm sheriff, you don't have no idea what kind of trouble you can have."

"Parker, are you soliciting a bribe?" Buck asked in a blunt voice.

Parker had not seen Buck come in and he jerked around in surprise at the challenge.

"Because if I thought you were actually doing something like that, I'd have to put you in jail."

"I was just teasin' 'im," Parker said, "I wasn't really expectin' a drink for free. I, uh, had better be makin' my rounds now."

"You do that," Buck said.

Before he left, Parker turned to Sean Kelly and Dub Wilk- erson, both of whom had come to town, and were waiting for Buck's report after visiting with Hampton.

Parker pointed to the two men. "Don't neither one of you forget that you got less 'n a week to get all them cows back where they belong. 'Cause iffen they ain't moved in time, I'll be comin' out there to confiscate 'em. 'N you can tell the others that too."

Satisfied that his warning to Sean and Dub had enabled him to recover a little of the dignity he had lost at Buck's challenge, Parker left the saloon.

"Sheriff Jones could be a pain in the ass at times," Ben said after Parker left, "but I'm afraid that one's goin' to wind up being a first class son of a bitch."

"I disagree with you, Ben," one of the bar patrons said. "Parker ain't a first class son of a bitch, 'cause there's nothin' first class about him."

Those within hearing distance laughed.

"What did Mr. Hampton say?" Sean asked when Buck joined them. "Will he take our case?"

"Yes," Buck said, his answer satisfying the two men.

After reading through the court order that would force the small cattlemen to break up their herd, Hampton began researching a strategy for fighting it. Once he came to a decision, he informed Buck that his first move in fighting Judge Fitzhugh's order, would be to get a superior judge to overturn it, and for that, they would have to go to Flagstaff.

"In Flagstaff, I'll put the case before Judge Lynch of the 3rd Federal Judicial District," Hampton told Buck. "But I'll want you to go with me."

Buck agreed to go, the trip to Flagstaff being no more than a half-hour train ride.

Hampton sat quietly beside Buck for the entire trip. It was some time now since Hampton had taken his last drink, and the symptoms of alcohol withdrawal were already beginning to exert themselves. He was unable to keep his hands from shaking, and he was sweating profusely. Twice, during the short trip, it had been necessary for him to go to the restroom and throw up.

When they reached Flagstaff, Buck had to help Hampton down from the train.

"Mr. Hampton, are you going to be all right with this?"

"I don't know," Hampton admitted. By now the shaking was affecting his entire body.

"I knew an old soldier once who beat his drinking problem, not by stopping all at once, but just by stopping a little at a time," Buck said. "He just sort of slowed down on his drinking until one day, he didn't need to drink at all. How much have you been drinking, per day?"

"I don't know, I quit counting," Hampton replied, "but if I had to guess, I'd say from ten to fifteen drinks a day."

"All right, why don't you start by cutting down to no more than five drinks a day? Do that for a week, then the next week make it four a day, then the next week three, and go on until you're not drinking anything at all."

"Is that how your friend did it?"

"Yes."

Hampton nodded. "No more than five drinks today. Yes, I would like to try it that way."

Buck smiled. "Before you meet Judge Lynch, I think you'd feel more comfortable if you could put the shakes behind you. Do you think a drink would do that for you?"

Hampton nodded. "I know it would."

Buck took Hampton to the North Star Saloon where he bought a single whiskey for himself and one for the lawyer.

"Let's get a table," Hampton said. "If I'm to limit my drinking, I'd like to drink very slowly."

"All right."

A moment later the two men were sharing a table, and Hampton lifted his glass to take no more than a sip.

"It was Parker," Hampton said.

"Yes, Parker is the one who served the court order," Buck said, sipping his own whiskey so as not to get ahead of Hampton.

"I'm not talking about the court order." Hampton took another drink.

"Then what are you talking about? What was Parker?"

"Parker's the one who killed those women—the ones in the barrio. And when Sheriff Jones found out about it and confronted him with the charge, Parker shot Jones and killed him."

"How do you know that?"

Hampton took another swallow before he replied. "Because I saw it."

"You saw it?"

"Yes, I did, and I'm relieved to get it off my conscience. Bustamante had told Sheriff Jones that the killer was *fue el ayudante.* I explained to the sheriff that what Bustamante was really trying to say, but was afraid to tell him, was that the killer was ayudante del sheriff, or assistant to the sheriff. He was saying that Deputy Parker was the one who was murdering all those Mexican women.

"I don't think Sheriff Jones believed me at first, but I told him that I'd given him the translation of the phrase, so he could use it however he wished. Then I left.

"Once I got outside, I started to head back to my office, but something made me stop. I turned around and started back to make certain that the sheriff knew what I was saying.

"When I approached his office, I saw Parker go inside. Parker didn't see me, so I looked in through the open window. The sheriff was holding out a tobacco pouch. I don't know where he got it, but I heard him tell Parker that there were earrings in the bag. Jones said Parker had jerked them off the ears of the women he had killed.

"That was when Parker drew his gun and shot and killed the sheriff," Hampton said, finishing the account of what he had witnessed.

"This confirms it," Buck said. "Parker killed those women, and he more than likely killed Bustamante, too. When we get back to Canyon Diablo, I will deal with Lanny Parker. You have done a great service to the town, Mr. Hampton."

Hampton took a deep breath, then finished his drink. He put the glass down resolutely. "But first, we have to deal with the cow problem. Let's go see the judge."

"Do you feel, uh . . ." Buck started, but Hampton interrupted him with a smile.

"Do I feel up to it? Yes, not only because of this," he lay the palm of his hand across the top of the glass, "but also because I told you about Parker. That's been bothering me, but I thought if I said anything, I'd be the next to die."

Judge Archibald Lynch was a big man with dark, slicked back hair, and a thick walrus moustache. At the moment he was examining the court order that Hampton had shown him. When he was finished, he glanced up at Buck and Hampton.

"Mr. Hampton, as I'm sure you know, I'm always loathe to overturn the decision, or the court order, of any judge below me without just cause," Judge Lynch said. "And to be honest with you, sir, I see no technical difficulties with this order. It certainly follows all the procedures necessary for it to be valid." He pushed the court order back across the desk. "I can see no justification for overturning the order."

"Your Honor, I have been retained by the ranchers named in this court order to plead their case for relief, if you would hear my petition," Hampton said.

Judge Lynch leaned back in his chair. "All right, counselor, make your case, I'll listen."

"The plaintiffs have sought relief based upon the published regulations of the two controlling agencies in this case, the General Land Office, and the U.S. Grazing Service.

"This is the criteria for involving those agencies in any interaction with rivers, streams or creeks."

Hampton read from a published pamphlet.

"Once a stream is classified, dam operators who regulate stream flow, divert water, or pump large quantities of groundwater from aquifers, must meet certain requirements. Owners or operators of

other structures or devices that divert water and impact surface water flow must also minimize stream flow impact.

"Now I submit to you, Your Honor, that the defendants use of Laroux Fork Creek, which is the stream cited by the court order, does not divert water in any of the ways as specified by this regulation.

"In addition, this act provides regulatory exemptions in case of, and again I am reading from the federal regulation, *extreme economic hardship or for agricultural diversions.*"

Hampton put the book down for his summation. "Your Honor, even without the authorized exemptions, both of which are met by the defendants' use of Laroux Fork Creek, the initial justification of the court order is invalidated, and I urge you to overturn the order signed by Judge T. Gordon Fitzhugh."

"Mr. Hampton, why don't you and Mr. Elliot have a seat and a cup of coffee, while I read through the rest of the document?" Judge Lynch said. And Mr. Hampton, if you would allow it, may I see the regulations you have cited?"

"Yes, of course, Your Honor," Hampton said, handing the book, with the marked page, to the judge.

Buck drew two cups from a coffee maker that sat on nearby counter top, then joined Hampton on a leather sofa as Judge Lynch continued to read.

He read for a moment longer then looked up toward Buck and Hampton.

"One of the demands of the order is that the gather of cattle will be dispersed according to ownership and returned to the lands of the individual defendants. What possible hardship would that work on the ranchers? Wouldn't they want their livestock on their own land?"

"By keeping the cattle together it's easier to deal with the rustling that's going on there," Buck said.

"Rustling? There are active rustlers in the county?"

"Yes, Your Honor," Buck said. Buck started to tell the judge that he was certain that Smythe was behind the rustling, but he feared that if he did so, it would complicate the issue at hand, which was to overturn the lower court order.

Judge Lynch lay the document down, then stroked his chin for a moment as he studied the two men.

"Gentlemen," he said, "I am inclined to agree with you. That was a brilliant presentation, Mr. Hampton. I will invalidate this court order."

"Thank you very much, Your Honor!" Buck said. He stuck his hand out to take the lawyer's hand. "And thank you. Mr. Hampton."

3 4

When Buck rode onto Eagleshire on Sherlons Fork, he was able to immediately separate the real workers from those who were but a part of Smythe's army. The workers were all gainfully employed, whereas Smythe's 'soldiers' were engaged in various pass times. Of the three actual gunfighters Smythe had hired, only Frank Corbett was still here, and Corbett came out to meet him.

"What are you doing here?" Corbett asked, the words little more than a growl.

"I've come to see Smythe."

"What do you want to see him about?"

"Well now, Corbett, that would be between Smythe and me, wouldn't it?"

"Yeah well, the thing is, Mr. Smythe hired me to keep people like you away from him," Corbett said.

"People like me? And what sort of person would that be?"

"You've done kilt Lodeen 'n Stillwell that we know for sure. How do I know you don't want to see Mr. Smythe on account of maybe you're a' plannin' on killin' him?"

266

"Because if I had it in my mind to kill Smythe, I would have killed you by now," Buck said.

Corbett blinked a couple of times, and the look of belligerence changed to an expression of apprehension.

"Yeah, all right, wait here 'n I'll go tell Mr. Smythe you've come out here to see him."

Buck nodded toward a nearby watering trough. "If you don't mind, I'll give my horse some water."

Corbett didn't respond but hurried into the ranch office to carry the news that Arizona Ranger Buck Elliot was here to pay a visit. As it turned out, it wasn't necessary for him to inform Smythe of Buck's presence, because his employer already knew.

"Why is Elliot here?" Smythe asked.

"He wants to see you," Corbett said. Then, in a bit of bravado he added, "I don't think you have to worry none, I mean, I told 'im this had better be nothin' no more 'n you 'n him just a' talkin' 'n he agreed."

"Thank you Mr. Corbett, you may show him in."

Corbett stepped outside, then crooked his arm toward Buck.

"You can come on in," he called.

Buck led his horse back from the watering trough then wrapped the reins around a hitching post. Without bothering to knock, he pushed open the door and stepped into the office. Smythe was in the process of lighting a cigar.

Buck stood quietly until Smythe had the cigar lit. Not until then did Smythe look up at him.

"If you have come to plead for more time for the ranchers to disperse the herd on Laroux Fork, I'm afraid there is nothing I can do for you. It is out of my hands now."

Buck smiled. "You've got that right, Smythe. It is out of your hands."

Smythe's confident smirk was replace by a look of uncertainty. "What, what exactly do you mean by that?"

"Fitzhugh's order has been overturned by a higher court." Buck showed Smythe the decree signed by Judge Lynch.

Smythe lay the cigar in the ashtray to look at the paper given him by Buck.

"So as you can see, the cattle stay where they are, and I will consider any further attempt at dispersion to be a direct violation of established law, and as I am an officer of the law, I'll not allow it."

"Where is Deputy, I mean, Sheriff Parker?" Smythe asked. "Does he know about this?"

"I don't know if he knows about it or not," Buck replied, "but it won't matter to him after we meet later today."

"Why will it not matter?"

"I don't know if you have ever heard of Juan Bustamante."

"Bustamante, yes, of course I have heard of him. If one is going to do any business at all with the Mexicans, one must first deal with Juan. He is a smart businessman."

"I've heard that he was."

"Was?"

"Juan Bustamante is dead. So are four Mexican women. And, I might add, so is Sheriff Jones."

"Yes, I knew about the four murdered prostitutes, and about Sheriff Jones, of course. But I knew nothing of poor Juan Bustamante's passing.

"I see why you are saying that the court order won't matter to Sheriff Parker. No doubt he will be busy dealing with the murders."

"Dealing with it? You might say that," Buck said. "By the way, do you still have the address of that fancy lawyer you hired to get McGee and Logan acquitted of the arson charges?"

"Of course I do. Why do you ask?"

"Parker might be needing a good lawyer."

While Buck was informing Smythe of the fact that the Fitzhugh Order had been overturned, and that the cattle would remain where they were, Parker was across the tracks in the Mexican area of town. At the moment he was in the cantina which had belonged to Bustamante.

"So, who owns this place now?" he asked the bartender.

"I suppose it is Senora Bustamante, Senor Sheriff."

After giving Parker the tequila he had ordered, the bartender had withdrawn to the far end of the bar and he stood there now, in fear of Parker. By now, like every other citizen of the barrio, he knew that Parker had murdered the women, and they suspected he had also murdered Juan. Their suspicions had not yet connected Parker to the death of Sheriff Jones.

"So you've got a rich widow in town, huh? Whoee, I'll bet a lot of men are goin' to be after her now, ain't they? Is she good lookin'? Hell, I might be payin' her a few visits my ownself." Parker laughed out loud, but the bartender didn't join in the laughter.

Except for Parker and the bartender, the cantina was empty. When Parker looked around and saw that, he was a little surprised. He was certain there had been other people here, when he had first come in. He also noticed that there were no bar girls.

"Hey, where are all the damn *putas*?" Parker asked.

"I don't know," the bartender replied in a voice that was thick with fear.

"You know where they are, you Mexican son of a bitch. You just ain't tellin' me."

Parker drew his pistol and pointed it at the bartender.

269

"Now I'm goin' to ask you one more time. Where are the *putas?*"

"Parker, you won't be killing anybody else today. You're going to jail."

At the unexpected sound of Buck Elliot's voice, Parker whirled around to see him. At first he was frightened; then he realized he had the advantage. Parker's gun was in his hand. Elliot's gun was in its holster.

"The hell I am!" Parker shouted, extending his gun hand.

In a lightning move that startled Parker, Buck drew his gun and fired before Parker could pull the trigger. Parker felt a blow to his chest, and a sudden loss of breath. He tried to pull the trigger, but his finger didn't respond to the order from his brain. Then he was lying on the floor of the cantina, though he had no idea how he got there. He saw Buck standing over him, looking down at him, and he tried to speak, but he couldn't form the words. It grew dark.

"Is he dead. Senor?" the bartender asked.

"Yes."

The bartender started to cross himself, but stopped in the middle, "No," he said, "No prayer for this evil one." He spat on the body, *"Arde en el infierno."*

"Burn in hell," Buck repeated, "Yes, I expect he is."

35

EAGLESHIRE ON THE SHERLONS FORK

"You're sure of this?" Smythe asked. "Parker is dead?"

"Yeah, Buck Elliot shot 'im on account of it turns out that Parker is the one that's been killin' them Mexican whores. He's also the one that shot Sheriff Jones," Corbett said.

"Disgusting man," Smythe said. "We are better off without him."

"Yeah, but it was kind of good to have a sheriff on our side."

"You have a point, Frank. And to that end, how would you like to be the new sheriff?"

"How can I be sheriff without I get elected?"

Smythe smiled. "I can arrange that."

"How?"

"It's quite simple. Yavapai County is without a sheriff now, and there must be a temporary occupant of that office until the next election. That is the responsibility of Judge

Fitzhugh, and I can make it profitable for him to make whatever appointment I suggest."

""Yeah, yeah," Corbett said, a big smile spreading across his face. I'd like to be the sheriff."

"First I must have your guarantee of absolute fealty."

"What?"

"You must understand that your first loyalty will be to me, rather than to anyone else, since I, and not the voters, will be responsible for your position."

"Yeah, I'll be working for you, just like now, only it'll be more legal," Corbett said. "When can we do it?"

"I'll take care of it, and I already have your first assignment. Now, that the small ranchers have managed to get the court order overturned, they are planning to take their herd to Winslow."

"Well, at least that'll get 'em away from that creek like you was wantin'," Corbett said.

"No, no, my dear man, you don't understand. There is a buyer in Winslow, but he is limited by his employer as to how many animals he can acquire. If the small ranchers get their cattle there before I do, it will shut me out of the market. It will also give them sufficient funds to resist any future economic obstacle I may place before them in my quest to put them out of business. Therefore it is imperative that I deny market access to this . . . this gaggle of riffraff who have been my Achilles heel. If I can stop them, they will either be forced into a long, difficult, and costly trail drive, or they will have to sit it out on their land with cattle that have become a financial liability rather than an asset. I had hoped that the court order would so disorient them, that I would have no difficulty in preempting their market. Unfortunately the order was overturned, so I must try some newer and more drastic tactic."

"Yeah, but Mr. Smythe, I don't see no way how you're

going to get your cows there first," Corbett said. "Them ranchers is a hell of a lot closer to Winslow than you are."

"They have a combined herd formed of cattle from eight different ranches, do they not?"

"Yeah, that's what they got all right."

"With such a diverse gathering of cows that are unfamiliar with each other, it is quite likely to make them uneasy. It wouldn't take much to put the cattle into such a disoriented state that they lose cohesion, and while the small ranchers are busy rounding up their displaced cattle, I will be able to reach Winslow before they get do. Once there, I can sell enough Eagleshire cattle to preclude any further purchases from the buyer."

"Yeah," Corbett said in agreement, though he had no real idea what Smythe was talking about.

"First, we must visit Judge Fitzhugh to get you sworn in as the new sheriff, then, you can swear in your deputies."

"Where am I going to find deputies?"

"Why, look around you, my good man. They are right in front of you." Smythe swung his arm out with a sweep."

"You mean your men are going to help me with the stampede?"

"Oh no, Mr. Corbett, there is to be no stampede; intentionally causing a stampede would be illegal."

"Then how are we going to stop 'em from getting' there first?"

"You and your deputies will have court authorization to check the cattle for tick fever. If during the course of that inspection the cattle are disturbed to the point that herd integrity can no longer be maintained, well I'm afraid that will just be an unfortunate by-product of cattle health awareness. After all, we can't be too careful, you know. An infection like tick fever can spread."

· · ·

Trailcross Ranch:

By now everyone in the valley knew of the confrontation between Buck and Parker, and there had been universal approval for the outcome. Shortly after his encounter with Parker, Buck was invited out to Trailcross where they could discuss with him their plans for their drive to Winslow.

"Roan and I have the most cattle," Sean said. "I have just over fifteen hundred head, and Roan has twelve hundred head give or take a couple."

"Dub is next," Roan added. "He's got a few over a thousand, the others, except for Sara Sue, are close to a thousand. Sara Sue has six hundred head, so that makes a total of about seven thousand head."

"The buyer in Winslow is paying thirty dollars," Sean said.

"Seven thousand head at thirty dollars each, that's," Buck paused for a moment to make the calculation, "damn, Sean, that's a lot of money! That's two hundred-ten thousand dollars!"

"Yeah," Sean said with a big smile. "And with that much money and all of us working together, I'd say that Smythe has about run out of tricks with all his double-dealing and monkey business."

"But," Roan said, holding his finger to emphasize his point, "in order to get them to market, we first have to get them to Winslow."

"That's not a very long drive, you should make it in two days," Buck said.

"If we don't have any trouble from Smythe's men," Roan said.

"Which is why," Sean added, "that Roan and I have talked to the others, and we are all in agreement. We'll give you a dollar a head to make sure we get our cows through."

"That's seven thousand dollars," Roan said. "What do you say, Buck? Will you do it?"

"Yeah," Buck agreed with a pleased smile. "Since I was going to help you anyway, it would be a little dumb of me to turn down the money, now wouldn't it? When do we start?"

"First light tomorrow morning," Sean said.

Very early the next morning Buck and the others were preparing to get the drive underway. Somewhere in the pre-dawn darkness a calf bawled anxiously and its mother answered. In the distance a coyote sent up its long, lonesome wail, while along the bank of Leroux Creek, frogs thrummed their night song. The moon was full and the night was alive with stars...from the very bright shining lights, all the way down to those stars which weren't visible as individual bodies at all, but whose glow added to the luminous powder that dusted the distant sky.

At the moment Buck, Moe Peters, George Baker, and Pete Connors, were riding around the milling shapes of shadows that made up the herd.

"This drive to Winslow sure ain't goin' to be nothin' like the drives I used to make back in Texas," Connors said.

"You don't miss those long drives do you?" Buck asked, with a little chuckle.

"No," Connors said. "Well, maybe just a little. I mean once we got all the cows all delivered, they was always some fun to be had in Dodge or Caldwell or some such place."

"I'm surprised none of Smythe's men are here watching the herd," Moe Peters said.

"They're here," Buck replied.

"What? Buck, have you seen somethin'?"

"No," Buck answered.

"Then, what makes you think there's anyone out here watchin' us?"

"I can feel it," Buck said.

The calf's call for his mother came again, this time with more insistence. The mother's answer had a degree of anxiousness to it.

"Sounds like one of the little fellers has wandered off," Connors said. "Maybe I'd better go find it and get it back to its mama."

"Leave it," Buck said. "We need to get the herd moving as quickly as we can."

"Ah, I'll do it real quick," Connors said, and slapping his legs against the side of his horse he rode off, disappearing in the darkness.

Less than a minute later a gunshot came from the darkness.

"What the hell is Connors doing?" Moe asked. "He'll spook the herd."

"I don't think that was Connors," Buck said.

"What do you mean?"

"I think we've got company."

They heard the sound of galloping hooves, then from the darkness, Connor's horse, its nostrils flared wide, and its eyes wild with terror, came running by them, its saddle empty.

"My God, where's Pete?" Moe asked.

Now, several gunshots erupted in the night, and the muzzle-flashes lit up the herd.

"Jesus! What's happening? What's going on?" Roan asked as he, Dub, and Sean joined the rest of them.

The cattle, spooked by the gunfire, started running.

"The cattle are stampeding!" Sean said.

"No, look, they're running in the right direction. Keep them going!" Buck called as he pulled his rifle from the scabbard.

"What are you doing? Where are you going?" Roan asked.

"I'm going after the ones who fired those shots, and then I'm going to find Pete."

"By yourself?"

"Stay with the herd!" Buck shouted again, already starting toward the sound of the guns.

Sean and the others were more than anxious to comply with that order, and they fell in beside the herd, shooting and yelling, urging the cattle to run faster.

Buck rode at a gallop to a near-by ridge, leaped from his horse, and lay on his stomach on a flat rock.

He saw them then, four mounted men, moonlit and silhouetted against the star-bright sky. They were riding hard in pursuit of the herd, their right arms extended in front of them, pistols in their hands, firing toward the thundering herd.

Buck fired at the one who was at the rear and saw him tumble from the saddle.

Because of all the noise, the four men did not realize that they were, themselves, under attack, nor did they know one of their number had been shot.

Buck fired a second time, again taking out the man who was riding at the rear. Not until he took out the second man were the two remaining riders aware of what was happening. They suddenly realized that they were no longer the hunters, they were the hunted, and they broke off their chase, turned, and galloped away as fast as they could. Buck threw a couple of long-distance shots at them, purposely missing them now, because they no longer represented a threat. But he put the bullets close enough for them to hear them passing, and to keep the men running.

With the danger now gone, Buck rode back over the ground, looking for Pete. He found him about a mile back, lying belly down. When he dismounted for a closer look at him, Pete suddenly rolled over with his gun in his hand.

"No, Pete, it's me!" Buck shouted quickly, holding his hand out.

Pete lowered his gun.

"Where are you hit?" Pete asked.

"In the leg," Pete replied. "It's just a grazing wound, but it was enough to knock me out of the saddle."

"Think you can sit a horse?" Buck asked.

"I don't know what happened to my horse."

"We'll catch up with him. Right now we're going to ride double."

Buck helped Pete up onto his horse, putting him just behind the saddle.

"Riding double like this'll sure slow us down, if those guys come after us," Pete said.

"They won't be doin' that."

"They won't? How do you know?"

"Because I ran them off," Buck answered without further elaboration.

From the Book Legend of a Gunfighter, by Ernest Haycox:

> *Shortly after the small ranchers were able to deliver their cattle to the buyer in Winslow, Ranger Buck Elliot arrested both Sheriff Frank Corbett and Judge T. Gordon Fitzhugh. Both men were tried, convicted, and sentenced for malfeasance in office. Corbett was killed a year later, trying to escape prison. Fitzhugh died in prison in the fourth year of his ten year sentence.*
>
> *Nigel Smythe became badly overextended and wound up losing everything. He returned to England where he failed to have his title restored. There, he had an unsuccessful run for a seat in parliament, then failed in a business venture that dealt with land in Australia. In January of 1915, in the very first German*

Zeppelin attack of World War One, Nigel Smythe and nine others were killed when bombs fell on the small seaport and market town of Kings Lynne, England, about 98 miles north of London.

36

"Gentlemen, I have good news, and the deal is signed, sealed, and delivered," Jacob Parnelli said. With a wide smile he dropped a folder on his desk.

"What did you get worked out?" Haycox asked.

"Ernest, you'll return the fifteen thousand dollars you were paid for the rights for your book, and the rights will revert to you. And, Buck, you'll be returning the four thousand you've been paid for your consultant's fee, and, the best thing, your name will not be used," Jacob said.

"That's wonderful," Buck said, "but what does Starburst get out of this? I know Alcy Harris didn't just fade away quietly in the night."

"He seems to be happy with the deal. He's agreed to give up the title *Legend of a Gunfighter,* and the movie which is in production will now be called, *Law of the Arizona Desert.* And, I'm sure it will come as no surprise that in *Desert,* Clive Malone will portray Clive Malone."

"The news is good," Ernest said.

"Ernest, I thought you would be ecstatic," Jacob said. "You don't seem all that enthused."

"Oh, but you're wrong, I am pleased, but contrary to what the public believes, writers don't have bags of money lying around. The fifteen thousand dollars—frankly, I'm going to have to float a loan to pay it back."

"No you won't, unless you want to of course. Fox is willing to pay you twenty-five thousand dollars for the rights to *Legend of a Gunfighter*."

"What? Are you serious?" Ernest asked his eyes widening. "I can't believe it! Their initial offer was for twelve thousand."

"I know, but John Ford says that since there's been so much publicity surrounding this picture, he has no doubt that the picture will pay out in a big way. He talked William Fox into increasing the offer.

"Ryan, they want your screen play, and they want to hire you as a staff writer. Are you interested in the job?"

"Absolutely!" Ryan said enthusiastically.

"And, Buck, there's a place for you as well. Are you willing to give this movie business another try?"

"I will, with one condition," Buck replied.

"Buck, wait a minute before you say something you might regret," Ernest said. "And besides, what condition could you possibly want? Jacob has gotten everything we wanted."

"There's a young man I've come to know. He works as a janitor at the Hotel Normandie, and he came out to Hollywood to break into the movies. His name is Julian Throckmorton, but he's taken the screen name of Tim Curtis. If it would be possible I'd like to see him get a part in the movie." Buck held up his hand to stop any immediate protest. "Now, before any of you say anything, I ask with the caveat that if he can't handle it, fine. But I'd really appreciate it if he could be given a chance."

"I'll take care of it," Jacob promised. "You know, Buck, I can see why the people love you. You didn't ask what you were going to get out of this—you asked for a favor on behalf of a kid you met pushing a broom in a hotel."

Fox Studios Stage Six

"If this looks like a real ranch instead of a studio set, that's because it is a real ranch," Jacob told Buck. "This ranch once belonged to Tom Mix."

"I understand it was more of a hobby than an actual ranch, though," Ryan said.

"That may be," Jacob said. "But it's still a ranch. What do you say, Buck? You're the consultant on this picture. Will this pass as a ranch?"

"Move the cars out of the way and I'd think I'm back on Trailcross," Buck said.

"Oh, here comes John Ford," Jacob said.

There were two men with Ford as he approached, one was tall with broad shoulders, and the other was the young man Buck had recommended for a role in the movie.

"Hello, Julian," Buck greeted.

"I've got a part in the movie, Mr. Elliot," Julian said excitedly. "And Mr. Ford says it's all because of you!"

"I just mentioned your name, Julian; the acting part is going to be up to you."

"Right, but it's Tim, remember? I'll be credited in the film as Tim Curtis."

"Then Tim it is," Buck agreed.

"And this young man will be portraying you, in the movie," Ford said.

"Wait, he will never do," Buck said. "Why he isn't wearing

white, and he doesn't have a brace of pearl handled, nickel-plated pistols."

Ford and the tall young man got surprised looks on their faces, but Ernest and Ryan laughed out loud.

Then Ford got the joke as well. "He's teasing you son. He's joking about Clive Malone."

"So, you're going to play the part of Buck Elliot, are you?" Ryan asked.

"Well now that's—a mighty tall order I mean me playing the part of—a genuine Western hero like Buck Elliot, someone I've—heard about for just about my whole life," the young man replied in a low voice that had a peculiar cadence of frequent pauses between words. "But Mr. Haycox here has written a very good book and—Mr. Ryan has turned out a really good script. So if Tim and I can't make it with what we've got to work with, well—I reckon we just aren't going to be able to make it in this business."

"You know what?" John Ford said. "With that attitude, I've no doubt that you'll make it. I've got an idea that you and I will make quite a few movies together before we play out our string. Yes, sir, I'd be willing to bet that one day everyone in America will know the name John Wayne."

A LOOK AT LONG ROAD TO ABILENE, THE WESTERN ADVENTURES OF CADE MCCALL BOOK I

LONG ROAD TO ABILENE, is a classic hero's journey, a western adventure that exemplifies the struggles, the defeats, and the victories that personify the history of the American West. After surviving the bloody battle of Franklin and the hell of a Yankee prison camp, Cade McCall comes home to the woman he loves only to find that she, believing him dead, has married his brother. With nothing left to keep him in Tennessee, Cade journeys to New Orleans where an encounter with a beautiful woman leads to being shanghaied for an unexpected adventure at sea. Returning to Texas, he signs on to drive a herd of cattle to Abilene, where he is drawn into a classic showdown of good versus evil, and a surprising reunion with an old enemy.

AVAILABLE NOW FROM ROBERT VAUGHAN AND WOLF-PACK PUBLISHING.

ABOUT THE AUTHOR

Robert Vaughan sold his first book when he was 19. That was 57 years and nearly 500 books ago. He wrote the novelization for the miniseries *Andersonville*. Vaughan wrote, produced, and appeared in the History Channel documentary *Vietnam Homecoming*. His books have hit the NYT bestseller list seven times. He has won the Spur Award, the PORGIE Award (Best Paperback Original), the Western Fictioneers Lifetime Achievement Award, received the Readwest President's Award for Excellence in Western Fiction, is a member of the American Writers Hall of Fame and is a Pulitzer Prize nominee. Vaughn is also a retired army officer, helicopter pilot with three tours in Vietnam. And received the Distinguished Flying Cross, the Purple Heart, The Bronze Star with three oak leaf clusters, the Air Medal for valor with 35 oak leaf clusters, the Army Commendation Medal, the Meritorious Service Medal, and the Vietnamese Cross of Gallantry.

www.ingramcontent.com/pod-product-compliance
Lightning Source LLC
Chambersburg PA
CBHW060604030726
47498CB00005B/1533